P9-BBO-891

APPLEWHITES COAST TO COAST

Also by **STEPHANIE S. TOLAN**

GRANDPA—AND ME
THE LIBERATION OF TANSY WARNER
THE LAST OF EDEN
NO SAFE HARBORS
THE GREAT SKINNER STRIKE
THE GREAT SKINNER ENTERPRISE
THE GREAT SKINNER GETAWAY
THE GREAT SKINNER HOMESTEAD
MARCY HOOPER AND THE GREATEST TREASURE IN THE WORLD
A TIME TO FLY FREE
THE WITCH OF MAPLE PARK
PRIDE OF THE PEACOCK
BARTHOLOMEW'S BLESSING
SOPHIE AND THE SIDEWALK MAN
SAVE HALLOWEEN!
ORDINARY MIRACLES
PLAGUE YEAR
A GOOD COURAGE
WHO'S THERE?
THE FACE IN THE MIRROR
WELCOME TO THE ARK
FLIGHT OF THE RAVEN
LISTEN!
WISHWORKS, INC.
SURVIVING THE APPLEWHITES
APPLEWHITES AT WIT'S END

APPLEWHITES COAST TO COAST

STEPHANIE S. TOLAN
and R.J. TOLAN

HARPER
An Imprint of HarperCollins*Publishers*

Applewhites Coast to Coast

For information address HarperCollins Children's Books, a division of HarperCollins Publishers, 195 Broadway, New York, NY 10007.
www.harpercollinschildrens.com

ISBN 978-0-06-213320-5 (hardcover)
ISBN 978-0-06-213321-2 (library bdg.)

Typography by Erin Fitzsimmons
17 18 19 20 21 CG/LSCH 10 9 8 7 6 5 4 3 2 1
❖
First Edition

For our family who went on ahead.
See you on the other coast.

The Cast of
APPLEWHITES COAST TO COAST

At Wit's End

E.D. (Edith) Applewhite–
the only organized member of the Applewhite artistic dynasty

Jake Semple–
the bad kid who was sent to the Applewhites' home school, the Creative Academy, when he was thrown out of every other school

Winston–
a basset hound

Lucille Applewhite–
E.D.'s aunt, a poet

Archie Applewhite–
E.D.'s uncle, a sculptor

Destiny Applewhite–
E.D.'s little brother, a talker

Cordelia Applewhite–
E.D.'s big sister, a dancer

Hal Applewhite–
E.D.'s big brother, a recluse

Sybil Jameson–
E.D.'s mother, an author

Randolph Applewhite–
E.D.'s father, a theater director

Zedediah Applewhite–
E.D.'s grandfather, a craftsman

Jeremy Bernstein–
a writer, the Applewhites' biggest fan

Melody Aiko Bernstein–
the new girl, Jeremy's niece

Govindaswami–
Aunt Lucille's spiritual advisor and yoga master

Wolfie and Hazel–
two goats

Bill Bones–
a biker

On the Road

HADDOCK POINT, NORTH CAROLINA

Simon Rathbone–
an actor

CLAYTON, TENNESSEE, AND VICINITY

Marianne Quintana–
head librarian

Michael Lyons–
assistant librarian

Rabbit Girl–
likes to bite

Farmer–
a farmer

VALLEY VIEW, ARKANSAS

Joe the Blacksmith–
a sculptor, member of the Ozark Art Co-op

Suzi–
a dog, Winston's new best friend

SAUNDERS, NEW MEXICO

The Organic Academy–
competitors on the Education Expedition, including Michaela, Gary, Tyler, and the "French Fries"

SEDONA, ARIZONA

Madame Amethyst–
a shaman and pilot

RUTHERFORD ART CENTER, CALIFORNIA

Larry and Janet Rutherford–
creators of the Education Expedition

Hector Montana–
a TV producer

Trudy–
a mime

Chapter One

E.D. Applewhite could no longer put off confronting the problem of the Kiss.

She had wakened early in the morning from an intense dream she couldn't quite remember. All she knew was that Jake had been in it. Jake. She stared out her bedroom window into the thick canopy of trees, their late-summer leaves pocked with holes chewed by caterpillars, and sighed. What was she going to do about *Jake*?

The art camp her family had run all summer was over. The campers had departed yesterday, amid hugs and tears and promises to come back next year. No one in the family had to teach or encourage or share with someone else's children their own love of art anymore. Wit's End, her family's home and creative compound, was back to normal. Jake had come into her life only a little more than a year ago as the "bad boy from the city," who joined the Applewhites' home school because he'd already been kicked out of the whole public school system of Rhode Island for burning down his school, and then out of Traybridge Middle here in North Carolina, and had no place else to go. How could she possibly have known when he showed up with his scarlet spiked hair, his multiple piercings and black clothes and nasty attitude, that he would turn out to be the first boy to kiss her?

But he was. And she'd kissed him back. She had most definitely kissed him back. And had been unable to get the whole evening out of her mind ever since. They had been alone on the porch of the main house, with the sound of the campers singing down at the campfire rising above the summer-night sounds of crickets and cicadas. There had been a moon. And a slight breeze. And then the hoot of an owl.

Nothing had come of it, really. In fact, they'd both sort of pretended ever since that it hadn't happened at all. But she was pretty sure Jake had no more forgotten it than she had. There had been moments now and then through all the rest of camp when they would accidentally make eye contact and she would feel a kind of shock, like static electricity. She could just tell he felt it, too. She had taken to looking purposely away whenever Jake came near.

And now without the campers in their faces all the time, they would have to figure out what it meant, wouldn't they?

Maybe she was being silly, E.D. told herself fiercely. Maybe it hadn't meant all that much to Jake. He'd probably had lots of girlfriends in his life. She could imagine flighty, hormone-ridden girls all over Providence, Rhode Island, throwing themselves at the scary guy with the crazy, spiked, dyed hair and eyebrow ring. Even with his current look—the rather more ordinary floppy brown Mohawk, cutoffs, and rock-band T-shirts—one of the twin eleven-year-old campers had developed an instant crush the day she met him. For Jake, what E.D. called *the Kiss* was probably a perfectly ordinary thing.

Not so for E.D. Homeschooled since the age of nine, she'd had almost no opportunity even to meet boys, let alone kiss them. There was David, of course. Even thinking about David, the camper who had left yesterday proclaiming that he might *consider* coming back to camp to star in next year's end-of-camp show, made E.D.'s cheeks burn with chagrin. She'd made a fool of herself over him just because he looked like an angel, and he had turned out to be the total opposite. Maybe this whole thing wasn't really about Jake. She was thirteen, after all. Maybe the only reason she couldn't get the Kiss out of her mind was that it had been her first.

Nothing has changed, E.D. told herself. *I'm moving on with my life.*

She got out of bed and headed for the bathroom. No one else seemed to be up yet. She thanked goodness, as she did every morning, that Jake didn't live in the Applewhite main house, so she didn't have to worry about running into him in her pajamas on the way to brush her teeth.

Which reminded her that the whole situation was impossible! Her five-year-old brother, Destiny, regularly called Jake his "bestest brother," a title their real older brother, Hal, never bothered to argue with. "I don't like little kids any more than I like regular people," Hal had told E.D. once. "I'm not nearly as useful a big brother as Jake."

The fact was, *everybody* treated Jake like a member of the family. And you just couldn't date a member of your family! There were whole Greek tragedies written about that sort of thing.

E.D. locked herself in the bathroom and stared at her reflection in the mirror. She might not be as gorgeous as her teenaged big sister, Cordelia, but she wasn't all that bad, she thought. Her hair was bleached from the sun, and in spite of the sunblock she'd used every day of camp, her cheeks had the slightest tint of bronze. She smiled at herself, trying to look confident and grown-up. *Moving on with my life!* she thought.

Suddenly the dream she'd wakened from flashed into her mind. She and Jake had been sitting together on his secret boulder in the woods. An owl had called from the trees above them. What was it with owls? Jake had leaned toward her and their lips had met. Just like the first time. Except that this time, he'd taken her into his arms and kissed her again. And again.

Reliving that dream, E.D. squeezed toothpaste onto her toothbrush. Maybe it *was* possible. Jake wasn't *really* her brother, after all. He was smart and talented and reasonably well organized. And even if she didn't have anybody to compare him to, there was no doubt at all that he was a good kisser. She wrinkled her nose, grinned at her reflection, and stuck her toothbrush into her mouth. And gagged.

She spat and spat, then turned on the water and lapped it into her mouth with her hand, but her mouth was still full of something nasty and oily. It tasted completely horrible! She turned her head and stuck her face right under the faucet, letting the water pour directly into her mouth. Little by little the taste faded and she dared to swallow.

The tube lying there on the vanity wasn't toothpaste at all. She'd covered her toothbrush with Hal's zit cream instead!

That's it! she thought. This whole thing was *totally impossible!*

Even thinking about having a relationship with Jake Semple had turned her brain to mush. She sloshed her mouth out with water one more time and spit again. She would just have to break up with him, that's all. Could you break up if you didn't actually have a relationship? Whatever. She had to tell him there was nothing—nothing whatsoever—between them and never could be, in spite of the Kiss. Right now! Well, not now, of course, but today. The first chance she got. She had her sanity to consider.

Moving on with my life, she thought again. She saw that nobody seemed to be getting up to make breakfast. It was the end of August, nearly time for the Creative Academy home school to start its fall semester, and the schoolroom was still set up as *Eureka!*'s camp office. At the Applewhites' home school, the kids decided for themselves what they wanted to study. E.D. usually spent the summer organizing her curriculum notebook for the fall, but here it was, almost September, and she hadn't even thought about it. The least she could do was start gathering the school stuff that had been stored in the shed behind the barn for the summer.

She was on her third trip from barn to office, puffing, sweating, and staggering under the weight of a massive carton of books, when she ran into Winston, the bassett hound. Right behind him, as usual, was Jake.

He was wearing a swimsuit and T-shirt, with a towel over his shoulder. On the way to the pond for a swim, she thought. E.D. shuddered—she didn't like swimming in water that could hide the approach of a snapping turtle. Then she pictured Jake stripping off his shirt and diving into the still, cool water, and almost dropped the box she was carrying. *Totally impossible!*

"You want some help with that?" Jake asked, grinning.

She kept walking. "I can manage." Much as she wanted to get the necessary breakup conversation over and done with, she didn't want to have it with Jake in a bathing suit.

"Come on, you're about to drop it." He flipped his towel around his neck and took the box from her, hoisting it easily onto one shoulder.

E.D. followed him up the side porch steps and into the office, absolutely refusing to notice the way the muscles of his shoulders moved under his shirt as he shifted the weight to open the door. He plunked the box down on the office counter next to the two boxes of supplies she'd already brought over, then looked around at the camp notes and messages that still covered the walls. "Camp's over," he said meaningfully, raising the eyebrow with the silver ring. "It's just us now."

There was that little shock again as their eyes met.

She looked away and stared fixedly at the map her brother Hal had painted of Wit's End that occupied most of the schoolroom wall.

Suddenly, without meaning to say a word, or planning anything, she heard herself saying, "There isn't any *us*. I mean, even if there ever *was*, which there probably wasn't—even if there *was*, it's over. It *should* be, I mean. It has to be. It wouldn't work. We're practically family. It's *totally impossible*."

And then she turned and ran out of the office.

She didn't dare look back and risk seeing the expression on his face. What if the Kiss hadn't meant anything to him? What if he didn't even remember it? Maybe he had no idea what she was even talking about. What if—she could feel her cheeks burn with the thought—what if right now he was laughing at her?

E.D.'s only thought was to go back to her room and pull her sheets over her head, and maybe her pillow, too. But in the kitchen Aunt Lucille's guru, whose name was Govindaswami and who was a frequent houseguest of the Applewhites, was standing at the stove, dressed in his usual voluminous pants and tunic, stirring something richly aromatic in the big frying pan. E.D. stopped. Moving on required sustenance, after all.

Aunt Lucille and Uncle Archie were seated at the table now, steaming coffee mugs in front of them, and E.D.'s mother, Sybil, lured by the delicious smell, had come down to join them. Destiny, clutching the patchwork possum one of the campers had made for him, his face streaked with tears, appeared in the doorway just as Govindaswami said, "I am at work on a very special breakfast to celebrate the successful completion of a glorious camp experience."

At that Destiny burst into sobs, through which, after a moment, a few words could be made out—"gone" and "alone" and "never, never." Finally, he threw himself on the floor and wailed, "All gone forever and ever and ever . . ."

E.D.'s mother set her mug on the table and hurried to comfort him. "Destiny, dear, camp's over, but you're not *alone*," she said. "You're right here in the midst of your whole, loving family."

As she reached down for him, he kicked his feet on the tile floor, narrowly missing her ankles. "I don't want to be by my ownself with just my family. I want the campers back! If I can't have the campers back I'd rather be dead!" he shrieked. "Like Cimmamon's possum!"

Suddenly, out of nowhere, an engine roared up outside the house. A great klaxon horn sounded from the driveway, echoing across Wit's End. *Aaah-oooo-gah! Aaah-oooo-gah!*

A door slammed. "Yoo-hoo," came a voice that E.D. recognized immediately. "Yoo-hoo, Applewhites! Anybody home?"

Chapter Two

After E.D. rushed out of the office/classroom, Jake stood for a moment, doing his best to breathe, and then sank to the floor, where Winston tried immediately to climb into his lap, licking Jake's chin and slobbering on his neck. Jake shoved him off and wiped his face with his towel.

He felt exactly the way he had felt one time back in his days as the Terror of Rhode Island. There had been a fight—not much of one, just some name-calling and shoving—between Jake and his tough-guy companions and some others who'd been smoking out back of the local mall, when out of nowhere a wiry, little shaved-head kid had socked Jake in the stomach. Hard. Really hard. *Whump!* And he'd gone down.

Turns out, you didn't have to get hit to feel that way, Jake thought. Turns out, all it takes is for a girl, one you had started to let yourself think of as possibly, maybe, just maybe your first actual *girlfriend*, to tell you that she's not. Whatever he'd been thinking might happen between them was over, she'd said. Before it even started. *Whump!* And down you go.

Come on, Semple, he thought. *Get up off the floor.* Winston's tail thumped against his leg. The bassett hound looked at him as if to say that there wasn't any point just sitting there.

So E.D. didn't want to be his girlfriend. So what? A month or two ago the idea wouldn't even have occurred to him. A month or two ago he would have thought it was ridiculous. Sure, he hadn't liked it much when she had gone moony over David, but that was because David was a jerk. "This is just E.D. we're talking about," he said to Winston. "The one who never wanted me here to begin with." Yeah. Just E.D., the girl he had been thinking about every day since that night on the porch. Just the first girl he had ever really kissed.

With tremendous concentration, Jake sucked down a deep breath. *Acceptance.* That's what Govindaswami told the campers in yoga class. How important it was to *accept* whatever was happening in your life no matter how it felt in the moment. Not to fix it, not to fight it. Accept it so you could move on. It was a "practice," Govindaswami said, which meant you had to work at it.

Jake would have to work on accepting that E.D. didn't want to be his girlfriend. He forced another breath. Accepting that the moment he'd been looking forward to ever since the Kiss—when the campers would be gone and there would finally be time for him and E.D. to be alone and figure out what it was like to actually have somebody who wanted to kiss you—that moment wasn't going to happen. The Kiss wasn't going to end up meaning anything at all.

He was breathing, but it didn't help much.

He patted Winston on the head. "No pond today," he told him. He didn't feel like swimming now. Or anything else.

Aaah-oooo-gah! went an incredibly loud horn from the driveway. *Aaah-oooo-gah!*

Winston leaped to his feet and tore out the door of the classroom, barking his furious anti-home-invasion bark. Jake sighed and pushed himself up off the floor. He didn't want anybody to see this wimp of a Jake Semple who had let a girl get him down. He ran a hand through his Mohawk, pulled his shoulders back, said a couple of words that were longtime favorites of Paulie, Zedediah Applewhite's potty-mouthed parrot, and went to see what was going on.

"Yoo-hoo, Applewhites!" a familiar voice was calling from just out of sight. "Anybody home? Anybody—*waughh!*" Jake rounded the corner to a remarkable sight.

Winston had flung himself bodily onto the visitor, knocking him straight to the ground and covering him in slobbery kisses. The guy on the ground was Jeremy Bernstein, the Applewhites' biggest fan; he had stayed with the family for a whole year to write a book about them. And behind him was the most remarkable vehicle Jake had ever seen.

It was a gigantic, fantastically painted school bus. It wasn't just paint, Jake realized as he got closer. It had textures on it, too—some of the swoops and swooshes of color rose off the sides of the bus in fins and ridges, like a sculpture. Some parts were covered in mosaic. He saw tiles, pebbles, and even little bits of broken ceramic dishes worked into a swirl that went all along the side like a racing stripe. On the roof, sticking up between what looked like a half-dozen solar panels, was a flagpole dragging a long triangular flag. It was tattered and wind-torn, but Jake could just make out the motto, painted on the pennant in flowing script letters: *Art can save the world.*

People were coming out onto the porch to see what was going on, and Jake saw E.D. at the back of the pack. He felt his stomach flip over, and hurried around to the other side of this crazy-looking vehicle. He wasn't avoiding her, he told himself, he just really wanted to see what the back of the bus looked like.

As it turned out, the back was just as interesting as the rest—there was a whole porch welded onto it, complete with a railing. Across the back was a yellow-and-black warning sign. Rotten as he felt, Jake couldn't help grinning at it. CAUTION, it read. WEIRD LOAD.

"Jake!" cried Destiny, running around the bus to check it out from every angle, his eyes popping in five-year-old wonder. "Did you see this bus that Jeremy's got, Jake? Isn't this the most amazing thing ever? Jeremy says he'll take me on a tour and I can even take a *ride* on it! Come and see the rest!" Jake found himself being dragged back around to the side where Govindaswami was staring with wide-eyed appreciation, while Archie, Lucille, and Sybil barraged Jeremy with questions.

"It's an Art Bus," Jeremy was saying over their questions. "The official vehicle of the Rutherford Foundation. Have you guys heard of the Rutherford Foundation? I work for them now."

Everybody looked puzzled except for Uncle Archie. "Rutherfords. Aren't they that eccentric billionaire couple in California? The ones who give all that money to artists?"

"The nation's foremost private arts philanthropists,

as we at the foundation like to say," Jeremy added.

"Phil-anthro-what?" asked Destiny.

"It means they give people money," said Archie.

"Basically!" agreed Jeremy happily. "And now they've decided that—"

"What on earth is going on out here?" cried E.D.'s father, Randolph Applewhite, bursting out the front door of the Lodge with his hair sticking up on one side and a threadbare plaid robe clutched around him. "It sounds like someone has docked a cruise ship on our lawn! Decent people are sleeping here—does nobody realize that? Oh, hello, Jeremy."

"Randolph!" Jeremy cried, and ran up the porch steps to fling his skinny arms around him. "I've just been telling your family, I have the most fabulous news!"

"News? What news? Has anybody made coffee? I hope this news doesn't require any kind of sane response from me. Not, at least, without caffeine!"

"Where are the others?" Jeremy asked now. "This involves all of you. Here, hang on a second!" Jeremy scrambled down the porch steps and into the bus. The giant air horns mounted on top blasted out again: *Aaah-oooo-gah!*

"Jeremy! Jeremy! Can I blow the big horn?" cried Destiny, clambering up the stairs after him.

"For heaven's sake, don't show him how to—" began Randolph, but he was too late. Everybody clapped their hands over their ears as Destiny grabbed the pull string for the horn. *Aaah-oooo-gah, aaah-oooo-gah, aaah-oooo-gah!* bellowed the bus, again and again. Eventually E.D.'s brother Hal and sister, Cordelia, emerged, blinking, from the house, and their grandfather Zedediah came from the direction of his cottage, muttering a whole string of "parrot words."

"So what is this earth-shaking news of yours, Jeremy?" asked Randolph after Destiny had been dragged from the bus and all the greetings were done.

Jeremy clasped his hands in front of himself. "It's so wonderful I barely know where to begin. First, I need to thank you all. It was because of you that I got this fantastic job!"

"Us?" Sybil said. "What did we do?"

"You let me stay here with you and write my book! *Art, Education, and the Meaning of Life: The Story of an Artistic Dynasty.* My publisher showed the Rutherfords the manuscript and that's why they hired me! They were inspired by the story of a whole family of artists. And Jake, too! I guess you could say Jake was sort of the linchpin."

Everyone was looking at Jake now, except E.D., who was staring fixedly at the bus. Jake felt his cheeks getting hot.

"They were just blown away by the story of how you turned around a troubled kid with the uplifting power of art! It made them realize that to save the world you really have to begin with the kids. It started them on a push into a whole new field. And now I've got—they've got—*we've* got plans for you! Big plans!"

"Jeremy, darling," said Lucille gently, "whatever you have to tell us, perhaps we should all go inside and you can explain over Govindaswami's splendid breakfast."

"Ah, of course. But first there's . . . well, there's somebody you should meet." He stopped and rubbed at his face with both hands. "That's the *other* thing," he said, oblivious to the fact that he hadn't yet explained the first thing. "My brother and his wife, when they found out about the wonderful influence you all had on Jake, well, their daughter has been"—he struggled for the right word—"troubled? I guess. What you could call a troubled child. Anyway." He stepped up onto the bus, leaned in, and shouted toward the back. "Melody! You can come out now!"

There was a groan from the depths of the bus, and some shuffling in the darkness. Jeremy stepped aside from the bus doorway like a magician pulling the cloth away from the lady he had just sawed in half. "Applewhites, may I introduce you to my niece, Melody Aiko Bernstein."

Reluctantly, a girl stepped out into the light. And for the second time that morning, Jake found himself unable to breathe.

Chapter Three

What happened to E.D. when Melody Bernstein—her tall, slim body dressed only in a halter top, extremely short shorts, and flip-flops—stepped out of the bus and swept her eyes across the assembled Applewhites was seriously weird. A wave of cold, almost as if someone had just opened a very large freezer door, swept over her. She actually got goose bumps. It was the *look* the girl gave—a look of such distaste as she took in the Applewhites, assessed them, and dismissed them, all in the space of a heartbeat. A moment later E.D.'s cold feeling had passed, the way a cloud's shadow passes when the cloud drifts past the sun. But she wasn't likely to forget it.

She looked around at her family, but nobody else seemed to have noticed anything. Then her eyes landed on Jake, who was staring at Melody like a puppy that has just caught sight of its first biscuit.

E.D. had to admit that Melody was beautiful. She had dark eyes, high cheekbones, and perfect, glowing skin, and when she tipped her head, a curtain of straight, shining, almost blue-black hair swung forward in a way that seemed somehow both accidental and well practiced.

Aunt Lucille opened her arms wide. "Welcome to Wit's End, Melody!" she said, starting down the porch steps toward her. "Just as I told Jake on his first day with us, you are a radiant light being. If some cannot see it, you may have been standing in shadow."

Melody didn't say anything. She just crossed her arms across her bare midriff, let that cascade of sleek hair fall across her face, turned her gorgeous, dark eyes toward Lucille—and glared.

Or maybe, thought E.D., *it wasn't so much a glare as a sneer.*

Lucille stopped at the bottom of the steps as if she'd run into a wall, her arms still outstretched to give the girl a hug. *Sneer* for sure, E.D. decided, judgmental and hostile. Aunt Lucille often said, "Thoughts are things." If this girl's thoughts were things they'd be daggers.

Destiny was impervious to thought daggers. "Hi, Melody!" he said, bouncing up and down on his toes. "I'm Destiny Applewhite. That's a pretty name, Melody. It means like a song. I love to sing. Do you love to sing?" As usual Destiny barely finished one sentence before he was rushing into the next. "And your middle name, is that *Eye-co*? That's pretty, too. I never heard a name like that. Did Jeremy tell you about our pond? Is that why you already gots on your bathing suit? I can go get my suit on, too—I'll be really, really fast—and we can go to the pond, and you can see the goatses on the way—"

"Kid?" said Melody Aiko Bernstein. Destiny stopped mid-ramble and looked at her questioningly. "Shut. Up."

A ripple of shock went through the Applewhite family. Destiny blinked up at her. She looked around at them all. "I'm starving. What have you people got to eat?"

Jeremy sighed. "Melody, I offered you breakfast and you refused."

Melody looked at him as if he were something that had slithered out from under a rock. "That green slime you drink isn't breakfast. Breakfast is something you *chew*!"

Govindaswami, who was standing just inside the

screen door, beamed a benevolent smile in the direction of this radiant light being. "In that case, Miss Melody Aiko Bernstein, it would seem the Universe is blessing you. Our own breakfast is ready now to begin." He opened the door, and Winston, who recognized the word *breakfast*—or any other word related to food—thundered up onto the porch and pushed his way between Govindaswami's silk-slipper-clad feet to get inside first.

Zedediah nodded. "Yes, of course, breakfast. You're welcome to join us, both of you. Govindaswami's cooking does require chewing." His eyes were twinkling as he stared down Melody Bernstein. She stared right back. "You, young lady, might wish to find some sort of wrap. The house is air-conditioned." He turned toward the house. "Jake, make sure there are enough chairs in the dining room for everybody."

Jake didn't respond. He was standing exactly where he'd been standing when Melody Bernstein stepped out of the bus. Like a statue, thought E.D. Like a big, dumb stone statue.

Zedediah noticed. "Jake, the chairs? *Jake!*"

Jake startled, as if he'd just been wakened from a dream.

"*Chairs,*" E.D. hissed at him through her teeth. "You're supposed to check on chairs." If she had had any regrets about having broken up with Jake, the way he was making goggle-eyes at Melody erased them. He looked as if his brains had dribbled right out the back of his head. He was clearly blind to the overwhelming vibrations of malice the girl radiated.

Yes, she was beautiful, E.D. thought, but so were the evil queens in fairy tales.

E.D. followed the rest of the family into the house. She glanced back as the screen door closed behind her. Melody and Jeremy had disappeared inside the bus. She found herself wishing as hard as she could that they would just drive away.

But, of course, they didn't. They showed up in the dining room ten minutes later, Jeremy with a fat notebook emblazoned with the name and logo of the Rutherford Foundation and stuffed with papers, brochures, and pamphlets, which he set on the buffet. Melody had thrown a large, rumpled white linen shirt over her shorts and halter. Loose and unbuttoned as it was, it didn't cover her or provide much protection against air-conditioning.

Everyone came to the table, including Hal. E.D. had expected him to revert to his hermit self after camp. She'd thought it would take months for him to recover from a summer of living in a cottage with three other humans.

As Melody took the chair Jeremy was holding out for her, Aunt Lucille stood up from her own place across the table. "Before we begin we should make formal introductions! Melody, the Applewhite family welcomes you—and Jeremy, of course—to our family table." She waved a hand toward Zedediah. "I'd like to present Zedediah, the patriarch of our clan." He nodded. Melody barely glanced his way. "Next to him is Randolph, his older son and renowned theater director; then Randolph's wife, Sybil Jameson, author of the bestselling Petunia Grantham mysteries." Melody reached for her napkin. "They're the parents of Cordelia, Hal, E.D.—which is short for Edith . . ."

Wrinkling her nose, Melody gave E.D. a look that reminded her of why she had changed her name.

". . . and, of course, Destiny," Lucille continued.

"That's me!" Destiny said, waving at Melody. "They used to call me the baby, but I'm not a baby anymore. I'm five years old and I likes to draw. . . ."

"And this is Archie," Lucille went on, overriding Destiny. "Archie is my beloved husband, and the creator of the famed Furniture of the Absurd."

Melody sighed loudly, as Govindaswami came into the dining room balancing four plates of something as aromatic and tantalizing as everything else he cooked.

"And *this*," Lucille said, putting her hands together and making a little bow in Govindaswami's direction, "is my guru, Ravi Govindaswami."

"*Guru?*" Melody said. She could, it turned out, make a single word into a sneer.

"Yes, indeed! He's a master in more ways than any of us can know."

"*My* favorite," Randolph said, as Govindaswami set one of the plates down in front of him, "is master chef!"

"I'll help serve," Cordelia said, getting up and heading for the kitchen as Govindaswami passed the other plates.

Melody wrinkled her nose when Cordelia brought her serving. "This is *breakfast*?" She poked with a fork at the steaming golden mixture on the plate in front of her. "Peas? Carrots? Potatoes?"

As he took his own seat at the table, Govindaswami nodded and added, "Cashews. Peanuts. Noodles. And peppers, of course, to help the body's cells awaken. It is vermicelli upma!"

E.D. perked up. Melody was looking at her plate with grave suspicion. The Applewhites were all used to Govindaswami's cooking, and they had trained their taste buds to handle the heat. Maybe it would be too much for Melody Bernstein?

Randolph, who had begun eating as soon as he'd been served, wiped at the sweat under his eyes with a napkin. "Spectacular!"

Good, thought E.D. *Looks like it's a spicy batch!* She watched hopefully as Melody took her first tentative bite.

The girl's eyes grew round, and her cheeks went pink. But instead of howling in pain, as E.D. had hoped, she broke into a huge smile that made her look even more beautiful than she had before. "This is *amazing*!" she said, and took another bite, and then another. She didn't even reach for the glass of grape juice that had been provided at each place setting for cooling the tongue. She had finished her first serving by the time E.D. had taken her first bite, and held her plate out. "Is there more?"

"The Universe is blessing you once again," Govindaswami said, his face wreathed in a smile as broad as his ample body. "My intuition told me this morning to make extra."

When everyone had eaten, Lucille asked all the kids to clear the table so Jeremy could spread out the contents of his notebook. Melody ignored her entirely, burped loudly, and wandered off. She didn't even clear her own plate. By the time she came back, the table was clean and Jeremy was ready to plunge into an explanation of his mysterious plans.

Melody went directly to the stove and was busily scraping Govindaswami's large frying pan with a wooden spoon to get the last crispy bits of vermicelli. As Jeremy got ready to speak, she sighed loudly. "Hey, Uncle J," she called, "do I really have to hear all this again?"

Lucille raised a hand. "Maybe someone can take Melody for a tour of Wit's End? 'The woods are lovely, dark and deep,'" Lucille said. E.D. wondered whether Melody knew Lucille was quoting a famous poem.

"And the pond is wonderfully inviting."

"I want to swim!" Destiny shouted, leaping from the step stool. "I'll go put on my suit. You get yours, too, Melody!"

Jake sat up quickly. "I'll take her on the tour. You don't have to swim," he told Melody. "I mean, unless you want to. Which you might not. But it's . . . um . . . pretty nice."

Look at him, thought E.D. with disgust as they left the dining room. *He can barely speak*.

"All right, Jeremy," said Randolph when they were gone, "what on earth are these plans you're talking about?"

"My new employers, the Rutherfords," Jeremy said, "agree with you all that the best education comes from creative exploration. They saw what you did, and what art and creativity did, to change the life of a problem kid, and they were so inspired by Zedediah's definition of education—"

That definition played itself like a recorded message in E.D.'s brain as Jeremy talked: *Education is an adventurous quest for the meaning of life, involving an ability to think things through*.

"They want their money—and they've got billions—to support art-based education. They want nothing less than a total reinvention of what school can be! So they're creating an *Education Expedition*, where groups of artists and creative types will take students across this vast country on an adventurous educational quest."

"'Across this vast country'?" Zedediah said.

"Yes. In a bus. Or rather buses. Like the one I'm in! That's the expedition part."

"And this concerns us how?" Randolph asked.

"Well, you'll be going, of course!"

"Going on an expedition," said Zedediah.

"That's right!" cried Jeremy. He was so excited he seemed not to notice how perplexed everyone else was.

"Driving across the country?" Zedediah said. E.D., whose head was spinning, thought he sounded admirably calm. "In school buses?"

Jeremy waved a pamphlet with a photo of the Art Bus on the cover. "The details are all in here. It's an adventurous quest—a kind of monumental field trip—that each group will document with video logs that will get national coverage. They're even working with a producer to make it into a television show!"

Sybil groaned. "Oh, Jeremy, not *television* again. . . ."

E.D. winced. It had been Jeremy who arranged for the television crew to come film the Applewhites' production of *The Sound of Music* and interview the whole family. That experience, with the horrible perky television personality, had been a disaster none of them would ever forget!

"This is ridiculous," said Randolph, standing up. "I

don't have time for field trips, and I have no interest in television; I'm a theater director!"

"The winning group's educational plan will be showcased nationally, and it will serve as the foundation for a national charter-school franchise," Jeremy continued quickly, as Randolph rolled his eyes and started out of the room. "And the winners will also get quite generous funding for their *own work*."

Randolph stopped in his tracks. "Funding?" he asked, turning back.

"Generous!" repeated Jeremy. "In the form of a grant and individual fellowships for the artists!"

The room was quiet for a moment. "Not to be crass," Randolph said at last, "but can you give us a dollar amount—or at least a general neighborhood. . . ."

Jeremy grinned. "The grant will be somewhere in the mid six figures."

"The mid WHAT?" hollered Randolph, incredulously.

"Six figures," said Jeremy. *Six figures*, E.D. thought. Hundreds of thousands of dollars. She worried her father might faint. He opened and closed his mouth a few times, before finally squeaking out a strangled "And fellowships, you say? Individual grants for each artist?"

"Ten, fifteen, maybe twenty thousand dollars. Each! The Rutherfords are extremely wealthy and extremely generous."

Randolph sat down at the table again.

"Doesn't that make the whole program a *competition?*" Zedediah asked. "I mean, if we decide to participate—"

"For that kind of money, we'll participate, all right," Randolph said.

"It would be like the Creative Academy, on wheels," Jeremy said, his eyes flashing. "You'd need to buy buses—you'll probably need two!—and outfit them. The Rutherfords will provide funding for that, and each group will fix them up in their own particular style. Then you take to the road, making your way to the Rutherford Art Center on the coast of California, north of LA. Learning and teaching as you go!"

"Will they provide some kind of curriculum?" E.D. asked.

Jeremy shook his head. "No, no, no! They believe life itself is the true curriculum. The whole point is for each group to creatively use what they find along their particular journeys to craft their own!"

This sounded like E.D.'s worst nightmare and everything that had always worried her about the Creative Academy. If nothing was planned, and nothing was required, how were you going to be sure anybody was actually learning anything? Or learning something that would one day get them into college?

Jeremy's cheeks were pink with enthusiasm. "Plus, you can show how art really can turn a life around, just like you did with Jake! The timing is almost miraculous. My brother and his wife were at their wits' end with Melody, but I've promised them that what happened for Jake will happen for her. Being with all of you, how could it not?"

Melody! E.D. wondered what that girl and Jake were doing out at the pond right this minute. If those short shorts and that skimpy halter top were what she considered fully clothed, what must her bathing suit look like? E.D. found herself imagining a massive snapping turtle grabbing Melody's toes.

Jeremy was passing out brochures with glossy pictures of the Rutherford Art Center around the table. "Who would we be up against?" asked Randolph, his eyes glinting.

Jeremy squeezed his eyebrows together as he thought about it. "So far the competitors are a charter school for the arts in Florida, an arts colony slash commune in Maine, a co-op school in Brooklyn, and a group of homeschooling visual artists based in San Diego—they'll make a big loop around the western states. I'm still working on getting this really interesting mime group from the Midwest and a music camp in Idaho. But if you do this, I can't see anybody else beating you. Not that I can make any promises, of course. I have to stay completely neutral."

"You're talking about a great deal of money," Zedediah observed. "But it's also a massive undertaking, and extremely disruptive to our lives. . . ."

E.D. tuned out the conversation. She was the

family's designated organizer, the only member of the clan who could be relied on to hold things together in times of crisis. She had overseen the transformation of their barn into a theater and stage-managed *The Sound of Music.* She had been the main planner of the art camp and practically single-handedly kept it going. The responsibility of organizing a roaming school, which the family was *sure* to hand over to her, made her dizzy. The thought of how much chaos the Applewhites could create, all traveling across the country together, made her palms sweat. And with Melody Aiko Bernstein along? That made her want to throw up.

Chapter Four

Jake had never been more grateful for Destiny's ability to talk endlessly without interruption or encouragement. Because every time Jake tried to talk to Melody Bernstein, it all came out wrong.

"This one is Wisteria Cottage, which is named for the flowering vines," Jake found himself saying as they toured Wit's End on the way to the pond. "Wisteria is an invasive species, actually, that was brought over from—" *Stop talking, Jake,* thought Jake.

Destiny galloped past them and onto the porch of the cottage, tottering under the pile of towels he was carrying. He already had his life jacket on. He dropped the towels and pulled open the door. "Come in, Melody, come in! You gots to see Uncle Archie's coffee table and Aunt Lucille's meditation corner and Jake's room and everything!"

Melody followed him in and looked at each thing Destiny pointed out, as Jake attempted to explain it. "Come down here, come down here!" Destiny yelled, bouncing off down the hallway. "Come see Jake's room! It's my favoritest place to be in Wit's End except for *my* room, and the goatses' pen, and the pond and the woods and the theater." Melody followed him and stared in through the door at Jake's room, which Lucille had painted and decorated entirely in lavender. Jake wished he hadn't left a pair of underwear lying right there on the floor next to the laundry hamper.

"Lavender?" Melody asked, looking at him.

"It's supposed to be calming, I guess? Lucille left it lavender when I moved in, you know, because I was . . ." He trailed off.

"Because you were a *troubled kid*," she said. Her head was tipped to the side and her hair fell across one eye. She stared straight into his eyes, and his heart went *bump-thump* against the inside of his chest.

"Okay, now let's go meet the goatses," Destiny cried, and banged back out through the cottage door.

Melody made a sound that could have been a

cough, or could have been a laugh, and walked out onto the porch. Winston went out after her and Jake followed, picking up the towels Destiny had left there.

"So," he said, as he fell in behind Melody on the path Destiny had taken toward the goat pen, "how old are you?"

"Older than you," Melody called back over her shoulder.

"Are you in high school or middle school or, well, there aren't any grades or anything in the Creative Academy, you know—nothing like eighth or ninth or—of course, it isn't really a school. Or it is, sort of. But—" *Jake,* thought Jake, *seriously, just stop talking.* He stopped talking.

Destiny had reached the goat pen and was yanking handfuls of the weeds that grew just outside the fence and holding them out for Hazel, the female goat. She chewed at them thoughtfully. "This is Hazel, short for Witch Hazel," said Destiny. "She's the lady goat and Wolfie, short for Wolfbane, is the boy goat, but he's in their little house right now, which is good because Wolfie can be kind of mean sometimes. My aunt Lucille says it's from being abused before she rescued them."

Jake hadn't thought that Melody Bernstein would have much interest in the goats, but she went straight over to the fence and knelt down directly in front of Hazel. Destiny had to scramble out of her way. Melody tucked her hair behind her ear.

"Cool eyes," she said. "Scary."

Which was exactly what Jake had always thought about the goats' eyes. They were wide, and dark, with glimmering golden irises and rectangular pupils. It was those pupils, Jake thought, that made them look scary. Blank, somehow, or empty, like a shark. Or a devil.

Melody leaned toward Hazel, staring into her eyes, her forehead an inch or two from the gate.

"Um," said Jake, "you might not want to get so—"

He was too late. Wolfie exploded through the open door of the goat hutch and charged straight for Melody, head down, his whole body at full stretch. His horns smashed into the gate just inches from Melody's face with a terrifying crack. Destiny shrieked and dove out of the way, Winston started barking, and Jake flinched even though he was standing several feet back.

Melody, however, barely moved. Wolfie rebounded from the impact and stood, glaring at her, his front feet a little bit apart, his haunches tensed for another battering attack.

"Oh yeah?" said Melody, so quietly Jake could barely hear. Then, to Jake's utter astonishment, she pulled her head back and smashed her own forehead into the gate. The crash wasn't quite as loud as Wolfie's, but it made a significant bang. She tipped her head forward and stared straight at Wolfie, totally unfazed.

The big goat slowly began to back away. Keeping an eye on Melody the whole way, he slipped back into the hutch and out of sight.

"Whoa!" breathed Destiny, from where he was still sprawled in the grass.

Melody uncoiled herself smoothly from the ground. "So," she said. "Where's this famous swimming pond?"

Destiny darted off ahead. Melody followed him, but not before Jake saw a red spot growing into a welt on her forehead. She didn't even seem to notice. Her long legs sliced easily through the tall grass of the field, which was starting to turn brown and smell like hay under the baking late-summer sun. Grasshoppers scattered, buzzing, in front of her, and Jake, towels clutched to his chest, trailed along in her wake.

They reached the pond and Destiny began a well-practiced recitation of the rules for swimming. "You gots to wait half an hour after you eat before you swim," he said, "and you can only dive off the end of the dock where it's deep—" Melody didn't even pretend she was listening. She shrugged out of her flimsy shirt and slid off her shorts, revealing a simple blue bikini underneath. She ran the length of the wooden dock and dove, knifing into the water and out of sight.

"She didn't wait for me to finish telling her the rules," said Destiny.

"No, she didn't, buddy," said Jake, dropping their

towels onto the grass. "No, she didn't."

Melody broke the surface and struck out across the pond with smooth, clean strokes. She paid no attention to them at all. Jake shrugged at Destiny, and the two of them ran, whooping, off the end of the dock.

Destiny's favorite pond game was to make Jake jump off the diving platform in the middle of the pond in various funny ways. As Jake pulled himself up onto the platform, Destiny shouted, "Do a new one! Jake! Jake! Do a new one!"

Melody was doing a lazy backstroke around the edge of the pond. Jake couldn't tell if she was watching, and wouldn't let himself look to see.

"All right," said Jake. "I've been saving this one—crisscross applesauce!"

Destiny giggled and clapped, bobbing up and down in his life vest. Jake took a running start and leaped as high as he could over the water, pulling his legs up so it looked like he was sitting cross-legged in midair. He crashed into the water butt-first and made an excellent splash, but then the water slammed in on his head, driving quite a lot of the pond straight up his nose.

He came to the surface choking and laughing, and swam back to hang off the side of the platform and cough it all out. Destiny was shouting with laughter and saying, "Again! Again! Crisscross applesauce again!" and then suddenly Melody was hanging on the side of the platform next to Jake.

"Race you back to the dock," she said, and started swimming.

Jake swam after her.

"Where you going, Jake?" Destiny hollered. "Aren't you gonna do it again?"

Melody got to the dock well ahead of Jake and began climbing the ladder. "Hey, little kid," she called.

"My name's Destiny," said Destiny.

"Yeah, yeah. I bet you don't know what kind of plant that is sticking up by the bank," she said, pointing over Destiny's head at the other shore of the pond.

Destiny turned around to look where she was pointing. "That tall one with the brown tops? That's a cattail. Cattails are my favorite because when they dry out you can break off the little puffs and let them blow away."

"You know any of the other ones?" Melody asked as Jake, who had finally caught up, climbed the ladder.

Destiny was launched now, showing off what he knew. "Jake and me knows just about all of 'em! Those big flat ones floating by the cattails are lily pads, and the green stuff near those is duckweed, and . . ."

"Come on," said Melody, heading toward the shore.

"Um, where?" asked Jake, but she was already off the end of the dock. She stooped to grab her shorts. "Mel—Melody?" called Jake, as she pulled a cigarette pack out of her shorts' pocket and waggled it at him. She winked, jammed her feet into her flip-flops, and headed toward the woods. "Um, hang on," said Jake. "I can't leave Destiny; he's not allowed to swim alone."

Melody stopped just at the edge of the trees. "He's fine," she said. "Anyway, that dog is there to watch him." Winston was lying on his back next to the dock, sound asleep. "We'll be right over here and back in like two seconds." And she stepped behind a tree.

Jake could feel his heart pounding in his chest. *I really shouldn't*, he thought. He looked back at Destiny, who was still conducting a solitary nature tour of the pond and didn't even notice they had gone. *He's fine,* Jake told himself. *He's got his life jacket on. And I'll be back in like half a minute.* Barefoot, he headed after Melody into the woods.

She was lighting the cigarette with a Zippo that looked a lot like his old one, and held it out to him seriously. "*There* he is," she said, blowing a lungful of smoke out of the side of her mouth. "I was starting to think all this bad-boy-from-the-city stuff was a big fake." Jake took the cigarette, and her fingers brushed his. He couldn't tell if it was on purpose.

It had been almost a year since Jake had smoked. Smoking wasn't allowed at Wit's End. Come to think of it, it had also been almost a year since Jake had broken the rules. Any rules. And right now he was breaking a couple of big ones. He was supposed to be watching Destiny. He wasn't supposed to be smoking, especially while hiding in the woods with a stunningly gorgeous girl. He had forgotten how exciting it could be to break the rules. He took a drag on the cigarette. It tasted great.

Then he took another drag, and his head spun and the forest floor went all spongy under his feet, like a trampoline. Suddenly the cigarette didn't taste good at all. There was a rushing sound in his ears, and he couldn't tell if it was wind, or his own heart racing, but either way he couldn't hear Destiny anymore.

"I've got to go check on Destiny." He handed her back the cigarette, and turned and headed for the dock.

Destiny was still paddling happily in the middle of the pond. He had finished identifying the freshwater flora and had moved on to the clouds. "That one there is a cumulus, and those feather ones are cirruses, and way up there . . ."

Jake sat down on the dock and watched him, and tried to catch his breath. His fingers were tingling the way they did when he was about to go onstage.

Tingling the way they used to when the old Jake Semple used to break rules.

Eventually Destiny had enough swimming, and they both dried off with the towels that were warm from sitting in the sun. When they looked for Melody, she was nowhere to be found.

Chapter Five

E.D. Applewhite was on strike.

The whole family, she thought, had always been so quick to turn to her. To organize all the things they didn't want to think about. To do the things they didn't want to do. Or find out how to do what they didn't know how to do. They just assumed E.D. would handle it. And handle it she had, holding everything together in times of crisis.

But now how did they thank her for all the times she'd done just that? All the times she'd saved them from catastrophe? They *completely ignored* what she had to say about the Education Expedition.

When the family met to discuss whether they should go, E.D. had pointed out that Wit's End needed tending, the goats needed feeding, the whole place could fall into disrepair while they were gone. But then Govindaswami agreed to stay and host his annual yoga retreat there and look after the place. She reminded Hal that he would have to live and travel and eat and sleep in close quarters with the whole rest of the family just after he—a total recluse!—had spent the summer living in a cabin with a bunch of campers. And Hal, clearly already under Melody's spell, said *that was all right*. All right! Even Zedediah, the one person she could always count on to be sensible, was so burned out from building and selling his handcrafted wood furniture to support the family and their camp that he was suddenly willing to just toss everything aside and rush off across the country in some rattly old school bus!

Nobody noticed, as they all voted yes, including Melody, who shouldn't have had a vote at all, that E.D. hadn't participated. That she wasn't smiling, she wasn't cheering and predicting a win like her father, or jumping up and down like Destiny about this so-called adventure. Nobody even noticed that E.D. didn't want to go. *She didn't want to go!*

She loved Wit's End. She loved watching the seasons change. She loved planning her curriculum for the year and then working through it one step at a time, handling every detail, completing every project, pushing herself to do better and better, genuinely earning the A's she gave herself. Most of all, she loved having everything under control. Now she was supposed to throw all that away? Drive across the whole country? How was she supposed to control *the whole country?* She couldn't create a curriculum without knowing exactly where they were going, what they would see, who they would meet, or what they were supposed to do on the way!

No. It was impossible. So she was going to sit this one out. If the family was going, she'd have to go, too. And she would take care of her own education. She'd make her own plans—somehow. But she wasn't going to lift a finger to get this Expedition on the road, or to do anything for anybody else. They could just figure it out without her.

To her horror, over the days that followed, they began to do just that.

Jake had been assigned to bus research, and he found them a gigantic modern bus for very little money at a nearby private school that had gone out of business. Archie and Zedediah set about fixing it up, and now, just a week later, it was starting to look like an RV that people could actually live in. On its outside, Cordelia and Hal were adding paintings and designs, and Archie had gotten in on the act with a big stripe made of beautiful wood siding. Even Destiny had been allowed to paint an enormous purple possum on part of one side.

Then Randolph had driven up in a smoking, shuddering, rusted-out old disaster of a bus he'd seen in a churchyard with a For Sale sign under its windshield wiper, and announced—just announced, like nobody else even had a say!—that he was going to mount a stage on the side and turn it into a traveling theater. "It's a pageant wagon!" he shouted. "Like in medieval times. They would roll giant wagons from town to town doing plays—the wagons were their stages! Theater was absolutely central to everyone's lives, and on this Expedition we're going to bring that back!"

As far-fetched as that sounded, nobody raised any objection. Randolph told Jake and Archie to build stage platforms, and two days later, there they were, sitting alongside Randolph's "Pageant Wagon." To E.D.'s growing horror, little by little, with no lists and no charts and no calendar, the Applewhites were getting ready to hit the road.

E.D. Applewhite was determinedly on strike, and the worst thing was, nobody even seemed to notice.

After a while, she started to feel seriously left out. Even worse, the "school year" ought to have started by now, and though she'd done her best to begin creating her own curriculum, just as she would have done if she were going to follow it right there at Wit's End, she couldn't keep her mind focused on it. She'd ended up reading novels instead, just to keep herself occupied. Probably everybody else was learning more than she was, just by having to get the buses ready. Except Melody, of course, who was mostly swimming and sunbathing and watching people work (especially Jake, it seemed to E.D., who, she was pretty sure, was watching Melody right back). The only person E.D. was hurting with her strike seemed to be herself.

Finally, she holed up in the classroom and got out the huge box of materials and supplies from the Rutherford Foundation that Jeremy had left behind when he drove off in the Art Bus—leaving Melody as well. She opened it and found it packed full of papers, booklets, and equipment. She felt her heart begin beating faster. *It's not like it's a treasure chest,* she told herself sternly, *it's just a box of supplies, and I don't find it at all exciting.*

First there were the maps. A full set of beautifully detailed paper maps, one for every state. She unfolded North Carolina and found Traybridge. Her finger slid across the smooth paper toward the ocean. There had been no specific instructions so far from the Rutherfords, and Randolph had announced—announced!—that the Applewhite Expedition was to be literally coast to coast. Their first stop would be a small town on the Outer Banks of North Carolina called Haddock Point, where an actor friend of his had just finished doing summer theater and where Randolph was going to debut a new production he was planning to produce on the stage of their Pageant Wagon. He had named this production *Randolph Applewhite's Theatrical Portrait of America*, and as far as E.D. could tell it had *nothing* to do with education. If she wasn't on strike, she would have said something.

At the top of the map a big gray area caught her eye. It extended up into Virginia, and it was huge. It had the most amazing name: *the Great Dismal Swamp*. E.D. was irritated. How could there be this huge place with a name like that just a few inches on a map from where they lived and she'd never even heard of it? She went to the computer and tapped in the words *Great Dismal Swamp*.

Half an hour later, her head was swimming. *This* was educational! There was so much to *know*! A young George Washington, before the Revolutionary War, had joined a survey crew as they explored and mapped the swamp. A colony of runaway slaves had hidden there for *years* during the Civil War! Not to mention all the plants and animals there were to study. All of it just map-inches away!

She couldn't help it. E.D. was hooked. After all, just because she was on strike from her family didn't mean her *own* education had to suffer. The lists, the outlines, the summaries, the projects about the Great Dismal Swamp started forming in her head. Maybe, just maybe, since she had no choice but to go along, she could get something out of this Expedition after all.

She dug back into the box of supplies. At the bottom was a big padded case with a dozen tiny video cameras, and some basic guidelines for creating video logs. That's how the Rutherfords wanted the groups to keep track of the Expedition—in videos. Fascinated, E.D. poked at the button on the top of one, and a little red light came on, winking at her. She turned it back off. Then she set it on the desk across from her, ran her fingers through her hair, and pressed the button again.

"Hi, uh," she said into the camera, and immediately felt ridiculous. "Hi," she started again, trying to sound more confident. "E.D. Applewhite here, video log number, um . . . number one. I guess." *Smooth,* she thought. "So, my first proposed stop on the Expedition will be the Great Dismal Swamp. It's interesting to note," she added, trying to smile into the camera, "that the water there is the color of iced tea, and you can drink it right out of the lake, because it has so much tannic acid in it that no bacteria can grow there. So," she ended, fizzling out somewhat, "I just thought that was interesting. Okay, let's see how the buses are coming along, I guess."

She paused the recording and headed out across the compound. She filmed the Pageant Wagon, where power saws and drills sat among mounds of sawdust piled up like snowdrifts. She filmed Aunt Lucille stitching rainbow-colored fabric into curtains, to cover the opening to the back of that bus where she and Uncle Archie would share a bed. E.D. filmed the narrow bunks, one mounted above the other, where Zedediah and Jake were to sleep.

Uncle Archie grinned into the camera. "Just like on a submarine," he said, and then went back to screwing the bunks to the wall.

E.D. paused the recording and walked over to the big bus, which everyone had for some reason started calling Brunhilda. Inside Brunhilda she found Zedediah installing a tiny refrigerator. She started filming him.

"Check out the bathroom!" cried her grandfather, pointing to a tiny room that had a small sink bowl and a showerhead directly above the toilet. E.D. panned the camera down to show the drain in the middle of the linoleum-lined floor. "The whole bathroom is waterproof," Zedediah told her happily, "and doubles as the shower stall. Clever, huh? I'm stringing up a hammock for Destiny. I told him he can sleep like a real pirate; he loved that. Hal put a platform on the roof, says he's going to pitch a tent up there. And check out your space! The dining table folds down and becomes part of a regular double-sized bed. At night you and Melody just fold it down, flip the cushions, and it becomes the bunk you two will share."

E.D. snapped the camera off and, her heart beating a mile a minute, headed back to the schoolroom. She would not—*would not!*—share a bed with that girl. Cordelia, maybe. Even Destiny. But absolutely and certainly not with Melody!

Three days later, E.D. had begun to think she was going to be saved from the Expedition after all. One thing after another was going wrong.

The work wasn't finished. The Pageant Wagon, it turned out, wouldn't go more than fifty miles per hour, and even at that speed sounded like someone was murdering a barrel full of cats. Jake tried to explain to Randolph that there were two kinds of school buses, one for city driving and one for highway driving, but Randolph just shouted "Details!" and went into his room to sulk. Nobody could figure out how to mount the stage on the Pageant Wagon, either—with just two platforms bolted to it, the whole bus leaned over like it was going to capsize. Neither bus had air-conditioning, and they got so hot in the sun that work had to stop each afternoon. "It's like an oven!" Archie shouted, swiping at his forehead with an already-soaked handkerchief.

Worst of all, one morning Destiny came out of Brunhilda holding his nose and looking green. "Poopy!" he declared. Sure enough, the RV toilet they had installed, and had been using while they worked, to save time, was making the whole bus smell like an overheated porta potty.

Zedediah, his face dark and cloudy, announced they'd have to postpone the beginning of the Expedition. Their intended departure day came and went, and the Applewhites were still at Wit's End.

But then, just as it seemed certain the whole Expedition would end before it even started, the postponement turned out to save the day. Because the very next morning, Bill Bones came into their lives.

Govindaswami's yoga retreat had been scheduled to start that morning, since the Applewhites thought they'd be gone already. When E.D. woke up, the grass parking lot next to their barn theater already had a scattering of cars. She went out to where Destiny was moving among the vehicles, most of them old and funky and covered in political or spiritual bumper stickers. "Visualize Whirled Peas," read one. "Something Wonderful Is About to Happen," read another. Destiny was standing by a rusty orange VW van staring at the biggest, ugliest motorcycle E.D. had ever seen. It had spikes on it, and long tailpipes that looked likely to drag on the ground. The handlebars stuck way up in the air and had long leather tassels. Startlingly realistic flames were painted on the side of the gas tank. At the end of each handgrip was a chrome skull with rubies for eyes.

"Whoa," said Destiny quietly. "Is there *pirates* at Govindaswami's retreat?"

Just then E.D. saw Lucille's guru bustle out onto the porch of the main house. She hurried over to him, Destiny tagging behind. "Govindaswami," she said, "where are all the people for your retreat going to stay? We aren't out of the cottages yet!"

Govindaswami beamed at her. "It is a complication to be sure, but when you trust in the Universe, the Universe will provide. Last year the retreat center I had used before burned to the ground—an accident with the incense—and my meditation retreat had to take place at a campground. You see? The Universe has already ensured that I am well provided with tents." He waved toward the far side of the parking lot, where a dozen or so people, clad mostly in homespun shirts and yoga pants, were bustling around setting up tents.

"They look like they're taking it in stride," E.D. said.

Govindaswami took a long, slow breath. "Most are skilled at the practice of *acceptance*, and are, as you say, taking it in their stride. But not all." A look passed over his round face that E.D. had never seen there before—a look that on anyone else might be irritation.

From inside there was the sound of large boots pounding slowly across the floor, and the screen door banged open. A gigantic man with a thick mane of white hair and a drooping silver mustache that reached down past his chin strode onto the porch. Rings shone from each knuckle, and tattoos reached up his neck from the collar of his dirty white T-shirt.

He had black leather pants and a heavy chain that ran from his belt to his back pocket. Destiny stared at him with eyes like pie plates, and E.D. found herself taking an involuntary step back.

"Swami!" he bellowed. "All the bedrooms are occupied! I signed up for an air-conditioned room, not a tent!" He noticed E.D. and Destiny and pulled up short. "Why, you must be some of the Applewhites!" he cried. He strode toward E.D., and it took all her concentration not to turn and run.

The man stuck out a hand the size of a large steak, but his handshake was surprisingly gentle. "Heard lots about the famous artistic clan; it's a pleasure to meet you. My name's Bill Bones. Thought I wasn't going to get the chance to meet you in person—Swami said you'd be on your way by now."

"Yes," said E.D., "we've had some delays—"

The giant man roared with laughter. "Swami told me! Bus trouble, is it? Well, I happen to know a little bit about that. Let's get a look at your rigs." And without a backward glance, he stomped off across the yard toward where the Pageant Wagon and Brunhilda were already starting to bake in the morning sun.

"Let me guess," E.D. said quietly to Govindaswami. "He belongs to the motorcycle out there in the parking lot."

"Your guess is indeed correct." Govindaswami sighed. "Sometimes we have to accept a good deal of spice before the sweet."

By the time everyone, family and retreat participants alike, had gathered that night for dinner in the dining tent, now strung with colorful Tibetan prayer flags, Bill Bones had met the rest of the Applewhites and Jake and Melody, had been invited to share Zedediah's air-conditioned cottage, and had begun sketching out fixes for the buses with Archie and Zedediah.

Govindaswami blessed the food and reminded the assembled members of his retreat group that the meal was to be eaten in silence. Bill Bones—who had seated himself among the Applewhites—immediately began talking in a loud stage whisper. "Spent many a year living out of an old diesel Blue Bird bus back in the sixties. Converted the thing myself—and did a couple later for some other folk. I can probably get yours fixed up within the week. If Govindaswami will let us borrow some of the fine folks from his retreat to help with the work . . ."

"You, too, are on the meditation retreat, Bill Bones," said Govindaswami quietly.

"Why, that I am! And what better way to grow spiritually than through the mindfulness of manual labor?"

Chapter Six

Four days after the arrival of Bill Bones, the work crew, which included a few recruits from the meditation retreat, had the buses shipshape. A new vent was in Brunhilda's bathroom. "No more poopy smell!" cried Destiny, who had taken to following the big man around all day and whose arms and legs were now decked with tattoos of his own Magic Marker design. A pair of army surplus generators were wired into the electrical systems of Brunhilda and the Pageant Wagon, and a pair of RV air-conditioning units Bones had salvaged from a junkyard nearby were humming away, cooling them nicely. Along with everything else he could do, Bill Bones turned out to be an experienced welder and had managed to fashion a metal-framed fold-down stage for the Pageant Wagon that tucked up against the side when it was time to get on the road. When that project was finished Randolph looked, Jake thought, ready to weep with joy.

On the fifth morning, Jake woke up to the sound of the Pageant Wagon roaring to life just before dawn, as Bill Bones drove it away without any explanation. Randolph had a meltdown when he got up a few hours later, thinking the man might have stolen his beloved rolling theater. Sybil managed to keep him from calling the police, and by midafternoon Bones and the Pageant Wagon were back. "Swapped out the rear end—" he began to explain when everyone came to see what he'd been doing.

Destiny giggled. "The bus has a rear end?"

"Indeed it does, little man—but not like a butt," Bones added, and Destiny choked with laughter. "It's the big thing on the axle between the wheels in the back; it's got a set of gears in it that turn the wheels. It needed one with different-sized gears, which my guy at the junkyard found for me. You can run that beauty on the highway any time now." Jake had told Randolph that some school buses were made for city streets and some were for highways, but this was the first time he'd really understood how that worked.

"Bill Bones," said Govindaswami, "you have achieved wonderful things. But I must ask that you and your helpers return to our meditation and spiritual practice before any more time has passed from our retreat."

"Swami," said Bill, "I've known a number of gurus in my day, and you're among the best. But I believe these buses have put the old travel itch back in me, and sitting around breathing slow just won't cut it anymore. I'm getting back on my bike and heading west."

An hour later Bill Bones had packed up his bags. "Where're you headed when this Expedition of yours starts?" he asked the family, who had gathered to say good-bye.

"To the Outer Banks, then west as well," said Randolph. "Destination: California."

"Maybe I'll catch you all somewhere out there." He went over to Govindaswami and pressed his hands together for a solemn little bow. "*Namaste*, guru."

"*Namaste*, Bill Bones."

"What's *nah mahz tay?*" asked Destiny, putting his hands together and bowing.

Melody, who was standing next to him filming Bill's departure with one of the Expedition video cameras, turned it off. "It means the spirit in me bows to the spirit in you," she said.

Govindaswami looked in amazement from Destiny to Melody, to the driveway where the dust Bill Bones had kicked up drifted in the air. "Let this be a lesson to me," Jake heard him say softly. "Human people have always the capacity to surprise you."

And finally, it was time to get the Education Expedition on the road. Jake looked at the buses and had to admit they were a sight to behold. Every member of the Applewhites with a talent for the visual arts had contributed some design to the outside of Brunhilda, and the side of the Pageant Wagon was painted to look like an old-fashioned stage, complete with painted-on red velvet curtains and an ornate archway around the stage Bill Bones had mounted on the side. No one seeing them would even for a moment think *school buses*.

The plan was to leave the next morning at nine o'clock, drive to Haddock Point, set up, and rehearse for the *Theatrical Portrait of America*. They were to do two shows and a weekend matinee, and that would be their first Expedition stop.

The big morning came and it quickly became clear that this schedule, too, was going to be disrupted. The buses, cool as they looked, didn't actually turn out to have much storage space, and every single Applewhite had brought more than enough to fill all the available space. Everybody except for Melody, who had just a backpack and a small duffel bag, and E.D., who was sitting on the porch with her own small bag, watching everybody bicker.

For about the thousandth time, Jake wondered what the heck was going on with E.D. She should have had lists of what to pack, and limits on what everybody could bring, and packing plans to make it all fit! But she hadn't said a word, hadn't lifted a finger to get the Expedition going. Bossy, hyperorganized E.D. had been locked in the schoolroom, surrounded by notebooks and maps and outlines, but she never said anything to anybody. It was like she didn't want the Expedition to happen at all!

The only person who had been *less* helpful was Melody, but Jake suspected that was pure laziness. The only thing she'd taken any interest in at all were the video cameras—once E.D. had gotten them out, Melody always seemed to have one in her hand, and at least once a day she dragged Hal away from his work to show her the video-editing software he'd installed on his computer. Other than that, she hadn't done a single thing. While everyone else worked, she worked on her tan, or swam laps in the pond, or ate serving after serving of Govindaswami's cooking.

Jake, who had been sleeping maybe six hours each night and running around like crazy the rest of the time, found himself thoroughly fed up with both of them.

Eventually, somehow, with much shouting and argument, everyone's stuff was either packed aboard or left behind. Things were piled on every available surface in both buses—Jake found his entire bunk in the Pageant Wagon stuffed full of giant boxes of groceries—but the Applewhites, including Winston, were ready to get on the road.

Randolph declared that he would drive Brunhilda, since that's where he and Sybil would be sleeping. "Typical," Jake heard Archie mutter as he climbed into the Pageant Wagon's driver's seat and yanked on the handle to slam the door shut. "He buys this rattling rust bucket and leaves *me* to drive it." He cranked the key and, with a roar, the wagon sputtered to life.

They waved good-bye to Govindaswami, Randolph hollered "FORWARD!" out his window and shifted Brunhilda into gear, and the Applewhites' Education Expedition rattled down the driveway and out into the world.

Looking back on it later, Jake would be amazed at how little he remembered of the details of the first stop of the Expedition. His brain felt so full of new experiences that everything else just tumbled out like his head was an overstuffed grocery bag.

He remembered the feeling of rumbling down the road in the Pageant Wagon. It was so loud that conversation was almost impossible, so everybody did their own thing. Archie drove, Zedediah sat reading a book and periodically consulting a map in the "copilot" seat, and Lucille lay down on the bed in the back "to recover from the exhaustion of these last days." Jake mostly just stared out the window and watched everything go by, as they passed from the farmland around Traybridge, through the woods, and eventually out into the salty marshes of the coast. It was late when they got in, and the sun was setting behind them as Brunhilda and the Pageant Wagon roared across the causeway and descended on the sleepy beach town of Haddock Point.

He did remember his first sight of Randolph's actor friend, Simon Rathbone. As they pulled the buses to a stop in the town's main square, an alarmingly tall and thin figure seemed to unfold out of the shadows in front of the little theater, raising a bony arm in greeting. As Randolph clambered down from Brunhilda, Rathbone drew him into a spidery embrace and intoned, in a voice that was surprisingly deep and rich from such a thin frame, "Randolph, my dearest boy, many welcomes. Do come and meet your troupe."

That night was a blur, as they found parking places for the buses and set up the stage, unpacked enough to free up the bunks, ate a hurried dinner that Lucille insisted on cooking over the camp stove they'd brought but which mostly consisted of canned beans, and settled in for a restless first sleep. As Jake lay in his bunk, the hum of the generators and the air-conditioning wasn't quite enough to mask the sounds of other people settling into bed, rolling over restlessly, making the springs of the bus squeak with every movement. Finally, just as he was drifting off, someone farted. From the bunk above, Jake heard Zedediah chuckle quietly, and then sigh.

They had arrived so late that the only rehearsal was crammed into the day of the first performance, so that, too, went by in a rush. In his hurry to put the show together on short notice, Randolph had accepted just about anything proposed by the actors who had agreed to stay after their summer season in Haddock Point, so there was a grab bag of songs, scenes, and speeches. Two young actors from a nearby community college were doing the balcony scene from *Romeo and Juliet*, which Randolph justified as part of a *Theatrical Portrait of America* by having Jake do a song from *West Side Story*, the musical based on *Romeo and Juliet* but set in New York.

As to the performance itself, Jake wished he *didn't* remember it. The afternoon sun glared down on the town square, and if Haddock Point had crowds during the summer, they had all gone home now that the season was over. A picnicking family, some confused-looking teenagers, and a handful of kids who quit playing soccer to come see what was going on were their whole audience. Jake sang his song, the actors did their scenes, and overall nobody seemed particularly interested.

The last part of the show was to be Cordelia, dancing the solo ballet she had choreographed. By that time the audience had started wandering away. But then, just as Jake was wondering whether Randolph was going to step in and stop the whole thing, Melody appeared from behind the Pageant Wagon and started mimicking Cordelia's every movement. Jake could tell she was making fun of Cordelia, but she looked so serious about it as she flung herself back and forth that he couldn't help but chuckle. So did what was left of the audience, including those who had started away but now turned back to watch. Soon they were all laughing outright, and Cordelia finally stopped in confusion and looked behind her. Just in the nick of time, Melody stopped dancing and started a round of applause for Cordelia, which the audience happily joined. Cordelia, still looking baffled, smiled graciously and bowed, then brought the rest of the troupe out for a final curtain call. The tiny crowd clapped gamely and then dispersed.

As they went, Jake saw Melody making a beeline for one of the video cameras, which she had set up on a tripod facing the stage.

Destiny came running around from behind the Pageant Wagon. "Nine-one-one!" he yelled. "Daddy says I gotta get everybody together at the theater across the street for a 'mergency meeting, nine-one-one!"

"That," cried Randolph angrily, once the whole team had assembled, "was a fiasco of the highest degree. Troupe, I thank you for your service, and I release you from the obligation of putting yourself through that again. It was a pleasure to meet you, but you may go."

The actors, looking puzzled, stood and said their good-byes and slowly drifted off. Simon Rathbone came around and shook hands with each of the Applewhites, pausing to stare intently into Jake's eyes. "You, young man," he said quietly, "have a splendid voice and a wonderful stage presence. Working with you was a very great pleasure indeed." Jake, whose favorite part of the thrown-together show had been Rathbone's performance of a speech from a play called *Death of a Salesman*, blushed deeply and nodded his thanks.

"Thank you, Simon," said Randolph, gripping his friend by the shoulders. "I will make this up to you."

"I'll hold you to that," Rathbone answered with a sly grin, and then slunk away down the street.

Randolph was still standing as if he had something to say, and for once the Applewhites waited quietly. Everyone looked glum. Applewhites, Jake thought, were used to succeeding in what they did.

Jake noticed that Melody, on the far side of the stage, had her camera out, its red light on.

"This," Randolph began at last, "was an unmitigated

disaster! It was my fault—I should have known better." Jake wondered if anyone else was as stunned by this admission as he was. "In the rush to come up with a performance of some kind, I neglected the fundamental requirement of great theater—narrative structure."

"What's narrative structure?" Melody called from behind her camera.

"*The arc of story.* Beginning, middle, end. Rising action, climax, resolution. There's a protagonist, of course. A hero. With clear needs."

"Needs?" Melody repeated. Surprisingly, Jake thought, she seemed to be really interested. Her camera was focused on Randolph.

"What the protagonist *wants*—intentions, motivations. And those needs are opposed by clear obstacles. The audience is pulled into the action because they are following the dramatic question. Will he—or she—manage to overcome those obstacles? Suspense!"

"Fascinating," said Melody.

"Well, it is!" cried Randolph. "That structure has underpinned the art of theater since the Greeks! An audience wants story! In the pressure of the moment, I let myself be lured into presenting a mere hodgepodge of entertainment. No *story* for an audience to sink its teeth into!"

"Well," said Zedediah, rubbing his face thoughtfully. "Isn't this what this Expedition is supposed to be about? Learning through life experience? You seem to have learned something here."

Randolph glared at his father. "Maybe what I've learned is that I can't afford to take time out of my *real* career to be dragged across the country in a parade of rattletrap garbage cans on wheels!" He drew himself up to his full height. "If anyone needs me, I will be down the street at the dining establishment so quaintly entitled EAT."

There was a stunned silence before Zedediah pushed himself to his feet. "And thus concludes the first stop of the Education Expedition. I think we can all agree that, if we choose to continue, we have a lot of work to do. Or, of course"—he paused dramatically—"there is also the choice to abandon the whole thing altogether!" Jake realized he had stopped breathing. "Everybody take some time to consider this, and we can make a decision at dinnertime."

Jake watched the others leave. He did *not* want this Expedition to end when it had only just begun!

"What's with the face?" asked Melody, who had come up beside him so quietly that he jumped. She laughed and punched him on the shoulder.

"I don't want them to give up on the Expedition."

"So what are you going to *do* about it? Weren't you listening to Big Randy up there?" As down as he felt, Jake had to grin at that. He wondered how Randolph would feel about being called *Big Randy*. "You want to do this Expedition, right?" Jake nodded. "Right. Me, too. So that's our *want,* our *need,* our *intention*. And it looks like Randolph, at least, is giving up, right?" Jake nodded again. "There you go. Obstacle. What that means"—she leaned in conspiratorially—"is that we have everything we need to build ourselves some *dramatic structure*."

Jake took a deep breath and tried to share her confidence. "Okay, so what do we do?"

"Maybe we get ourselves a table in that restaurant before dinner. We meet up and talk."

"Who?"

"*Us*. The young'uns—the *protagonists*. The heroes. The kids. Education Expedition. This will be *our* story."

Destiny had lagged behind when the others left. "Can I meet up, too? I'm a kids! Do I gets to be a hero? Can I wear a cape?"

"Sure, runt," said Melody, and he skipped away happily. "You," she pointed at Jake, "tell Hal and Princess."

"Oh, jeez," said Jake. "Is Cordelia even talking to you? You made fun of her pretty bad out there."

"Not as far as she knows," Melody said. "I found her right afterward to tell her how hurt I was that the audience laughed at me."

"Laughed at *you*?"

"Yup. When I was just trying to dance as wonderfully as she was." Melody's deep, dark eyes twinkled.

Jake shook his head. "You mean she bought that?"

Melody leaned way in. He could smell her shampoo. Coconut. "Oh, kid. Don't you know by now? I can be very convincing. Besides, most people will believe you if you tell them what they already hope is true. By the time I was done she had agreed to give me lessons." She snorted and then winked at him. "We'll get together and see about overcoming some obstacles."

Chapter Seven

E.D. hurried after her father's emergency meeting, wanting very much to get back to Brunhilda before anyone else. She needed to be alone. She could already tell that *alone* wasn't easy to accomplish on this Expedition that she had *so* wanted not to happen. And now, again, there was a possibility it might not happen after all. That should make her happy. Very happy. There was *so* much she hated about it. Sharing the dinette-bed with Melody had been horrible, all elbows and knees and tossing and turning! And she had no idea how Hal had survived the brutally hot night in his tent on Brunhilda's roof.

She opened Brunhilda's door and Winston greeted her, whuffling. "Come on," she said to him, grabbing his leash from the dashboard and her video camera from the dinette table. "Let's walk!"

They started across the patchy grass of the town park, Winston stopping to sniff at every tree—"checking his pee-mail," as her grandfather called it. E.D. looked from Brunhilda, parked on the street, to the Pageant Wagon, still standing in its painted glory next to the town's little war memorial. The two buses stood out in Haddock Point like flamingos on a chicken farm. If it weren't for the Expedition, these flamingos wouldn't exist, she thought.

"Beach," she said to Winston. "We haven't seen the beach yet."

The town was so empty she half expected to see tumbleweeds rolling down the streets like an old western ghost town. Other than the park and the theater, the "downtown"—such as it was—boasted a bank; a tiny library; a gas station; a church; a wood-fronted building that seemed to be a combination grocery, drugstore, and post office; the restaurant whose sign just read EAT; and a souvenir shop that specialized in T-shirts, saltwater taffy, and souvenirs made of shells. E.D. pulled Winston to a stop and panned her camera along the street, trying to get every detail of the town. "The bustling town of Haddock Point," she narrated.

She was starting to enjoy using the camera instead of taking notes.

They walked on, then, past two bed-and-breakfasts and a couple of blocks of houses up on stilts before they found the beach. The vast ocean stretched, in multiple shades of blue, to where it met the sky and she caught her breath at the sight. A few families were there, getting the last out of the afternoon, the kids digging in the sand or running back and forth in the unimpressive waves. There weren't any dogs but there weren't any signs forbidding them, either, so E.D. let Winston off his leash. He padded down toward the water to check it out, his heavy paws sinking into the wet sand where the last wave was on its way back to sea.

As she watched him pad around, E.D. sat in the sand. She dug her fingers into it and picked up handfuls, even though it was hot enough to burn her, almost. She let it slip through her fingers. There was no sand, no beach, no *ocean*, at Wit's End.

She felt totally unsettled. She felt lost. And somehow, some small piece of her felt an unexpected tingle of pure delight. Haddock Point was new. It was different. She thought of all the other *different* places there were between this ocean and the one on the other side of the continent. But she didn't *want* this Expedition! Did she?

Just then a wave, bigger than the rest, ambushed Winston and sent him tumbling, ears flapping, through the foam. The startled dog struggled to his feet, shook himself, and sneezed three times.

That's how I feel, thought E.D. as she went to put him back on his leash. *I feel like I've been picked up and turned over.*

E.D. got back to the buses, put Winston back in Brunhilda, and was headed for EAT when Melody suddenly came up behind her, grabbed her arm, and pulled her over toward the building. E.D. shook herself loose. Melody was standing uncomfortably close, staring at her intensely with those dark eyes.

"Hi," Melody said after a long moment.

"Hi," said E.D. tentatively.

"Okay, so . . . you won."

E.D. blinked. "What do you mean, I won?"

"I mean," Melody continued, "this whole deal doesn't work without you. We're just a few hours from home, the Expedition hasn't even successfully completed the very first stop, and it's already a wreck. You win. You didn't want to do it, so you killed it."

"It isn't a *wreck.*"

"Yeah? So what kind of a grade would you give it?" Melody asked.

E.D. really didn't want to answer. She had the uncomfortable sensation that she'd fallen into a trap Melody had set. Finally she sighed. "Maybe a C," she said.

"That is being super generous," Melody said. "How many nationwide education competitions do you think could be won with a C?"

"*I* didn't even want to do this Expedition. I'm not going to work my butt off for something I didn't want to do in the first place. So yes," E.D. spat back, "I've just been worrying about my own self."

"Fine, then. This is *your* home school. So what grade do you give *yourself*?" E.D. blinked again. "Come on," Melody insisted, "I know you grade yourself, because you're a gigantic nerd. What's on your own report card right about now?"

E.D. swallowed hard. She hadn't done any of the work she would have already done—notes, reports, presentations, outlines—in a regular school year. All she'd done was make some plans about the Great Dismal Swamp, and they might not even end up going there. She squelched a ridiculously childish impulse to stick her tongue out at Melody.

"Okay, okay. Point taken," she said at last. "I'd give myself a C, too." She paused and her stomach sank. "Maybe a C minus." She groaned. Never in her life had she had a grade that low.

"Okay, then," Melody said. "There's a whole lot riding on this Expedition, for a lot of people. We all win. Or we all lose. Think about what you *really* want." She turned, whipping her long black hair in E.D.'s face as she went. "And then come to the kids' table in the restaurant and let us know what you've decided. We want to make this happen and we've gotta know where you stand."

E.D. smacked a mosquito that landed on her arm, and wondered if the smear of blood it left behind was her own. She remembered how she'd felt at the beach, how it felt to be in a new place with the prospect of a trip across the whole continent, with new places all the way. And new stuff to learn about in every one of them. She could learn, and she could probably even organize it so that everyone else did, too. It's the kind of thing she could do, and do well—and give herself a good grade for it when she did. All she had to do was give up her strike.

She sighed a deep sigh, waited a bit to make the point that Melody couldn't order her around, and then followed her, aware that the tingly feeling in her stomach could only be excitement.

Cordelia had already settled at a table in the small dining room at EAT and the other kids were joining her, taking all the chairs.

From the adjoining bar came the sound of Applewhites arguing and a general background hum of other voices.

"Here's the thing," Melody said after the waitress had taken their order and left. "Your dad is really smart."

E.D. was so surprised she wondered if her mouth actually fell open.

"Dramatic structure. Arc. *Story*. That's how we're

gonna win this competition."

"I hate competition," growled Cordelia.

"Only when you *lose*," Melody said. "You are really, really *good*! Do you want to keep dancing, alone, in a shack in Bumblebutt, North Carolina? Or do you want the whole country to notice you? Money and attention and offers pouring in from all over the place to dance, do your choreography, compose your music, paint—whatever." Cordelia opened her mouth, then shut it again. "Yeah, that's what I thought."

"Do you really think the Expedition is such a big deal? I mean beyond the prize money," asked Jake.

"Uncle Jeremy's told me all about these guys—the Rutherfords. They have so much money it'd make your eyes water. And they get their kicks out of giving it away to make the world 'a better place.' *Their way*, of course. Through *art*. Believe me, this is a *very* big deal! Nationwide television exposure. A chance to be *stars*!"

"Your uncle Jeremy is a flake," huffed Cordelia.

"Says the Crown Princess of the Flake Empire," Melody shot back. "So, what's our motivation here? Do you *want* to do this Expedition? Do you want to *win* this Expedition? The only ones who'll get the big-deal TV thing will be the *winners*. Nobody cares about the guys who lose."

Jake looked at his fingertips. The front of his floppy Mohawk fell into his eyes, and E.D. had a sudden impulse to reach out and brush it away. She caught herself with a shiver.

"I want to go," Jake said at last. "I want us to do it."

"Yeah," said Melody. "Me, too." Jake looked up at her and smiled with what looked like gratitude.

That smile went into E.D.'s heart like an icicle.

"What about the rest of you? Do you want to do this Expedition?"

"Oh, my gosh, yes I do," said Destiny, his eyes big and wide. "I wants to see that other ocean. And mountains! This is the greatest thing that's ever happened in my whole life ever."

"Noted. Princess?"

Cordelia sighed dramatically. "I'd be willing to give it another try." Hal was nodding along with her.

Just then the waitress brought their food and everyone's attention shifted. When they'd finished eating, Melody turned her most evil-queen look on E.D.

"So. How about you, Professor? This is it. The moment of decision. You gonna go for an A plus?" Melody reached out, then, and touched her lightly on the arm. "Honestly, my plan needs you most of all." She smiled a smile so warm and infectious that E.D. had to concentrate to keep from smiling back. "This whole Expedition, this whole competition—it's just a story, like one of your father's plays. Whoever tells the Rutherfords the best story is going to win. I've been telling stories my whole life, making everybody—parents, teachers, boys—think what I want them to think."

"Your parents think you're a delinquent," E.D. objected. "They pulled you out of school and sent you to us."

"Bingo, genius. *They pulled me out of school.* Do you think school is where I wanted to be? If we're going to win this thing we have to tell the Rutherford Foundation the *story they want to hear.*"

"So what is that?"

"I've got that part, don't even worry about it." Melody waved her hand dismissively. "Think arts and education. The adults in your family are into the art part. What happened here shows how much we need *you* for the education part."

Everybody was looking at E.D. hopefully.

"I . . . I'll consider it." She would have said yes—*wanted to say yes*—but it was Melody asking. It felt as if she'd be working for Melody. Then she thought about the Great Dismal Swamp. If she took over, that could be their next stop.

"Okay, moving on," Melody said. "Our *intention* is to get this Expedition back on track and win it. Our *obstacles*? It looks like the adults might be just about to quit the whole thing. Will they? Won't they? Suspense!"

Jake shook his head. "But how do we keep them from quitting?"

"If you believe dear Aunt Lucille and her guru, we don't *have* to. We just set our *intention* and turn it over to the Universe. This disaster here was just 'the spice before the sweet.'" Her eyes were twinkling but she didn't sound entirely sarcastic. "This is going to be *our* story. Agreed?" The others all nodded.

Destiny was talking now, and E.D. tuned him out. She was near the doorway into the bar, and she scooted her chair closer, hoping to hear what the adults were saying. But they seemed all to be talking at once, and she couldn't make out the words. Her eyes drifted to the television over the bar, which was showing a newsperson doing an interview. It took her a minute to realize the person being interviewed was Jeremy Bernstein.

She jumped up from the table and ran into the bar. "Everybody, look!" she shouted, pointing up at the television. The bartender and the other patrons turned around to see what the fuss was about. "Can you turn the sound on?" On-screen, Jeremy was still talking, with a caption below him that read, "Education Expedition."

The bartender got the sound turned on. ". . . instead of a bus taking you *to* the school," Jeremy was saying, "the Rutherfords propose that the bus can *be* the school!"

The camera cut to an older couple, with the caption "Larry and Janet Rutherford." E.D. didn't know what superrich people were supposed to look like, but whatever it was, the Rutherfords didn't look like it. They looked like they worked at a health food store.

"Education in America is dying," said Larry Rutherford forcefully, "and it needs a radical plan to save it."

"As we speak," said Janet Rutherford, "teams of world-renowned artist-educators are preparing to set off across the country with their students, in a competition to see who has the best new ideas to revive American education!"

The shot cut back to the reporter, a tall young woman with elegant hair and a nice suit. She was standing in front of Jeremy's Art Bus. "We'll be following this Expedition for the next two months," she said. "Keep an eye out in your town for buses like this one."

The story ended, a commercial started, and the bartender muted the TV again. "Hey," he said, "is that what those funky buses parked out there are about? Are you guys famous?"

Randolph cleared his throat. "Yes," he said. "And yes."

The bartender nodded and smiled. "Cool," he said, and went back to cleaning glasses with a rag.

Melody had been right about everything after all, E.D. thought. Even the *Universe* seemed to be on her side. After that there was no doubt that the Expedition was on!

Half an hour later, on the way back to Brunhilda, E.D. asked her grandfather about stopping at the Great Dismal Swamp to start the education part right away. "We could get some great video logs."

"That would be an excellent plan," he said, "except that they've started handing out *assignments.* We just got our first one from Jeremy," he said. "Your mother is going to run the next stop. She's making plans with a library there already. There's no time for an unnecessary side trip."

E.D. stopped in the middle of the sidewalk. Her grandfather had called the swamp an *unnecessary side trip.* Suddenly, she didn't care one bit what Melody's plans for the kids to take over the Expedition were. *She was all in.*

Chapter Eight

They managed to get on the road by eight thirty the next morning, with Archie driving the roaring Pageant Wagon in front, Randolph driving Brunhilda behind. Destiny wanted to ride in the Pageant Wagon this time and was perched precariously on the rolls of cable on Lucille and Archie's bed. He insisted that Jake sing songs with him until Zedediah asked them to please stop.

At the first rest area, Melody came bursting out of Brunhilda with E.D. in tow. She grabbed Jake by the hand and led them back into the Pageant Wagon's bedroom, pulling the curtain closed across the doorway and wheeling around to face them with conspiratorial zeal.

"Okay," she began without any preface, "what do we know about this next stop?"

E.D. squinted at her for a moment and then spoke up. "Clayton, Tennessee. Grandpa said the assigned art form is literature, which is why my mother said she'd organize it. I think she's been on her phone with a librarian there."

Melody nodded. "I did some eavesdropping on that call, and as far as I can tell, her *workshop* isn't anything but her reading the chapters of *Petunia Possum, Detective* that she's written so far, with some time for the children to tell her how wonderful they thought it was."

E.D. sighed. "That's what I was afraid of."

"Not a winning program, and boring as death on camera," Melody agreed. "So now what?"

Jake looked from one to the other, both of them totally wrapped up in planning and paying no attention to him whatsoever. The sun at Haddock Point had brought out E.D.'s scattering of freckles and her eyes had the intense look they got when she was focused. Melody was tucking a long, sleek strand of black hair behind her ear, and her linen shirt was hanging loosely around her. Jake suddenly noticed E.D. staring at him over the pencil she was chewing on, and yanked his eyes away from both of them to peer innocently out the window.

"I mean," E.D. said after a while, "I do have *one* idea, but it feels risky."

"I like the sound of this already, Professor," said Melody, grabbing E.D.'s shoulder. "And I like the look on your face. If I didn't know you better, I'd say you've got some mischief in mind."

E.D. just smiled and pulled out her phone. She punched in a number, and while it was ringing she took a deep breath. When she spoke, her voice was deeper and more grown-up-sounding than usual. "Hello, Clayton Public Library?" she asked. "Yes, hello. This is Sybil Jameson's executive assistant. . . ."

Later that day, as they pushed on toward Tennessee, Jake just stared out the window as the North Carolina countryside rolled back the other way, and thought about Melody. Then E.D. Then Melody again. His life, he thought, had become very complicated.

It was their first night in a proper campground, and E.D. had (of course) taken care of everything. It was very good to have her back in gear, Jake thought. She had spoken to the lady at check-in about switching their sites to the kind you can pull a big RV straight through, so that Archie and Randolph didn't have to back them into place. ("They'd knock down every tree within a mile," E.D. had said). It was already getting dark when they pulled in. There were water, sewer, and electrical hookups, and they had to start working with flashlights, everybody bustling around to get set up—everyone, of course, except Melody, who brought out a portable light bar from the video equipment storage and wandered around recording everything with her camera.

At one point Randolph opened Brunhilda's blackwater tank—which held what Destiny cheerfully called the "poop water"—before Archie had gotten the hose into the campground's sewer pipe, and Archie got a flood of poop water all over his feet. Melody recorded all of it, including when Sybil and Lucille rushed in to pull the brothers apart.

Melody had figured out how to strap together two of the wheeled trunks that they carried sound equipment in, and hung up a curtain to cover it, so she was now sleeping in the very crowded Pageant Wagon with Jake, Zedediah, Archie, and Lucille. "The professor is all elbows and knees," she announced, rolling out her sleeping bag and hopping happily onto her new bed that night while Jake tried very hard not to notice how short her nightshirt was. "If we had to keep sharing a bed, one of us was going to die. Good night!"

As he lay awake well into the still, quiet night, Jake

learned that Melody Aiko Bernstein snored, just a little bit, in her sleep. It was kind of adorable.

They woke to a brisk and cloudy morning. Except for Randolph, who was still sleeping, they all gathered and ate the scrambled eggs Archie had made at the campsite's picnic table. "Almost civilized," Zedediah observed.

Melody helpfully pointed out that the coffee tasted burnt, and E.D. noted that the eggs were overdone in some spots and runny in others. But everybody looked oddly content.

"Perfectly splendid," Lucille decreed.

Jake was chilly, and some Haddock Point mosquito bites still itched, but he stared up into the leaves overhead and drank burnt coffee and ate runny eggs, and somehow had to agree. Yes. It was pretty splendid.

One downside to living in their buses, Jake thought, as everyone climbed down from the Pageant Wagon onto the tree-lined downtown sidewalks of Clayton, Tennessee, was that everything had to be packed up and all the hoses and plugs disconnected from the campsite before they could go anywhere. All the adults, except Sybil and Zedediah, who drove, had decided to stay behind in Brunhilda, but even so, it had been hard to fit everyone and everything into the Pageant Wagon for the ride into town.

The library was an old brick building with a stained glass window over large, carved wooden double doors. As they went inside, a small, eager young woman with very short hair, dyed bright red above dark roots, hurried over to them.

"You're here! You're here! I was afraid you might have difficulty finding us. Come right on in. Sybil Jameson, in our little library! I can hardly believe it! I'm Marianne Quintana, the librarian—we have everything set up in the children's room, just as your assistant requested." Sybil looked puzzled and opened her mouth to say something, but Marianne Quintana went right on talking. "We have every one of the Petunia Grantham novels! They're big favorites here in our paperback-lending area. I'm so excited to have an author of your *stature* visit us in person!"

"Well, of course, I'm not here to focus on myself," said Sybil, smiling proudly, and Jake felt E.D. let out a long-held breath by his side. "I'm here for the children of Clayton."

A young man stepped up next to the librarian. He reminded Jake of the boys on the swim team at one of his old schools. "This is Michael Lyons, my assistant," said Ms. Quintana. "He's been setting things up for you."

Michael Lyons, Jake noticed, was looking not at Famous Author Sybil Jameson, but at Melody and Cordelia, who were following Hal. "Can I carry anything for you?" he asked the girls, each of whom was carrying a roll of electric cable in one hand and a small device in the other while Hal staggered under two bags full of heavy equipment.

Melody handed Michael Lyons the tiny wireless microphone she was carrying. "Oh, thank you so much, that's so sweet," she said, and he beamed at her.

He ushered them forward, past Hal and through a door marked CHILDREN'S ROOM, into which the librarian and Sybil had already disappeared. Destiny went in behind them. Jake saw that E.D., briefcase in hand, was glowering at the young man, who had taken no notice of her at all. Jake wasn't surprised, given that E.D. was wearing faded jeans and a T-shirt while both Cordelia and Melody were dressed to be noticed, Cordelia in a flowing skirt and snug tank top, and Melody in very short shorts and a linen shirt.

Inside the room, Destiny had already dropped his heavy backpack on one of the low tables with small wooden chairs that were scattered around the edges of the room, and was pulling out his drawing pad and markers. The librarian was showing Sybil the rocking chair on the far side of the room, and Michael Lyons was asking Melody and Cordelia what he could do to help set up for the video recording, oblivious to the fact that it was Hal who was getting out the camera and setting up a tripod for it. "We're fine," said Cordelia, with a sly smile.

E.D. put her briefcase down on a table next to a stack of notebooks and a cluster of pens. Jake waved toward the tables, which also held notebooks and pens, all set up for a nice, educational workshop with the kids. "I'm sure glad the librarian paid close attention to Ms. Jameson's *assistant*," he said.

E.D. turned to him, grinning, and winked. Jake recognized the gleam of pride in her eyes—E.D. was, once again, feeling the joy of "handling things."

Fifteen minutes after the workshop had been scheduled to start, E.D.'s gleam of pride had been replaced by a look of sheer panic. Jake was feeling it, too. If they'd had too small an audience in Haddock Point, they actually had too *large* an audience here. There were almost two dozen children in the room, and the *oldest* of the kids looked about seven. They were running *everywhere*. The adults who'd brought them had been introduced to Sybil and then ushered out with strict instructions to be back to pick up their charges in two hours. There would be no help from the parents. *Two hours!*

"These kids are too young!" E.D. whispered urgently to Jake. "She wrote this book for kids ten and up! And they're going to be too young for any of the workshop activities I had planned!"

As the babble of children's voices filled the room, Jake had a distinct feeling of impending disaster.

Melody was already filming whatever caught her

attention. At the moment, that was a girl in pink overalls with her thumb in her mouth and a stuffed rabbit under one arm. Jake figured she couldn't have been more than four. Then Melody turned toward two of the boys, who were trading karate punches and kicks. Video like that would do nothing to impress the Rutherfords, Jake thought, and he began hustling the children to sit down in front of the chair where Sybil was sitting. E.D. came to help, as did Cordelia and Michael Lyons, who had been hovering near her. Together, they managed to get the kids seated.

"Good morning, children!" Sybil said. Her forehead was wrinkled with an uncharacteristic expression of concern. When a few of the children said "Good morning" back, she looked relieved and went on. "My name is Sybil Jameson, and I write books."

Out of the corner of his eye, Jake noticed Rabbit Girl, who had refused to sit, drifting toward the table where Destiny sat drawing. "This morning I'm going to read you a little of the book I'm writing now." She cleared her throat, told them the title, and began to read.

A girl directly in front of her raised her hand and spoke without waiting to be called on. "Does it have pictures? Can we see 'em?"

"This is a chapter book," Sybil explained. "And I'm a writer. I don't do pictures, I do the words."

"I do pitchers!" Destiny called from the table in the

back. "I'm a nillustrator!"

"Not now, Destiny," Sybil said. She went back to reading.

"I thought you said you write books!" a little boy called out. "All you got there is pieces of paper."

Sybil nodded. "That's because this is what's called a *manuscript*. It's what there is before a book *becomes* a book."

"Do you *make* it into a book? How do you get the hard front on it?" a girl asked.

"And how do you get all the words to fit on the page just right?" said one of the two boys who'd been punching each other.

"Let's save questions till I'm finished reading," Sybil said. "Just listen to the story for now."

"I don't like stories without pictures," the first little girl said. "When are you gonna be done?"

Sybil got through the second page and was halfway done with the third when the karate punching started again and Jake dragged the closest of the boys away to sit on a chair. Sybil had finished the third page and was about to begin on the fourth when screams erupted at the back of the room where Rabbit Girl had tried to take Destiny's blue marker and Destiny had snatched it back. "Mine, mine, mine!" Destiny shouted.

The kid sank her teeth into his arm, Destiny shrieked, and the entire room dissolved into pandemonium.

Chapter Nine

As far as E.D. could tell, it wasn't actually much of a bite. After his initial shriek Destiny was hollering more than crying, and there weren't even any teeth marks on his arm, just a little bit of slobber. But it was enough to send the room into utter chaos. "Somebody do *something*!" E.D. said in a low voice through gritted teeth.

It was Melody who sprang into action, putting down her camera and hurrying to the light switch by the door. The room, which had no windows, went suddenly dark. Very dark. A scream was cut short by

Melody's shout. "LIGHTS GO OUT AND MOUTHS GO SHUT!"

There was immediate quiet.

"When the lights go on again you'll need to listen to me and do what I say. Right?"

Still quiet.

"RIGHT?" Melody shouted.

"Right," came a scattering of subdued voices.

The lights went back on—and the children blinked, all of them remarkably still. "Okay, kiddies, turn around and face me!" Melody said. As the children scooted themselves around, she looked from Jake to Cordelia to E.D. to Michael Lyons. "Go with me here," she said to them, and focused again on the children. "Next thing is you're all gonna get into groups and be creative with—let's say the story of the Three Little Pigs!"

As much as E.D. hated the idea of just "going with Melody," she had to admit the girl had accomplished a lot in no time at all. The children's eyes were very round, and slightly frightened. "Who knows that story?" Melody asked. They all raised their hands.

Melody beckoned to E.D. "Let's do this, Professor!" E.D. glanced at her mother, who, frowning, was rooting in the bag next to her chair, seemingly oblivious to what had just happened. Whatever they did, they'd better get at it quickly, before the kids had time to go wild again.

Melody leaned in close when E.D. went over to her. "Groups!" she said. "Mini workshops. Dance. Drawing. Singing. Like that."

E.D. nodded. Jake could get a group singing, Cordelia would do dance. Destiny might be only five, but if kids here wanted to draw pigs and wolves and houses, he would surely be able to talk about doing it while he was doing it himself.

Lots of the kids wanted to do everything, so Melody lined them up and gave them all numbers from one to four, and then E.D. announced which numbers went with which workshop. The *ones* went to the table with Destiny to draw—E.D. noticed they'd accidentally put the biter in his group—the *twos* were sent to Jake, the *threes* to Cordelia, and the *fours* to E.D. Michael Lyons was given the job of roaming between the groups, keeping the children from punching or biting anybody, and Hal's job was to get it all, or as much as possible, on video.

E.D. pulled a legal pad and pencil out of her briefcase and told her group, three girls and a boy, that they were going to take turns telling the story of the three little pigs and she would write it down for them. She sat them all at her table. "Start," she said, pointing to the one boy, "with *once upon a time,* and after that you're on your own. Tell it the way you remember it. When I stop one person, the next takes the story on from there. You got that?" The children, still a little nervous from the lights having gone out, nodded solemnly.

Jake's group had gathered in a far corner, and it wasn't long before a ragged version of "Old MacDonald Had a Farm" began. As the children *e-i-e-i-oh*ed, E.D. realized suddenly that Melody hadn't taken on a group. Instead, she had her camera trained on Sybil, who was still in the rocking chair, ignoring everyone. She was going over her manuscript, frowning intensely, jotting notes and crossing things out with the total focus of her writer self. Sometimes when she was working, she'd forget to eat—so ignoring a roomful of children wasn't that surprising.

"You're not writin' nothing down!" a little boy in E.D.'s group said, and she turned her attention back to the task at hand.

"Okay," she said, "go on."

"So then," the boy continued in a rush, "the wolf comes back to the door again and this time he's gonna kick those pigs' butts. . . ." E.D. wished she had thought to bring a computer. She'd expected the kids—the imaginary ten-and-ups—to do what writing there was to be done.

When the parents returned, E.D. read aloud the pig story as the children had written it, which was a distinctly creative take on the original one, then the "nillustrators," as they were now calling themselves, showed their pictures. After that the dancers did their dance, which was about the wolf chasing the pigs and consisted mostly of running around the outer edges of the room, and Jake's group sang the pig part of "Old MacDonald" three times through. The parents shook hands with Sybil, who had finally put away her manuscript when they arrived. Two of the women had brought Petunia Grantham mysteries for her to autograph. The families all left looking happy.

Jake shot Melody and E.D. a thumbs-up sign, and Hal told them, as he gathered the video equipment and stuffed it back into the bags, that he thought his video would be a winner. Melody grinned in triumph and clapped E.D. on the back as the librarian thanked Sybil. "I would have loved to stay for your workshop, but I had a previously scheduled meeting. It must have been wonderful!" Sybil accepted the compliment with becoming grace—considering, E.D. thought, that she hadn't had a thing to do with the "wonderful" part of it.

"We did it!" Melody said. "Onward toward victory!"

"And then the librarian lady said our pitchers from my nillustrator workshop was *delightful*," Destiny said around mouthfuls of apple pie back at the campground that night, where the family was gathered in lantern light at the picnic table for the dessert they'd bought on the way back from town. "But I don't think that mean girl with the rabbit drew pigs good at all. They looked like bugs or hippos or something. My pigs were lots and lots better. They had really good curly tails."

"Now, now, Destiny," said Lucille absently, poking at the corner of her mouth with a napkin. "Everybody's artistic expression is valuable."

"Okay, but my pigs was way better," Destiny insisted. "And my wolf was bestest of all!"

Melody had just come back from the campground's shower house and, in spite of the evening chill, was wearing only cutoffs and her bikini top as she rubbed a towel in her hair. "Yours *were* better, squirt. No question!"

"Now, now, Melody . . . ," Lucille began. "Creativity is about expressing your artistic impulse. It shouldn't be a competition."

"Tell that to the Rutherfords," Melody answered. "Or the people who give out Nobel Prizes. Pretty much *everything's* a competition. Like how come your poems get published and most other people's don't?"

Lucille smiled and wagged a finger at her. "Very clever, Melody. You're very clever."

"All right, troops." Zedediah banged his coffee cup on the picnic table. "Jeremy says we won't get our next assignment until tomorrow night. So we have an extra day to fill in Tennessee. I'm thinking we might find something educational to do with this time. I spent the day scoping out the surrounding area. Unfortunately, there's not much else to do close to Clayton except see the 'famous fainting goats,'" he said with a chuckle, "so I'm thinking we might travel a little farther—"

"Fainting goatses?" Destiny asked. "Grandpa! Grandpa! We *gots* to see fainting goatses!"

Zedediah shook his head. "Destiny, I was kidding about them. There's no educational value to—"

"I want to see the fainting goatses!" hollered Destiny.

Melody, who had sat down at the picnic table next to E.D., leaned over to her and whispered in her ear, "The kids rule!" Then she spoke to Zedediah. "I thought the Creative Academy considered pretty much everything in life educational, just like the Rutherfords," she said. "I'll bet not a single one of you has ever seen a goat faint."

"I WANT TO SEE THE FAINTING GOATSES!" Destiny hollered again, loud enough that the dog in the next campsite started to bark, which sent Winston into full-throated answer.

That was how the family came to agree that the next day would be devoted to the pursuit of the highly educational activity of watching goats faint.

Destiny was in his hammock, singing softly to himself a song he had made up about fainting goats, as E.D. got ready for bed later. She was grateful that however much trouble it was to turn the dinette into her bed, it was, at least, all hers. This led, of course, to thinking about Melody. Again. No doubt the girl was very smart. And she had an amazing knack for getting things to go the way she wanted them to. But when E.D. thought about the way Jake had been looking at Melody when she came back from the shower, she sighed. What, she wondered, might Melody want with Jake?

"Fumes!" her father complained the next day as they drove away. "That wagon is emitting noxious fumes! This is the last time I agree to follow Archie!"

Sybil, in the passenger seat, didn't respond. She was bent over a sheaf of manuscript pages with a pen in her hand.

"Fumes!" Randolph said again.

E.D. shook her head. She had a feeling that in his own mind, her father had managed to rewrite the entire story of the Pageant Wagon and would from now on blame Archie for any trouble it caused.

"We're going to see the goatses faint! We're going to see the goatses faint!" Destiny was chanting, over and over, straining forward to see out the windshield, as if they might appear in front of the bus at any moment.

Chapter Ten

"We could have made this trip in the same amount of time before Bill Bones fixed it," Archie complained, when they'd been traveling for almost an hour. The road to the town that was famous for fainting goats turned out to be extremely narrow and hilly, with lots of twists and turns and sudden dips, and Jake was feeling a little sick as the Pageant Wagon lurched one way and then the other. Finally, though, they passed a sign, welcoming them to Duck Hill, Tennessee, population 732.

"Not sure how famous the goats can be," Zedediah

observed, "if they don't merit a mention on the welcome sign."

"You're just grumpy about having to live up to your 'life as education' principles," Melody said.

"And you're still trying to get a rise out of me, missy. Give it up. I've got six decades on you."

Jake remembered Melody staring Wolfie in the eyes, and then head-butting the fence of the goat pen. He hadn't figured Melody out yet, but he was pretty sure she wasn't going to just "give it up." If the Applewhites and this Expedition were supposed to change her, it definitely wasn't happening yet.

The town square was nondescript except for a small but historic-looking courthouse. There weren't any goats just standing around. Archie drove in big circles, getting farther from the center of town, until eventually they saw a hand-painted sign, nailed up on a telephone pole, that read FAMOUS FAINTING GOATS and had an arrow on it. They took that turn and followed a series of signs on smaller and smaller roads, until the buses were rumbling down a dirt track, kicking up huge clouds of dust behind them. "I sure hope we don't have to turn around," worried Archie. "If this road runs out we're going to have to back out the whole way. . . ."

Jake wondered what kind of folks lived out here. Folks with shotguns, he thought, probably. He remembered a horror movie that had given him nightmares for weeks, and had a sudden, fleeting fantasy of a deranged killer luring unsuspecting tourists out to the deep, dark woods, robbing them blind, then shooting them and burying their bodies in some wilderness ravine where no one would ever find them.

Silly, he thought, and pushed the movie out of his mind. Who would think of luring someone to their death with the promise of fainting goats?

They arrived at last at a little ramshackle farm with a weathered house, a tilted barn, and a big wire pen with six or eight medium-sized goats in it. As the buses fell quiet, a farmer came ambling out. Melody, who had spent the last half hour of the trip stretched out on her new bunk, came up and stood next to Jake with her camera focused on the scene outside. She put a hand on his shoulder and snorted with laughter. "Look at that," she said. "He's actually got a hayseed."

Sure enough, the balding farmer had a long stalk of grass sticking out of his mouth. Jake was relieved to see he didn't have a shotgun. This was not, Jake thought, anybody's idea of a deranged killer. The man smiled at them amiably as they all climbed down from the buses. If he was surprised to see these two ornately decorated vehicles in his driveway, he didn't show it.

Zedediah stepped forward to greet him, but Destiny was there first, his camera in his hand. "Are those the fainting goatses? Can we see them faint? What makes them do it? Can they do it now?"

The farmer looked him over and nodded. "Yup, they can. But it only happens when they's skeert. And I gotta warn ya, they've just about seen—and heard—it all, so it's harder and harder to startle 'em nowadays. You're welcome to try, young feller. Welcome to try."

Destiny ran to the fence and clapped his hands at the goats. They kept chewing at the tufts of grass inside the pen. Then he tried shouting "Boo!" and "Gotcha!" and kicking the fence post. Then he screamed loud enough to make Jake want to cover his ears. The goats just chewed and stared at him.

Soon the rest of the Applewhites were lined up at the fence. Melody and Hal each had video cameras out. "Hey!" yelled Randolph. "HEY, GOATS!" None of them even looked over at him. Randolph shrugged. He was not, Jake thought, used to being ignored. "I've got better things to do with my time," he said, and headed back to Brunhilda.

Archie disappeared into the Pageant Wagon and came back out with two lengths of pipe, which he banged together, making an astonishing racket. Nothing.

"Maybe it isn't just sound!" Cordelia said. "They're used to that. Let me try something. Everybody hold very still." Everybody did. "Quiet and still now," she whispered. "Don't move a muscle." Suddenly she leaped into the air, arms and legs spread as if she was about to launch herself over the fence at them. They ignored her. "I should've had a scarf I could wave at them," she said.

Destiny ran to Brunhilda then and came back with Winston on his leash. "Get 'em, boy," he shouted, pulling him close to the fence. "Bark, at least!" Winston sniffed the base of the fence post and then raised his leg and peed on it.

"I thought he'd scare 'em good." Destiny's shoulders drooped. "I really, really wanted to see 'em faint," he said in a quiet voice.

"You know," said the farmer in his slow drawl, "it ain't rightly faintin'."

Destiny blinked up at him. "It ain't?"

The farmer shook his head. "Nope. Just that when they gits skeert, their muscles go all stiff and they fall over."

Next to Jake, Melody snorted and elbowed him. "Oh, they don't faint, they just fall over," she said, her voice dripping with sarcasm.

Without thinking, Jake joined in. "But only when they gets *skeert*," he said, and Melody laughed some more.

The farmer turned sharply to Jake and squinted. "Welp," he said slowly, around his stalk of grass, "to call it by its right name, it's a neuromuscular condition. Myotonia congenita, they call it. But I find most folks got no problem sayin' they fall over when skeert."

Jake's face started to burn, and he noticed E.D. a

step beyond the farmer, looking at him in disgust.

"I'm sorry," he muttered. "I didn't mean to . . ." His apology trailed off and he looked at his toes. He hadn't really meant to say it loud enough for the man to hear.

"How'd they get to be like that?" asked Destiny. "We gots two goatses, and they don't ever fall over. Wolfie doesn't get scared of anything, either. Not ever!"

"These goats are born like that," said the farmer, turning away from Jake. "That's what the congenita part of the condition means—'born with it.' Every one of 'em is descended from four goats brought down by a feller name of Tinsley from Nova Scotia. You know where that is, little feller?" Destiny shook his head. "Way up in Canada. Area called the Maritimes. They call it that 'cause *mare* is the Latin word for ocean and the folks up there spend a whole lot of time in boats."

Zedediah leaned over to E.D. "I officially admit I was wrong," he said. "There's something to be learned here after all. I can think of a great many follow-up questions. Science, history, geography—"

Destiny looked out over the goats, still calmly munching away. His chin trembled a little. "Even if it isn't real fainting," he said, "I still wanted to see them do it."

The farmer looked at him thoughtfully, then ambled off to his barn. To Jake's horror, he came back out with a big old shotgun, hanging open where the barrel met the stock. For one wild second Jake thought maybe all this old man's chatter had been camouflage and he really was a deranged killer. As he returned, the man was staring right at him! Jake fought an impulse to step back.

The farmer turned his attention to Zedediah. "You trust this punky-lookin' youngster with a gun?"

Zedediah looked Jake up and down almost meditatively. "I suppose so, properly supervised."

The farmer nodded, fitted a shotgun shell into one of the barrels, and snapped the gun shut. He walked over and held it out to Jake.

Jake just stared at it, too scared to move. He had never even seen a real gun up this close, let alone held one. He wouldn't have dared to let the tough guys back in Providence know that, of course. Hard to do a good imitation of the "bad boy from the city" when you were terrified of so much as touching a gun.

"Go on, boy," the farmer said. "Take it. Jist keep yer fingers away from the trigger." His eyes twinkled a little as he added, "Don't be *skeert*."

Jake clenched his teeth, then as casually as he could manage, reached out and took the shotgun, the smooth wood warm in his hands. He was surprised at how heavy it was. The farmer showed him how to raise it to his shoulder, and helped him aim it off over the trees, then looked at Melody and Hal. "Might want to get those cameras runnin' again." Two little red lights came on, Hal's pointing toward the goats and Melody's pointing right at Jake. "All right, son," the farmer said, "let her rip."

Jake felt the trigger under his finger. He thought of all the movies and TV shows he had ever seen where shooting guns was nothing at all, and realized that his heart was pounding so hard he could hear blood rushing in his ears. But everybody was looking at him and he didn't want them to think he was "skeert." It took all his concentration to make his finger squeeze that trigger.

There was an almighty boom and Jake felt as if he'd been hit in the shoulder by a freight train. The next thing he knew, he was flat on his back in the Tennessee dirt. The farmer was laughing so hard he had to bend over and rest his hands on his knees.

As the ringing in his ears started to fade, Jake saw that Destiny was jumping up and down clapping, a huge grin on his face. Through the wire of the pen, Jake saw the goats lying on the ground, eight sets of goat legs sticking straight out, some to the side, some right up in the air like a cartoon animal. He sort of knew how they felt.

Before he had managed to sit up, the goats were already getting to their feet. E.D. walked over to Jake and looked down at him. "The Rutherfords are right, I guess," she said, her hands on her hips. "You never know when you'll run into a learning opportunity." With that she turned on her heel and walked back to the bus.

Chapter Eleven

E.D. was fuming. It wasn't *her* fault that her father had smashed the back of Brunhilda into the fainting goat pen and knocked down a whole corner of it (which was enough, Destiny was overjoyed to see, to make all eight goats fall over again). It wasn't *her* fault that the only campground within one hundred miles didn't have pull-through sites, or that her father was so unnerved by the accident with the goat pen (and the money he'd had to give the farmer to fix it) that he backed Brunhilda straight into a tree next to the campsite and got into a screaming match with Archie about it. It wasn't *her* fault nobody liked the canned chili they'd had for dinner—it was the only kind the last grocery store had in big cans! She definitely didn't appreciate Destiny announcing that it looked like barf.

Hal, already sulking that the campground didn't have any Wi-Fi, slumped down at the table next to her and announced huffily that nobody could get a signal on their phones. As if E.D., on top of everything else, was supposed to be responsible for the orderly distribution of cell phone towers throughout the state of Tennessee!

"How will we find out what our next destination and subject are?" Hal wailed. "Jeremy was supposed to e-mail that to us!"

"No doubt this place has a landline," Zedediah observed. "I'll just have to *call* Jeremy." He gathered up the cards he was using to play solitaire at Brunhilda's table and headed for the camp office.

Cordelia swept in, wrapped in a terry cloth robe and clutching her towel and shampoo. "Those campground bathrooms," she declared, glaring at E.D., "are not fit for swine!"

"What's swine?" Destiny asked.

"The three little pigs!" she answered, and closed herself into Brunhilda's tiny bathroom to try out the shower Archie had rigged. A few minutes later she emerged, wrapped in her towel, her hair covered in a foamy helmet of shampoo. "Something's wrong with the shower. *It ran out of hot water before I could rinse!*"

"It's a ten-gallon hot-water tank," Hal pointed out as she struggled, soaking wet, back into her robe. "Barely enough for a couple of goldfish."

"Next time, check out the bathrooms before you choose a campground," Cordelia said to E.D.

"Next time," E.D. answered, "*you* find the campground! Plan dinner and do the grocery shopping, too, while you're at it!"

"Maybe I will! Maybe *then* we'd have some *vegetables*!"

"VEGETABLES ARE REALLY EXPENSIVE!" E.D. shouted. She may have sounded angry, but she felt like she was going to burst into tears.

Then Zedediah came back from the campground office fuming about highway robbery. "Twenty dollars he charged me for a ten-minute call to California!" But the cost of the call didn't seem to be the only reason he was fuming. "Family meeting in the screen house in fifteen minutes!"

"Make it half an hour!" Cordelia yelled as she started toward the campground bathrooms with her damp towel over her arm and her hair still full of suds.

When everyone had gathered in the screen house they had set up around the splintery picnic table half an hour later, Randolph asked what the next destination was.

"Memphis," Zedediah said.

E.D. noticed that Melody, who had started filing her nails a moment after she sat down, looked up, her eyes suddenly alight with interest.

"That's still in Tennessee," Randolph protested. "How do they expect us to get all the way across the continent if we have to stop twice in one state?"

"And the subject area?" Sybil asked.

"That's one of the problems. There *isn't* a subject area," Zedediah said in an outraged tone. "They've started to call the stops *challenges* now. Like some sort of reality TV show. And they're naming them. The name of ours is 'Mining Memphis.'"

Now it was Destiny who perked up. "Does they gots mines in Memphis? *Gold* mines? If we go to a gold mine do we gets to keep some of the gold? Pirates always gots chests of gold! I really, really, really want some gold!"

"This isn't about real mines," Zedediah explained the moment Destiny stopped for breath. "We're to *mine* Memphis for interesting and creative educational challenges."

"Got one!" Melody said. "Beale Street! Home of the blues!"

"A strip of bars and restaurants is not an educational opportunity, Melody," said Zedediah with a sigh.

"*The Rock 'n' Soul Museum!*" Melody insisted. "It's a museum, it has to be educational." Zedediah pointedly ignored her.

"I have a friend who runs a theater company there," Randolph said. "We could see what show he has running. He does some interesting avant-garde work, very modern."

"The national ornamental metalworking museum is in Memphis!" Archie said. "I've been meaning to visit it for years!"

Lucille pointed out that Graceland, Elvis Presley's home, was also in Memphis. She was immediately shouted down by the others. "I didn't say we should go to it, I just pointed out that it's there."

"There's plenty of time to decide what we'll do in Memphis," Zedediah said. "It'll take at least half a day to get there from here. But Jeremy gave me some other news. It turns out that right now we're in fourth place."

"Fourth place? What does that *mean?*" Randolph said.

"It means that the video Hal sent in from the Clayton library workshop didn't get as many viewings as three of the other groups' first videos."

"Viewings?" Sybil asked. "What's a viewing? Where? By whom?"

"Online," Zedediah said disgustedly. "All the videos have been posted on a website called *Follow the Expe-*

dition and now they're out on social media."

"I didn't know they'd be public," Hal said. "Not before the end of it, on the big TV show they're doing in California! *Not before the final editing and everything.* I just sent raw videos. I thought they were just going to *Jeremy.*"

"You surely don't mean they're going to do the *judging* that way," Sybil said.

"Jeremy says no." Zedediah shook his head. "But even *he* didn't know they would be posted. Somebody in the foundation office made them public. Jeremy says the actual judging is still to be done by education and arts experts." Zedediah shook his head again. "Putting them online is just supposed to generate interest and begin to pull in an audience. He says they call it 'creating buzz.'"

"But we're in *fourth* place?" E.D. said. That, she thought, was like getting a C—no, a D! She had never even imagined having a D in her entire life!

"I told you," Melody said to Lucille. "Competition! *Everything* is competition."

"We need to see the ones that are first and second," Jake said.

"As soon as we can get online!" E.D. agreed.

"Absolutely not!" Zedediah banged his fist on the table. "We will *not* get ourselves into a *popularity* contest! What those other groups are doing on their Expeditions is their business, and the Creative

Academy is ours." E.D. wilted and felt her cheeks burning. All day everyone was treating her like everything was her fault, and now her grandfather was yelling at her!

"When we're on the road tomorrow," Zedediah continued, "E.D. will go online and check out what all is available in Memphis. Make a list, and we can decide how to 'mine Memphis' when we stop for lunch. But do *not*"—he looked around the picnic table at each of the kids in turn, his eyes narrowed threateningly—"*Do not* go looking to see what those other groups have done. We will do this our way or no way! You get me?"

E.D. just nodded silently. Across the table, Jake was looking as sheepish as she felt. Hal and Cordelia nodded, too. And Destiny nodded ferociously, even though he was the one kid who regularly ignored any adult rule he didn't care for, including his grandfather's.

Melody wasn't nodding. "No," she said, calmly and loudly.

Zedediah blinked. "What's that?"

"No," Melody repeated. "No, I don't get you. I don't get you *at all*. You say this isn't going to be a competition? Open your eyes! This *is already* a competition—and we're losing!"

"Not from where I'm sitting," Zedediah replied. "From where I'm sitting, this is a school!"

"Well then *where you're sitting* is in the *dunce* corner

for *old dummies*," Melody muttered. E.D. gasped. Even Jake goggled at Melody in disbelief.

"I'm sorry," said Zedediah evenly, "I didn't quite catch that. Would you care to repeat it?"

E.D. was sure he had heard every word.

"Nope," said Melody, flashing a sudden bright smile, innocent as the morning. "I'm good, thanks!"

"Well if that is everything," Zedediah went on, not once taking his eyes off Melody, "we have some planning to do."

"*Contentious*," E.D. read in her well-worn paperback dictionary the next morning, as the dinette table in Brunhilda vibrated beneath her. *Likely to cause disagreement between people with differing views.* This was an extremely useful word. Despite E.D.'s best efforts, the plans for their trip to Memphis were proving to be *contentious*. She read the second definition: *argumentative; frequently engaging in and seeming to enjoy disputes*. That one was a practically perfect description of her family.

Among the many educational possibilities she had found, she most wanted to visit the National Civil Rights Museum, which had been built on the site where Dr. Martin Luther King Jr. was killed. E.D. had done a whole history project on Dr. King last January. But Aunt Lucille immediately declared it "too traumatic" and nobody else seemed eager to argue with her, so E.D. had to let it go. A children's museum that had won some kind of big award was her next favorite. She had read the description aloud from its website and Destiny had been practically delirious about all the exhibits it had—his only regret was that it didn't have a gold mine. Cordelia, on the other hand, declared it worthless because she was not a "child."

Archie insisted on the Metal Museum, and Zedediah agreed that it would offer intriguing new possibilities for their work back at Wit's End. Not one single person other than Melody was willing to consider Beale Street and the Rock 'n' Soul Museum.

Eventually they had come up with a plan. Randolph would drive Brunhilda, with Lucille, Sybil, Destiny, E.D., Cordelia, and Hal (with the video equipment) and also Winston, to the children's museum, while Archie, Zedediah, Jake, and Melody would explore the possibilities of ornamental metalworking. E.D. strongly suspected that Melody's sole interest in metalworking was that Jake had chosen it. But she dared not go there herself after she had worked so hard to sell everybody on the children's museum.

E.D. closed her dictionary and her vocabulary notebook and put them on the seat next to her. Things had calmed down since the crankiness of the last campground stop. Hal was filming the countryside going past the window as they drove toward Memphis, Cordelia had earbuds in and was waving her hands gently in the air before her—probably, E.D. thought, choreographing a dance in her mind. Lucille was reading, with Winston upside down and snoring next to her, on the bed in her parents' bedroom. Destiny had taken out markers and a drawing pad to make a pirate treasure map to a gold mine.

When E.D. took a deep breath, and just really looked around, it was still pretty neat, rolling across the country in the big bright inside of the giant, loud, rattling bus. Seeing new places. Meeting new challenges.

A couple of little worries nagged at her, though. She wondered what Melody and Jake were doing in the Pageant Wagon. She wondered why the Applewhites were in fourth place, and who was beating them. And she wondered why it mattered to her so much.

Chapter Twelve

The weird thing was, Jake thought, the Metal Museum was really cool.

He'd been walking through with Archie, getting swept up in his enthusiasm. Archie was in his glory. "Look at the curve of that copper!" he'd shout, hurrying over toward a furled and folded bowl on one side with the video camera he'd brought. Then he'd rush across the room the other way. "Look at the intricacy of the etching on this lock!" he'd cry, or "How do you suppose he thought to use silver just here?" It was fun. And the exhibits really were beautiful. Jake could see why Archie would be considering expanding his work to include metal. Some of the pieces were as strange as his own Furniture of the Absurd, like the coffee table that was the first thing of Archie's Jake had ever seen—a sleek and shiny, elegant wooden object that looked somewhat like a hippopotamus, and couldn't possibly hold a cup of coffee.

Then Melody was next to Jake, her phone out. She slipped a hand into his and he felt a tingle go all the way up his arm. "Come with me," she whispered so close to his ear that he could feel her breath. Now he had a tingle and goose bumps, both. She tugged him down a hallway toward the bathrooms. Jake had the fleeting thought that she was going to kiss him. But she didn't. Of course not, he thought—that was just silly. Right?

When they were out of sight of Archie she said, "We're getting out of here."

"What? Why? Where are we going?"

"Adventure," she said. "Mining Memphis!" They reached the front doors without encountering Zedediah, and she pulled Jake outside, down the driveway, and out through the huge, ornamental gates. She let go of his hand then, and walked hurriedly down the sidewalk toward a taxi that was idling at the curb a little way away. "I told the driver not to pull into the museum so we wouldn't be seen," she said, waving her phone at the cabbie.

Jake stopped and looked back toward the museum, half expecting to see Zedediah coming after them. By the time he looked back at the cab, Melody was inside, holding the door open for him. *Adventure,* he told himself, and climbed in next to her.

"Beale Street," Melody said to the cabdriver in an imperious voice. She must be used to taking taxis, Jake thought. "Turn off your phone," she told him, as she turned her own off.

Jake pulled his out of his pocket and turned it off. It made him just the slightest bit uncomfortable to realize that now nobody would have any idea where they were or could reach them in any way. *Off the grid,* he thought, and was surprised to feel a bit of a thrill.

"Do you believe they brought us to Memphis and weren't going to let us visit *Beale Street*?" Melody cried, sounding outraged.

"I don't really know what Beale Street is," Jake admitted, even though it made him feel silly somehow.

"Don't mind him," she said to the cabdriver, who had looked up in surprise at his rearview mirror. "He's just a hick from North Carolina."

"Rhode Island," Jake corrected her. He had no intention of letting her know how much she had bothered him.

The taxi swung onto a highway for a while, then took an exit that went under a railroad overpass and began moving along the Mississippi River on their left. One of the few assignments Jake had actually done in school was read *The Adventures of Huckleberry Finn*, which was all about a trip down the Mississippi River. On a raft. Looking at it now, so wide and slow and muddy and powerful, he caught his breath. *We're off the grid and sneaking away, like Huck and Jim on that raft*, he thought. *Just the two of us!* Suddenly, he felt better than he'd felt in weeks.

Soon they were passing what looked like a long park along a slope above the river—grass and sidewalks and a few trees. Then the lawn swept upward, becoming part of the curved roof of a very long, modern-looking building. Rising from the middle of the sleek roof was a big red square tower structure. *Beale Street Landing*, it declared itself. As they turned and drove under the railroad overpass, heading uphill, the driver said, "Where on Beale Street were you wanting to go?"

"Just drop us at Handy Park," Melody said. "We can go wherever we want from there."

"Have you been here before?" Jake asked.

"Nope." She waggled her phone. "That's what the Internet is for, my friend! But for real is better. Way better!"

As the taxi pulled to a stop Melody pulled a credit card from her small leather shoulder bag and handed it over. "Add twenty percent," she told him.

"Where'd you get the credit card?" Jake asked.

Melody answered airily, "My parents gave it to me. Makes 'em feel better for giving up on me and shipping me off with Uncle Jeremy for *fixing*. It's about time I got away long enough to actually use it. Out!" she said. "Get out and see Beale Street. *Home of rhythm and blues.*"

Two things struck Jake the moment he got out. One was the smell of barbecue, which seemed to waft through the air from everywhere. The other was music, with horns and drums and a bouncing electric bass line, coming from directly across the street. He could hear other songs, too, fainter, coming from one or two of the bars up the block. Two, three, four different tunes all mingled in the afternoon air.

Melody waved at the driver as the cab pulled away and Jake noticed she was looking oddly serious as she stared at the entrance to Handy Park. A series of thick, square brick archways opened off the sidewalk on either side of the big concrete slabs that formed the main entrance. Dodging traffic, she headed across the street and Jake followed her as soon as it was safe. Inside the main entrance to the park stood a statue of a man holding a trumpet. Behind the statue was an open, grassy area, where a band was playing on a big square stage under a canvas roof. About a dozen people were gathered around listening, some of them moving to the insistent beat.

They stood at the entrance, listening to the band. Just up the block, sitting in the sun on the sidewalk, was a man playing an old, worn acoustic guitar; he seemed entirely oblivious of the band. He had the cut-off neck of a beer bottle on his finger, and it made mournful notes as he slid it up and down the neck of the guitar. A middle-aged man wearing a hat with a ribbon around it stood close, singing wordlessly along with the guitar music. Their song didn't sound anything like what the band was playing, and Jake took a step forward into the park so he could hear the big band better. But as soon as he did, he found he missed the guitar melody, the mix of two songs that weren't alike but somehow went together and became something more interesting, more *whole*, than he'd ever heard before. He stepped back again so he could keep listening to them both.

The big band finished their song, and Melody whistled and cheered. Jake asked where the Rock 'n' Soul Museum was, but Melody just laughed at him. "You don't go to Beale Street to go to a *museum*," she said. "We're going to a bar. I want a drink."

Jake immediately thought of about a dozen reasons why that was a ridiculous idea, but Melody seemed so determined that he found he couldn't even bring himself to object. He just followed her into a dark, beer-and-barbecue-smelling place a couple of blocks away, with recorded music pouring out into the street, and then followed her right back out when the man behind the bar said, "Out you go, little lady. Don't even bother showing me your fake ID."

"Idiot," she snarled when they were back on the sun-drenched sidewalk. "Never mind, they didn't have any live music anyway."

It turned out most of the restaurants advertised live music but it didn't start until evening. Melody was hugely disappointed.

The guy with the guitar was taking a break, mopping his forehead with a ragged handkerchief, but the band in Handy Park was still going strong. Jake couldn't stop looking at the huge signs out in front of the bars and cafés—every one of them covered with neon lights, pale in the sunlight. The street must be *amazing* at night, he thought, when all the music and signs went live. He made a mental note that someday, for sure, he would come back here—at night—with somebody at least as spectacular as Melody.

Finally, Melody led him into an expensive-looking place that specialized in "down-home southern cooking." "Give us a nice, private table," she said to the woman who greeted them, and they were led to a booth in a darkish place far in the back. Here the music, still with a beat that made him want to move, was softer than it had been in the bar, while the barbecue smell was all but overwhelming. Jake could feel his mouth watering, just thinking about a slab of ribs.

The trouble was, he didn't have so much as a quarter in his pocket, and nobody had ever given *him* a credit card of his own. He was thinking of just asking for water when the waiter arrived, and Melody, without so much as looking at Jake, ordered two hickory burgers, one with sweet potato fries, the other with regular. She pointed at him then, and said, "He'll have a ginger ale, and I'll have a beer."

The waiter looked from her to him and back again, his lips pressed together in a firm imitation of a smile. "One ginger ale, one *root* beer, coming up," he said.

Melody swore under her breath as he left.

The burgers cost about three times as much as any burger he'd ever eaten. He had never in his life been in a place like this with no adults, let alone with a girl like Melody. He became uncomfortably aware of his heart pounding in his chest. They sat for a while, listening to the music, feeling the breeze from the ceiling fan overhead, and soaked it in.

"Free at last," Melody said finally, blowing out a deep breath and leaning back in her chair. "I was suffocating with those people."

"The Applewhites aren't so terrible," Jake said. That, he thought even as he said it, was totally unfair. The Applewhites were way better than "not terrible." The last year-plus-a-little that he'd spent with them had been the happiest time in his life. He knew he ought to be sticking up for them more.

"Well what else are you going to say?" she said, as the waiter put her burger in front of her. She picked it up, looking at him over the huge, buttered bun. "You're their well-trained little lapdog."

Jake couldn't speak for a minute. He had just picked up his burger, doing his best to hold the whole giant thing together, but he put it back down. "Wait," he said at last. "*What?*"

She grinned and smeared some barbecue sauce off her cheek with the back of her hand. "Well, I mean, look at you! You're supposed to be this singer, right, but you've never heard of Beale Street. So I assume you don't know much about the blues. All your singing is like 'Old MacDonald' or songs from musicals, right? Randolph's precious *theater* music. The whole family's too snobby for Elvis! You heard their reaction to Graceland! We're in Memphis! And they don't want to see *Graceland*!"

Jake had never really listened to much Elvis Presley music, and didn't know why he should have wanted to see the guy's old house. But Melody was on a roll he couldn't manage to interrupt.

"You don't swear and you don't smoke, and you dress in stupid short pants and prance around onstage when they tell you to." She put down her burger and picked up a sweet potato fry and waved it at him. "Who *are* you—really? Basically you're just the babysitter for that motormouthed little kid." She bit into the fry, not even seeming to notice she was saying anything particularly mean. "I'm surprised you even get a bed. I'm surprised they don't just toss a pillow on the floor for you, like your buddy Winston the Wondermutt."

Jake wondered if the music had been turned up this high when they came in. It didn't sound mysterious and cool anymore; it just sounded loud. It made it hard for him to think. He put his hands flat on the table and took a deep breath to clear his head.

"Look at you," she said, quietly enough that he almost couldn't hear her over the music. "Our hands are on the table, not even four inches apart"—he hadn't even noticed, but now he saw it was true—"and it hasn't even occurred to you to touch me." She sighed dramatically. "I bet we'll do this whole cross-country trip, bunking in the same bus, and you won't even try to kiss me."

One time, Archie had taken Jake and Destiny fishing in the pond at Wit's End. They had caught only one tiny sunfish, and when they were getting it off the hook it fell on the dock and flopped around there for a couple of seconds before they could scoop it up and toss it back in the water. It struck Jake, at the time, how desperate the fish looked in the open air, its mouth opening and closing, suffocating out of the water. Out of nowhere, that image came back to him now.

I know how that fish felt, he thought.

He stood up before he really knew what he was doing. "I'm going to go take a walk," he said. Melody looked startled. For some reason that made him feel a little better. "I'm going down by the river. I'll meet you back here in an hour. Maybe." And he walked out of the restaurant without looking back.

Beale Street went down under a railroad bridge just before it ended at the river, and there was a freight train going over. Something about the clacking of the wheels over the rails sounded like the blues they had heard in the park. He walked under it, until the train was all he could hear, then out the other side and across Riverside Drive to the waterfront that was part of Beale Street Landing. He made his way down the grassy slope past two triangular kid park areas built like ships marooned on the hill, all the way down to the cobblestoned edge of the river. He could see where the water had reached when it was a little higher, marked by a line of tangled sticks and debris on the rocks.

Later on he'd have no idea what he thought about, even though he sat there on the stones, his knees pulled up under his chin, for most of an hour, watching huge barges push up and down the river, with the sun pounding down on him. He knew Archie and Zedediah were probably going crazy wondering where the two of them had gotten to. They must have known for a while that they were nowhere in the museum.

And how would he explain why they ran away and what they did? What he did? *I heard some music and looked at some signs and didn't eat a fantastic burger and fries. And then I sat alone by the river and thought about nothing.*

With a sigh, he powered his phone back on and texted Zedediah to tell him where to pick them up.

One thing he knew for sure, as he got to his feet and headed back to find Melody, knowing how mad she'd be that he was ending their little side trip. He really, really didn't understand girls. And he was beginning to think he didn't understand himself much better.

Chapter Thirteen

E.D. was used to almost constant squabbling and bickering. But what happened back at the Memphis RV park at the end of the day, when everyone finally gathered there, felt more like open warfare. Everybody was in full freak-out about something. All, actually, except Destiny, who had had "the bestest best day ever" at the Children's Museum—and Melody and Jake, who remained disturbingly silent about what had happened between the time they sneaked away from the Metal Museum and the time Archie and Zedediah picked them up on Beale Street.

E.D. was far too upset even to let herself think about what they might have been up to, and Melody had only offered a very unsatisfactory explanation. "We were *creatively but independently 'mining the city.'*"

"You turned off your phones!" Zedediah thundered at the two of them, his white mustache quivering.

Melody! E.D. thought. Jake would never have come up with that idea. Jake actually looked traumatized by the whole experience. He was sitting off to the side with his head hanging. Melody sat across the room and wasn't looking at him, either. *Interesting.*

Her grandfather took a breath now and spit out his next words. "Never. Ever. Ever. Again." He looked around at all the others. "That goes for everyone. *Do you understand?* There will be no turning off of phones!"

Sybil looked at Randolph, her eyebrows nearly meeting in a furious frown.

"What? What?" he asked with an air of injured innocence. "I *had* to turn it off. George and I were having a critical discussion. I couldn't very well allow interruptions."

Jake and Melody weren't the only members of the Expedition who had gone missing that day. When Randolph dropped them off at the museum, he had told them all he was going to park Brunhilda and would "catch up with them later."

"*That's exactly what I did!*" he had announced when

he finally drove Brunhilda up in front of the museum, a full hour and a half after it had closed. What he'd actually done was go find his old theater buddy, who worked nearby, and they had ended up chatting for the rest of the day. E.D. couldn't remember seeing her mother so mad. Sitting for more than an hour on the sidewalk in front of a closed museum was *not* Sybil Jameson's idea of a good time.

When he'd finally shown up, Randolph refused to accept responsibility for anything other than the large dent in Brunhilda's back bumper. "I didn't see that light pole. *I'd like to see one of you* park this monster on a busy street!"

They were only five days into the Expedition. This was what happened, E.D. thought, when you didn't have enough structure.

"I'm making my signature chili mac," cried Lucille above the bickering. *Comfort food*, E.D. thought. *Good. With lots of grated cheese on top!*

When they finished eating, Hal discovered that the Rutherfords' next e-mail had arrived. "Destination: *Valley View, Arkansas.* Challenge: *Cooperate with the locals.* And we're supposed to stay there for four days. Four days!"

Loud groans met his announcement. What would the locals of Valley View, Arkansas, be like? E.D. wondered. And what would they cooperate with them *about*?

"That cuts it!" Randolph said emphatically. "I'm opting out of this challenge to start working on the new Pageant Wagon plan. I have a great deal to do. And it will not—*not*—involve any random Arkansas locals."

"A writer does not *cooperate* in the creation of her work," Sybil said then. "I wish to finish *Petunia Possum, Detective* so that I can announce my new career as a children's author."

Packing up and breaking camp took a bit less time the next morning. E.D. could turn her bed back into the dinette in three minutes flat now, if she didn't count folding her sheets. Jake was helping Hal take down the screen house and pack up his tent as E.D. came out of Brunhilda to get Winston's food bowl from under the picnic table, and their eyes met. There was a split second of electricity before Jake's shifted away. There was something furtive in that shift, E.D. thought, as if he couldn't look her in the eye. Why, she wondered. *Why?* She wanted more than anything to ask him that, and she might actually have done it, if there hadn't been anyone else around.

Hal had just stowed the poles when Randolph and Zedediah came back from the campground's bathhouse, Randolph complaining that it was un-American to charge for a campsite and then charge fifty cents for a shower.

"Sounds *entirely* American to me," Zedediah said. "But," he said to E.D., "you might check what the nightly fee actually *covers* before you make our next reservation."

The problem with that, E.D. thought, was that she'd checked for campgrounds in Valley View before she'd gone to bed the night before, and there was only one. One that was "full up." She'd found another campground thirty miles away that had spaces, and she didn't even dare to question the facilities or the fee—the family would be grumpy enough about the distance. When she told them, she would just have to use one of Aunt Lucille's favorite expressions: "It is what it is."

She said it to herself several times as Melody and Jake once more climbed into the Pageant Wagon for the day's travel. E.D. had looked up Beale Street. It had bars and dark, shadowy restaurants with very private booths. *What had they been doing there all that time?* If E.D. was reading the signals right, Melody was actively ignoring Jake. That didn't make sense, though. It must have been her idea to sneak off—it just *must* have been! So why would she be mad?

As hard as it was not knowing what was going on, the hardest part was trying not to let it affect her. The real meaning of *it is what it is,* she thought, was *there's nothing I can do about it.* Even so, every time she thought about Jake and Melody together, she shuddered all over. His crush on her was so obvious it was pathetic. What if when they snuck away he took the chance to act on it? What if he tried to *kiss* her? *Shudder.*

E.D. was so preoccupied that she totally forgot to pay attention as they drove over the wide, mighty Mississippi River into Arkansas. *Only the most important geographical boundary in the whole of the United States,* she thought angrily when she realized it was behind them. *Only the most significant river in the history of the country, and I missed it!*

After a long drive into the Ozark Mountains, over gradually steeper winding roads, with two stops along the way—one to stock up on groceries and the other to get some lunch—it was midafternoon when they reached the outskirts of Valley View.

E.D. wasn't sure exactly what she'd been expecting from a small town in Arkansas, but Valley View was a total surprise. The main street, called Hawthorne Way, was lined with boutiques, galleries, and cafés. Along the sidewalks there were sculptures done in a variety of materials and styles. Some were made of metal parts that looked as if they'd been pieced together from farm machinery, others were covered in broken glass mosaics, still others looked as if they'd been carved from logs or tree stumps with a chain saw. The scattering of people on the sidewalks mostly smiled at their buses and waved as they drove by. E.D. wondered whether they'd heard of the Expedition, or whether they just thought the buses fit right in. Valley

View was certainly the only place on this trip so far where they did. *Jeremy must have picked this place for us*, she thought.

Archie had been leading the way in the Pageant Wagon, when he suddenly put on his turn signal and pulled into a gravel driveway that wound around the side of a sprawling building set far back from the side-walk. Just a few hundred yards farther down Hawthorne Way, the street itself dwindled into a wide meadow that ran up to a rock bluff topped by woods. The building was the last on the street. It could have been a factory once, but now it was painted in stripes and swirls of neon colors. Stained glass artwork hung in some of its windows, and a collection of sculptures flanked a massive and beautifully carved wooden sign that rose out of the grass almost as if it had grown there. And that was how they stumbled onto the Ozark Art Co-op.

Randolph followed the Pageant Wagon into the drive and pulled to a stop behind it. Lucille, who'd been riding in Brunhilda, clapped her hands as she read the sign. "Look at that! An art *co-op* when our challenge is *cooperation*!"

"Coincidence!" Randolph exclaimed.

"There's no such thing as a coincidence," Lucille answered. "It's a clear reminder that the Universe is on our side."

The building was surrounded by a raggedy lawn

that made it look as if the meadow might be trying to take it over. After a moment a gigantic man with bushy blond hair and a beard, who looked like E.D.'s idea of a blacksmith, came out to greet them, followed by a huge black-and-brown dog.

Winston, standing with his front feet on the back of the couch, saw the dog and started barking frenziedly from inside Brunhilda. "That a boy dog in there?" the man asked Archie, who had emerged from the Pageant Wagon. When Archie nodded, he laughed. "Tell him old Suzi's a pussy cat. They'll be fast friends in no time."

That turned out to be an understatement. The moment Brunhilda's door was opened Winston bounded out, nearly tripping over his ears, and went to sniff the dog, who was easily three times as tall as he was, tail wagging furiously. "Cooperating with the locals already," Lucille said, as Suzi licked the top of Winston's head. From that moment on Winston was like Suzi's shadow, following her everywhere.

The blond man, whose name was Joe, had actually heard of the Expedition and had even watched some of the videos online. When he found out they were supposed to be camping thirty miles away, he pointed to the meadow. "Nonsense! Just park yourselves over there, close to the driveway. We can hook you up with power and water. This town will be honored to have you here for a few days. I'll make a couple of calls and we'll get the whole co-op crew together here this evening to see what we can do for you. Soon as you get yourselves settled, Suzi and me'll give you a tour of the place." He turned, then, and pointed to a sculpture made of scraps of old farm equipment. "That's one of mine," he said. "They call me the blacksmith."

Ha! E.D. thought.

The co-op building, Joe the Blacksmith said, used to be a manufacturing plant for car parts. In one corner, behind a partial, paint-spattered wall, there were dozens of canvases stretched on frames and rack after rack of painting supplies. Paintings at all stages of completion were scattered everywhere. Some of them, E.D. thought, were really quite pretty—mountainscapes and valleys and vases of flowers—and some of them were the kind that she never really understood, all squiggles and scratches and blotches of color. She knew they were supposed to be very sophisticated, but she secretly thought they looked like something Destiny could have made.

In another corner was the sculpture area, which Archie exclaimed over, with wood- and stone-carving tools and some welding equipment. There was an upper level along one side, with a wall of Plexiglas windows "to keep out the dust," as Joe the Blacksmith explained. "That's our multimedia lab, lots of computers and musical instruments and stuff. We got a grant for all that!" Hal's eyes nearly doubled in size as the man described it. Melody, E.D. noticed, was particularly focused on that part of the building, too.

When Zedediah explained that the challenge for the four days in Valley View was simply to "cooperate with the locals," Joe laughed a great big laugh that just about filled the huge space and set both Suzi and Winston barking. "We call our group a co-op, but the truth is artists aren't always great at cooperating. Still, we'll do what we can!"

E.D. realized she'd left her notebook back in the bus. This cooperation project was going to need a lot of organizing, and she wanted to get started right away. She turned to go get it and almost shrieked out loud—Melody was standing *right* behind her, staring at her with those big dark eyes, her hair falling in her face. E.D. pressed her hand to her heart and took a deep breath. "Can I help you?" she said, trying to make her voice sound as dismissive and nasty as Melody's usually was to her.

"No," said Melody thoughtfully, after a long pause. "But I think I can help you." And without another word, she grabbed E.D.'s hand and dragged her away.

Chapter Fourteen

Two days later, Jake was on his way from the Pageant Wagon to the multimedia lab after lunch when Suzi the dog charged past him, followed by Winston and Destiny, headed for the meadow. "I'm taking a dog break!" Destiny shouted over his shoulder as he ran.

"Have fun!" Jake called after him as Destiny followed the dogs into the tall grass. Joe the Blacksmith had assured everyone that his dog wouldn't go far from the building, and Winston wouldn't go far from Suzi, so nobody worried about Destiny when he was off taking a dog break. It was a good thing, Jake thought, because *he* was way too busy with his project to be "the babysitter for that motormouthed kid," as Melody had put it.

The challenge was to cooperate with the locals, and everyone but Randolph and Sybil, who both steadfastly continued doing their projects alone, was working with one or another of the co-op artists. Archie and Zedediah had teamed up with Joe the Blacksmith, banging away throughout the day and into the night at his forge, working on a giant abstract metal sculpture. Lucille was flitting around with a photographer, composing poems to accompany the pictures he took of flowers, moss, rocks, and the like. Destiny had met an old puppeteer and built a possum puppet, then immediately they built five or six more and started writing a whole puppet show about them. "I wanna do our show for the publics," Destiny announced at the end of the first day. "I'm gonna get Dad to let me use the Pageant Wagon and we're gonna do our show for *everybody*. It's really good and I love our puppets." Clearly Destiny was *not* the kind of artist who was perpetually crippled by self-doubt.

The idea caught on, as it turned out, and plans were quickly put in place for a public showcase of all the cooperation projects on the last night of their stay. Signs went up around town and the collaborations went into overdrive.

Jake spent all his time in the computer video lab with Hal, Cordelia, and a heavily tattooed, self-identified "video geek" from the co-op, to do a video version of Cordelia's *Death of Ophelia* ballet.

But the strangest collaboration, by far, wasn't between the Expedition team and a local. It was between E.D. and Melody.

E.D. had been hostile toward Melody since the moment she set eyes on her—Jake guessed he could understand why. They were so different. Everything E.D. took seriously, Melody took lightly. Melody was comfortable being the center of attention—more than comfortable!—and E.D. liked to stay in the background.

The only thing he'd ever seen them agree on was that, ever since Beale Street, they were *both* refusing to talk to Jake. The one time Jake's and E.D.'s eyes had met, while they were breaking camp in Tennessee, Jake got the same little shock he used to get at the end of the summer, after the Kiss. But he'd immediately looked away. He was too afraid the intensity on her side, this time, was pure hostility. And Melody! Melody had been successfully pretending that Jake didn't exist, even when they were in the same room together!

But now, out of nowhere, Melody and E.D. had become a *team*. For days they had been almost inseparable. It started on the first morning in Valley View, when they were all walking together down Hawthorne Way, getting to know the town, and Melody had dragged E.D. into a women's clothing shop called Style.

That was where they found the "local" they were doing their cooperation project with. She was the owner of the shop and made most of the clothes she sold there herself. She was also a member of the co-op and called the clothes she made "wearable art."

Somehow, maybe by a kind of female energy he would never understand, the woman, whose name was Rainbow or Sunset or something, had gotten E.D. and Melody to cooperate *with each other.*

Only it wasn't just that. It was more than cooperation. They would go darting off together and close themselves into one of the art buses. When they were around other people—the co-op artists, people on the street, even the family, they started whispering behind their hands, casting long, appraising glances at them. Just today, they hadn't shown up for lunch, and came strolling in after everyone else was finished. They had "grabbed lunch at a café," E.D. explained. Whatever they were doing, they were keeping it a secret.

Jake opened the door of the media lab. Melody, with her camera in hand, was leaning very close to Hal, whispering in his ear. Hal's face was distinctly red, and Jake felt a twinge, seeing them together like that. Melody giggled, ruffled her hand in Hal's hair, and swept out of the room—right past Jake—without even making eye contact with him.

The public performance was scheduled for the evening of their last night in Valley View and everyone had scrambled to get ready. The Pageant Wagon stood in all its glory, with the stage unfolded from the side and the painted curtains glowing in the stage lights that had been mounted on telephone poles around the big yard of the Ozark Art Co-op. A fairly impressive crowd was gathered for the *Academy/Co-op Showcase*. Jake suspected most of the audience had come mainly for the food and drinks that were promised afterward. But maybe not. The town of Valley View, Joe assured them, had taken the Creative Academy on as their "home team" in the expedition competition. A banner had been put up across the driveway that read, GO CREATIVE ACADEMY!

Hal's official video would go off to Jeremy (and the rest of the world) when it was over, but there were lots of other people who had their phone cameras out. Some were gathered around the big abstract metal sculpture Archie and Zedediah had made with Joe.

At the back of the stage a white sheet had been stretched tight so that the nature slides Lucille's photographer had taken to go with her poetry reading could be shown, along with the videos Jake, Hal, and the co-op's special-effects guy had made for Cordelia's ballet. And a puppet stage made from a big cardboard box, decorated with Destiny's colorful animals, stood in front of it.

Destiny and the puppet maker were up first, with the puppet show the old man claimed in his introduction was entirely created by Destiny. Jake could certainly believe that. The story line involved a violently purple, very fuzzy possum, a white dog, and a caterpillar that got transformed into a butterfly while Destiny, as the possum, yelled, *"Fly, fly, fly,"* and the butterfly almost magically did. The audience cheered and applauded as if their football team had just made a spectacular touchdown in the last seconds of a tied game.

Next the special-effects guy, stationed at a computer to operate the technical side, put up a slide introducing "An Excerpt from Cordelia Applewhite's Ballet, *The Death of Ophelia*." Cordelia's discordant music blared from the speakers, and she danced onto the stage for a few moments before the lights on her faded and the video picked up. It looked like Cordelia had danced straight up onto the screen! The projected image continued to dance, and then gradually the special effects Jake and Hal had created started to take over. First Cordelia's dancing figure burst into flames, then it became a Cordelia-shaped flock of birds, and on and on through another dozen weird and interesting variations. When it was over, once again, the audience went wild. Cordelia took a bow and then motioned for Jake and Hal (who looked like he wanted to turn into a flock of birds and fly away himself) to stand up from the audience. After that, Lucille, accompanied by a local fiddler, read two poems in front of a series of nature slides, also to roaring applause.

Next up, Jake knew, were Melody and E.D. But he still had no idea what they were planning to do.

The lights went dark and a video came on, with the words ***The Art of Style*** stretching across the sheet in bright red. Music started playing, the word ***BEFORE*** scrolled across the projection, and a picture swung up onto the screen showing E.D., her hair pulled to the back of her neck with a rubber band, wearing a bulky, raggedy sweatshirt, worn blue jeans, and her usual clunky-looking hiking sneakers, climbing down from Brunhilda, carrying a clipboard, with a pencil shoved behind her ear. Then up swept a picture of Melody, her dark hair swinging loose, coming out the front door and down the porch steps back at Wit's End in her big white linen shirt over a turquoise halter top and short shorts. As usual she looked effortlessly glamorous. Her face and eyes were made up and on her feet were flip-flops. Who made this video intro? Jake wondered, before realizing that this must be what Melody and Hal had been talking about in the video room. He fought down a twinge of envy that Melody had asked Hal for help while she was still ignoring Jake.

Then the word ***AFTER*** scrolled across, the lights went down, and the music changed to something poppy with a heavy beat. Soon folks were bobbing their heads in time with it. Lights snapped up on the stage and Melody Aiko Bernstein, strutting like a runway model, burst out into the light. She carried a clipboard and there was a pencil behind her ear.

Jake stared for a moment and then gave a whoop of delight. Melody's hair was caught back just like E.D.'s had been in the photo, a rubber band holding it in a loose bun. She was wearing a big, baggy sweatshirt and a pair of Cordelia's jeans, which covered her snugly all the way to the ankle, where they disappeared into a pair of high-topped hiking boots. She took the pencil out from behind her ear and began tapping it on her clipboard in time to the music, swaying her hips as she walked. Whistles broke out from the crowd, and she wagged the pencil at them, as if she was scolding, but she had a devilish look on her face. She was dressed in E.D.'s usual way, but somehow an outfit that made E.D. vanish into the scenery made Melody look like a star.

Melody got to the corner of the other side of the stage and stopped for a moment, looking out across the audience, then put the pencil back behind her ear and flung the clipboard saucily into the audience, where one of the young co-op painters caught it and clutched it to his chest. Then she turned and pointed dramatically toward the other side of the stage. The music changed to something with an even heavier beat.

It took Jake a few seconds to realize that the glamorous, red-lipped, heavily eyelinered young woman who strode out into the light and across the stage was E.D.

Something had been done to her hair, though he couldn't tell just what. It hung loose, almost to her shoulders, and seemed to bend just a little, around her face. She was wearing loose black pants that seemed to flow as she moved, and a brightly colored snug silk tank top that made her skin glow and her neck look long and elegant. As she crossed the stage in time with the music, her feet, in what could have been red ballet slippers, peeked out from beneath the pants as she went. A lone whistle sounded from behind him, and Jake felt pretty sure it was the first one that had ever, ever been directed at E.D.

Afterward, when performers and audience were mingling, Melody was overflowing with pride about their presentation. Jake couldn't tell for sure how E.D. felt about it. She sat by herself in the corner of the co-op's lounge while people with plates of food and glasses of wine swirled around her. She kept pushing her hair back, and once or twice he saw her start to rub her face before remembering she had makeup on. She was smiling, and accepted the compliments people offered, but she seemed uneasy.

There was a loud clinking of a spoon against a glass, and a sleek, elegant-looking man with white hair asked for everyone's attention. People settled into instant silence. This, thought Jake, was somebody important. "Ladies and gentlemen, it has been the great pleasure of the Ozark Arts Co-op to cooperate with the Creative Academy these past few days. I'm sure you join me in wishing them the very best of luck in this competition. . . ." A smattering of applause and a general murmur briefly interrupted him. "As the founder and principal benefactor of this organization, which will—I'm not sorry to say—be getting some lovely national publicity from this event, I would like to offer the Creative Academy a complimentary day at my spa and resort if they can take tomorrow off before heading out to their next destination."

Cheers and more applause broke out. Jake looked at Archie, Lucille, and Zedediah, who were standing together at the refreshment table, to see what their reaction would be. They conferred in whispers for barely a second, and then gave the man a unanimous thumbs-up. There was yet another brief round of cheering. Jake felt a tug at his shirt and turned around to see Destiny looking up at him. "What's a spa?" he asked.

Chapter Fifteen

The spa was the most elegant place E.D. could ever have imagined. It even had a "doggy day care" for the pets of resort and spa visitors, where Winston ended up getting his first-ever massage and dog pedicure. The Applewhites were greeted as if they were visiting royalty, and in short order everyone had found things to do. Destiny wanted to go for a horseback trail ride, but was traumatized when they told him he was too little to go by himself. "But it's on my bucket list!" he cried. The idea of making a list of things he wanted to do before he died, or "kicked the bucket," was something he had picked up from the old puppet maker.

Zedediah said he didn't have a bucket list, but he'd go along. "You gotta make one quick," Destiny told him, "'cause you're way closer to dying than me!"

Sybil and Lucille suggested starting off with an "all-girl" mani-pedi. E.D. had never had either a manicure or a pedicure, and it took a while to get used to somebody holding on to her hands and feet and working on her nails and skin with an assortment of files, clippers, and lotions. She had first asked for a plain, clear nail polish, but Melody prodded her to "live a little," so she'd finally chosen a sparkly, pearly pale pink. Melody chose deep purple.

E.D. didn't know where Melody had gone after the mani-pedi, but she herself was now alone in the sauna—the first sauna she'd ever had. She'd chosen it because nobody else was doing it and she wanted to be alone, and also because if she didn't pour water on the hot stones, the sauna's heat was dry and the spiral notebook she'd brought in with her wouldn't get all damp.

She was doing her best just now, to write (using a surprisingly hot ballpoint pen and stopping every so often to admire her pink nails) about what had happened last night and how she felt about it.

The thing was, E.D. had never so much as *thought* about style in her life before. Whenever her mother or

Aunt Lucille had taken her shopping for clothes, she had just chosen T-shirts in the colors she liked and jeans or shorts and shoes that were comfortable to wear. She hadn't paid any attention to what anyone else would think of how she looked. After all, nobody in her family cared.

She'd always known, of course, that Cordelia and Lucille dressed in a way that was very different from her or her mother. They were all about flowing skirts and bright colors. Sybil favored jeans or slacks and oversized shirts, except when she had to go someplace to be a famous author. Even then, she tended toward plain dark slacks and elegant jackets. Sybil owned nothing whatsoever that was flowery or flowing.

"Style is way more than clothes," Melody had said when she'd first pulled E.D. into that boutique in Valley View. "Your style is everything about you—the story you're giving the world about who you are. Like an actor. You get the point of *costumes*, right? And playing a part?"

But E.D. hadn't fully agreed with the story thing when Melody said it, and even after all the research she'd done on the possible meanings of the word *style*, and what a great response their presentation had gotten, she didn't quite agree with it now.

Okay, she wrote in her notebook. *It's more than clothes, but it isn't just costume, either. It has something to do with who you really are, too.* Otherwise, she thought, Melody could not have pulled off wearing E.D.'s kind of clothes and come across nothing whatsoever like E.D.! She was still unmistakably Melody. What *was* that?

On the other hand, E.D. wasn't sure she had still been unmistakably E.D. when she dressed the way *she* had for their presentation. There was the very different way Jake had looked at her that night. And kept on looking at her now that she had taken Cordelia's and Melody's advice and learned how to manage her new hairdo and to put on some blush and some lip gloss when she got up in the morning.

A weird thing had happened when she'd come to the door in the spa that led to the sauna—a door with a window in the middle of it. She had automatically stepped back to let the girl on the other side of the door come through, until she'd realized that girl was her own reflection. It had been an unsettling moment.

Even Destiny had made a big deal about how she looked when she came to breakfast wearing one of the two new shirts she had bought at the boutique. When she'd tried them on, she'd hated looking in the mirror and being so horribly aware of her "bony" knees and elbows. But then Melody and Aurora, the boutique owner, had her get a bra that made her look somehow really different. How could those little bits of cloth and that tiny bit of padding make her same old body become something else? Since then, she'd suddenly become conscious of how she was standing. Or sitting.

Even when she was trying to get David Giacomo's attention back at camp, it somehow hadn't occurred to her to change something about herself.

When Jake showed up at Wit's End with his scarlet spiked hair and his piercings and his black clothes, E.D. never thought of the way he presented himself as a "style" choice. She had just thought of it as *him.* She had disliked him on sight, but she knew it wasn't just because of how he looked. How he looked fit what he'd done—burning down a school and getting kicked out of every other school that would have him. So what was the difference between a person's style and who that person really was?

Had Jake *changed* when he let his hair go brown and quit wearing that dog collar and those black clothes? Yes, but which came first? She didn't think she would have wanted to kiss Jake looking the way he did at first. But the Jake she kissed didn't just look different. He *was* different. Where could you draw the line between style and self? Jake had kissed her, she remembered, when she'd had no style at all.

Now she'd changed herself, at least a little, and everybody seemed to like it. But how much of it really felt like *her*?

As little as E.D. wanted to like Melody, there was something about the girl that was hard to resist. Something lively and particular and—*intense.* When the two of them started working together, E.D. had felt, maybe for the first time in her life, as if she had a real girlfriend, a person she could hang out and share stuff with. It felt like something *more* than just cooperation. "Between us, we're gonna rock this challenge!" Melody had said. Like she really believed in E.D.

But did she believe in E.D., or did she believe in what she thought she could turn E.D. into?

Check the dictionary for the right word to describe Melody. E.D. sighed. *There's a whole lot more I need to learn about style. Stuff I probably can't learn from the Internet.* She closed her notebook. It was all complicated and horribly confusing.

When the family gathered on the porch outside the spa's dining room for dinner, where fountains were playing gently and musically over stones, and wind chimes were tinkling in a light evening breeze, E.D. noticed that her mother looked no different than usual. Her face appeared freshly scrubbed and her hair was damp, as if she might have washed away whatever the makeover person had done to her. *Style,* E.D. thought. *Her own style and not somebody else's.*

Destiny was chattering on about the new things he had put on his bucket list while he and Zedediah were horseback riding. "Taking a shower under a waterfall—the guide girl wouldn't let me get off my horse and do it right then—and hang gliding. Did you all see those hang glider guys? They spooked Grandpa's horse and it's a good thing he used to be a cowboy or he might have got bucked off!"

Everyone looked at Zedediah, whose face was impassive.

"Cowboy?" Randolph said.

"*Cowboy?*" Archie echoed.

"Just because you're my sons doesn't mean you know everything about me," Zedediah said.

A waiter came to show them to a table. "How many will there be?" he asked.

Lucille began counting noses. After a moment, she said, "Somebody's missing." She looked from one to another, her eyebrows knitted. "Where's Melody?"

Everyone looked at everyone else. Melody was not among them. "Where'd she go after our mani-pedi?" Sybil asked.

"Don't look at me," E.D. said. "I was by myself in the sauna."

"We can't go to dinner without her," Lucille said. "We need to find Melody."

Five minutes later they hadn't found Melody, but they had discovered that the Pageant Wagon was no longer in the fast-darkening parking lot. "She can't have taken the Pageant Wagon," Lucille said. "She doesn't have a driver's license."

"Um," Jake said. "Um. Actually, she does."

"She can't," Zedediah said, "she's only fifteen."

"I didn't say it was a real one," Jake said. E.D. furiously told herself that she didn't want to know how Jake would know something like that.

"Call the state police!" Randolph shouted. "She's stolen my Pageant Wagon! She could drive it off a cliff! Or into a tree. We could be sued within an inch of our lives if something happens to that girl, to say nothing of the catastrophe of losing the Pageant Wagon!"

E.D. looked around at the circle as everyone began yelling at once. She realized that, even accounting for Melody, there were fewer people than there should be. Finally, she realized who was missing.

"Hey, everybody," she called, loud enough to get their attention through the squabbling. "Where is Hal?"

Nobody knew. Jake ran to check Brunhilda, but he wasn't there, and his tent was still packed neatly in her lower storage compartment.

"Well that explains it," said Zedediah, looking mightily relieved. "Hal has his license, and he drove the buses around some before we left Wit's End. They must have gone on an errand, or something." He waved to the waiter, who came over to take them to their table.

Randolph was still grumbling about "grand theft of a bus" but everyone else seemed willing to let it go. *This is something about style, too,* thought E.D., *in a way that has nothing to do with clothes.* As soon as they realized that Hal was along with Melody, they all immediately assumed that nothing *too* bad or dangerous could be going on. Looking at Jake, who actually seemed even more worried than he had before, she had to wonder if that was true.

The waiter had just come to take their dessert order when Melody strolled casually into the dining room and over to their table. She was wearing a spectacularly hand-painted silk shirt—all colorful birds on a black background—that E.D. remembered her trying on at Aurora's boutique, and a pair of ultra-skinny black jeans. She looked fantastic. In her hands she carried a box from Valley View's gourmet bakery, tied with a shiny ribbon. "Wha'sup?" she asked.

"Young lady . . . ," began Zedediah sternly, but Sybil broke in before he got going.

"Where is Hal?" she asked. "Isn't he with you?"

Melody smiled. "You betcha," she said, whipping out Hal's video camera, turning it on and aiming at the doorway to the dining room. "I am proud to present: *Hal Applewhite 2.0!*" She stepped back and gestured toward the entrance. Timidly, a figure stepped into the light.

He came through the doorway wearing skinny jeans, ripped on one thigh, held up by a belt with silver studs. He had on a plain white T-shirt with a short-sleeved gray work shirt over it, and motorcycle boots. A wide black leather cuff circled one wrist, stamped with patterns around the edges and held together with three enormous snaps. His hair, now a deep, rich cherry black, was buzzed on the sides and cropped into a single long slash, hanging down over one eye. He stood still for a moment so that everyone could get the full effect, and then threw his head back and smiled a triumphant, confident smile. It was so unlike any look E.D. had ever seen on her brother's face before that even though she knew perfectly well it was him, she could barely believe what she was seeing with her own eyes.

Melody had taken away Hal, the cripplingly shy recluse and oddball, and had brought back this . . . this rock star.

Maybe, E.D. thought, the word for Melody was *witch*!

Chapter Sixteen

"It was . . . I can't even describe it." Hal was holding up the video camera with the screen flipped around so he could see himself in it. He had invited Jake up to his penthouse tent on top of Brunhilda—which he insisted on sleeping in, even though all the others were in cushy lodge rooms inside. He was a contradiction in terms, Jake thought. A *rock star* hermit. "After the mountain biking I was so wiped out," Hal explained, "that I snuck into the Pageant Wagon to grab a nap. I had a dream that I was caught in a landslide, and woke up to find the bus hurtling down a twisty mountain road with Melody at the wheel. She didn't have any idea I was there. I think the most danger we were in was when I came out of Grandpa's bunk—I startled her so badly she almost went off the road."

"So wait, go back," said Jake. "Why did those kids help you again?" Hal had already explained that he got his haircut and his new clothes from a rough-looking pack of older teenage kids who had been hanging around the benches outside Valley View's coffee shop. They'd taken him to one girl's house, where they turned some music up really loud and the rest of them hung out while she cut his hair. Then another girl dyed it, and meantime two of the bigger guys had gone home to get some clothes they'd outgrown.

"That's the most amazing thing," said Hal, his eyes wide. "She walked right up to them. Melody. Just went right up and said, 'Hi, guys!' like talking to these total strangers was the most natural thing in the world. Told 'em she thought they'd be able to help her help me out. And they all got into it. Because she *asked*."

Jake knew he should be happy for Hal, who was still staring at himself in the camera's screen like he couldn't believe what he was seeing. He knew he shouldn't be jealous that Hal had had an adventure with Melody. He shouldn't be.

Hal was still talking and Jake realized he hadn't really been listening. "When I was in school,

Jake"—he shook his head—"it was . . . it was bad. That's basically why we started the Creative Academy. I couldn't handle school anymore. I never could figure out how to be around other kids. No matter where we went, it was like they knew they didn't like me, before I had even said anything, or done anything." He ran his hand through his hair, feeling the short sides and the long front, which fell right back down over his eye. "Dad said at the time it was because our creativity was being stifled, but they pulled us out of there and started homeschooling us because of me." He looked at Jake. "Do you know what that's like? To be hated, just on sight?"

Jake nodded. Of course, in his "bad kid" days he had looked as scary as possible to have that exact effect, on purpose. *Why did I ever want that?* he wondered.

"But these kids in town, they didn't do that. They looked at me and it was like they were just looking at another person. Like there was nothing wrong with me at all." Jake thought that was a terrible thing to say about yourself, but he kept quiet. "And she told them she wanted to help me out, with how I dressed and how I looked, and they just . . . they just did it! They had fun! And they were *nice* to me."

Hal looked so solemn, wide-eyed, and serious, that Jake thought he looked a little bit like Destiny—or as if Jake could see in Hal the little boy that nobody had ever liked, peeking out from under the rock star haircut.

"It was her," Hal said. "Melody. She's amazing." He smiled at Jake. It was a tentative smile, Jake thought, but it was a nice one.

And I'm not jealous, Jake told himself. *Not at all.*

An hour later, everyone was gathered in Randolph and Sybil's lodge bedroom for an Expedition check-in and planning meeting. Jeremy had told them to expect his call with their next destination. E.D. read his last e-mail: "'You've moved up to third place in the standings, for what it's worth. . . .'" Melody whooped and pumped her fist, then high-fived with E.D.

Zedediah looked skeptical. "What did you send as your last video report?" he asked Hal.

"It was our Art of Style presentation," E.D. answered instead, looking unsure. Melody nudged her in the back and she continued. "Melody . . . I mean, *we* figured, it was accessible and that folks would like it."

"And it worked!" gloated Melody. "We jumped up to third place!"

Jake could see what was coming, even if Melody couldn't. By the way she stared at her toes, he suspected E.D. could, too.

Zedediah was quiet for a while, but when he spoke, his voice was rumbling with suppressed anger. "This," he said. "This is exactly what I did *not* want us to get involved with. This . . . popularity contest!" Melody opened her mouth and he held up a warning finger. "This is not open to debate," he said. "We will maintain the academic standards of the Applewhites' Creative Academy, which means we will *not* be creating our video reports so that *people will like them.* If you only included your own work, then you left out a tremendous amount of value from our stop in Valley View. It will not happen again. Our reports will be complete, and they will be academic."

"And they will be *boring,*" Melody shot back, "and they will *lose.*"

"I refuse to believe," said Zedediah, his arms crossed, "that a program dedicated to education will penalize us for attempting to be *educational.*"

"But we've got the next video update already!" cried Melody. "Hal 2.0! The makeover and everything; you should *see* the footage I got in town—"

Zedediah was already shaking his head. "I see no educational value in that whatsoever. *It will not be submitted in this school's name.*"

E.D. finally spoke up. "Grandpa—" she started, but he cut her off.

"This discussion is over." Jake looked from her to Zedediah to Melody, and back. If anybody was going to say anything else, it was cut off by the phone ringing.

"It's Jeremy," said Randolph, and he put the phone on speaker.

"I'm sorry!" Jeremy said the very first thing. "I'm just so sorry!" His voice was shaky, almost as if he'd been crying, Jake thought. "I tried. I really, really tried! And besides, they *promised.* I *couldn't* have known . . ." And then, it was obvious he had broken down.

"Jeremy, dear," Lucille said, "*what* couldn't you have known?"

There was the sound of snuffling and nose-blowing. Then Jeremy spoke again. "The Rutherfords brought in this producer from a TV network, and they said he was *only* there for the TV show at the end of the competition! He's the one who started posting the videos online the minute they came in, and he's the one who started calling everything 'challenges.' He changed the whole *feel* of the Expedition. The whole point of it!"

"This is exactly the kind of thing I've been concerned about all along," began Zedediah, but Jeremy started talking again and he fell quiet.

"They're shortening the Expedition!" Jeremy moaned. "The producer says if we have the winner two weeks sooner, it'll be better for ratings! 'Stay away from the holidays,' he says! Then yesterday—this is the worst!—he said the education experts who were supposed to judge everything, and write up reports about what every group sent in, and visit different groups along the way, cost too much to be worth it. They're just going to use *online voting* and *celebrity judges* instead! I protested, of course! I stood up to him. To them. I did—I reminded them about art changing the world, about why they'd started the whole thing in the first place. I—" There was a sudden silence, a gulping sound, and then the nose-blowing again. "*They fired me!*" he wailed at last.

"But the competition is still on?" Randolph asked.

When Jeremy was able to speak again, he said it was. He said they should be getting their next challenge by e-mail the next day.

It was a very bad end to the spa day that had begun so well. Zedediah and Sybil said they should just pull out of the Expedition now. Lucille disagreed. "It's awfully hard on Jeremy, of course, but it would be a shame not to give the Rutherfords the benefit of the doubt. They do want to bring creativity to education, and we want that, too."

"To say nothing of the prize money," Randolph said.

"Keep your eye on the prize," Melody muttered under her breath. Jake had a feeling she wasn't just talking about Randolph. If there was one thing he knew about Melody it was that she had an absolute determination to finish this Expedition and get to California—and *win*!

Jake suspected she'd been checking out what the other Expeditions were doing all along. It was her idea to send only the makeover video and ditch the rest of what Hal had filmed, he was sure of it. For that matter, it probably played a part in what she'd done with Hal to begin with. Did Melody organize his new look just because it would make a great video?

After a considerable discussion, everybody finally agreed they should wait to see what explanation the Rutherfords offered the next day, and what the next challenge would be, before making any kind of decision about what they would do.

The e-mail that arrived the next morning didn't include any sort of explanation. It came from the same Rutherford Foundation e-mail address that Jeremy had been using, and wasn't signed. If Jeremy hadn't called to tell them the real story, they wouldn't have known anything had changed at all. "I wonder . . . ," Melody said, peering over Hal's shoulder at his computer screen.

"You wonder what?" Jake asked.

"Oh, nothing," she said.

The only thing that really mattered, Jake thought, was that whoever would be sending them their instructions from now on, it wasn't Jeremy. They were at the mercy of some television producer who had an agenda of his own.

This time, the Rutherfords' challenge had a catchy title: "Show, Don't Tell: Education Through Artistic Performance." They had a week and could do one performance multiple times, or multiple performances one time each. The subject area could be anything they liked and no destination had been provided.

"Perfect!" Randolph said. "We're going to Kansas City! I've directed there at the Missouri Studio Theater, so I have some useful contacts. And Simon Rathbone can fly out to meet us. It's the perfect time and place to try out the idea I came up with in Memphis. I need to get to a copy center! The Pageant Wagon is about to come into its own!"

Chapter Seventeen

Archaic, E.D. had titled the list of words her father had given her. It meant "no longer used in ordinary language." She sat now in blessed solitary silence in Brunhilda, looking up substitute words for the archaic ones in *Our American Cousin,* which was the play Abraham Lincoln had been watching the night he was assassinated in 1865—and which was also the play her father had chosen for the first "staged reading" in the Pageant Wagon.

The idea he had come up with in Memphis was to do plays people mostly didn't get to see in regular theaters, with actors carrying scripts so they didn't have to memorize lines and wouldn't need a lot of rehearsal. No big sets, no fancy costumes, just the characters and the words. They would do basic staging, like entrances and exits, and perform on the Pageant Wagon stage.

Randolph had chosen this play because it had "historical significance," so it fit the education part of the Expedition. It was a ridiculous sort of romantic comedy, and at the time of the Civil War it was the most popular play in America.

Simon Rathbone had come out to play the main funny character—a goofy old guy named Lord Dundreary—but most of the actors at MOST (the logo that was painted in huge letters across the front of the Missouri Studio Theater) were already doing another show, so Randolph's plan to cast them hadn't worked. That meant Jake and Melody and even Hal (who had surprised everybody by volunteering to act) were in it.

As she started to search for the first word on the list—*syllabub*—Brunhilda's door was jerked open. Destiny, his nearly grown-out Mohawk tousled, his face red and wet with tears, stormed up the steps. He rubbed at his face with one hand, leaving dirt trails on his cheeks.

"What happened to you?" she asked.

"I hate little kids!" he said. "They're mean and

stupid and I'm never going to play with them ever again. I don't gots to play with them if I don't want to!"

Destiny *loved* people, she thought. "You're a little kid," she pointed out. "And *you're* not mean and stupid!"

"Yeah, well, the ones with the mommy who runs the theater *are*! Nobody can make me play with them ever again! Not Daddy, not Mommy, not nobody!"

Not good, E.D. thought. The adults had all assumed that the presence of two kids—a four-year-old girl and a five-year-old boy—would be good for him. It was supposed to be a chance for Destiny to spend quality time with his peers. Because the children's mother, besides being the co–artistic director of the theater, had also agreed to play a small part in the play, Cordelia had been charged with keeping an eye on the three of them while the mother was rehearsing. Of course, E.D. thought, Cordelia had also been charged with designing the backdrops for the reading. That probably meant the children had been left pretty much on their own to amuse themselves.

"What happened?"

Destiny's hands were balled into fists and his eyes flashed with a kind of fire she had never seen in them before. "That boy wouldn't let me build with his Legos and then the girl kicked me and hit me and called me names. After that the boy stole my markers and wouldn't give them back."

E.D. sighed. She had always been afraid Destiny

would grow up uneducated, thanks to a family who didn't believe in forcing kids to learn what they didn't want to learn. How had she missed the fact that growing up homeschooled as the littlest kid in the Applewhite family could be sort of like being raised by wolves? Destiny was entirely unsocialized to his own kind. She would talk to her parents about this later. Meantime, it would probably be a good idea to keep Destiny here with her right now, no matter how much of a distraction he would be to her work.

"Go wash your face," she told him, "and then come back here. I need your help."

Destiny's face immediately brightened. "Do you gots something I can draw?" Then his eyes flashed again. "'Cept I don't gots my markers anymore!"

She showed him the legal pad with her list of words. "I need your help with words this time."

"I don't do words," Destiny said.

"You talk!" she told him.

He grinned. "That's right! I talk real good." With that, he went happily down the narrow aisle and into the bathroom to wash his face.

When he came back, she showed him her list. "See this word? You tell me its letters one at a time and I'll type them so the online dictionary can look it up for us." Destiny knew the alphabet and could write his own name, but it was about time somebody started teaching him to read, she thought. This was as good a time as any.

Destiny looked at the word on her list. "*D*," he said, "and *R* and *A* and *U* and *G* and *H* and *T*."

She typed *draught* in and clicked enter. "There," she told him, "it's pronounced *draft* and it has a bunch of different meanings. There's a scene in the play that's funny because they're all using the same word to mean different things."

Destiny looked from the screen to her list of words, frowning. "If it's *draft*, how come there's a *G* in it? *G*'s sound is *guh*! Like for *goose*. There's no *guh* sound in *draft*!"

"When the *G* is followed by *H* it can sound like *F*," she told him. "Like in *tough* or *cough*."

"So how come they don't spell 'em with *F*? *F!* Like in *fox*!"

"I don't know."

"So does *G-H always* sound like *F*?"

E.D. considered the question. *Through, though, thought.* She shook her head. "Never mind." Somebody else could teach Destiny to read, she decided. "Just give me the letters for the next word." As he read off the letters for *sockdologizing*, she typed them in. "No matches found," the screen said. She sighed.

When she'd done what she could, E.D. left Destiny playing with the computer and went over to the theater, where the actors were rehearsing. She listened for a while, glad to hear that the play, in spite of being so old, was really funny in some places, and when

Randolph called for a break she went over to Jake. He was clutching the black binder with his script in it to his chest and looking vaguely traumatized. "Would you be willing to hang out with Destiny for part of your break?" she asked him. "I have to meet with Dad, but it won't take long. Whatever we do, we can't just leave him alone with those two kids everybody wanted him to play with."

"What happened?" Jake asked.

"Remember when that little kid in the Clayton library bit him? This time Destiny got beat up by a four-year-old girl and the boy stole his markers. He's decided he hates little kids."

Just then the mother of the offending children came into the room, leading her daughter, her son tagging along behind. Both of the girl's arms were covered with what looked like brilliantly colored tattoos, and there were two jaggedy streaks of purple on one cheek. The mother looked around the room for a moment and then came over to E.D. "I need to know if those markers Caleb took from your brother were permanent ones."

"Doesn't Caleb still have them?" E.D. asked.

"He says he threw them in the Dumpster."

The woman did not seem particularly angry, E.D. was pleased to see. "Destiny doesn't have any permanent markers anymore. He can't really be trusted with them."

"So I see. I just wanted to know what I would need to get the purple off her cheek."

"I like dese ones," the little girl said, showing her arms. "He did 'em good. But I didn't want a possum on my face!"

"I gather she let him know that pretty forcefully. Emma isn't a particularly compliant child."

E.D. nodded. "Destiny said she kicked him and hit him and called him names."

"Sounds about right," the woman said. "I've taught her to stick up for herself."

"He stomped on my Lego truck and broke it all to pieces, and then knocked me down," Caleb piped up from behind his mother. "So I grabbed up all his markers and wouldn't let him have 'em again. He went away crying, and I climbed up that ladder on the big garbage thing and threw them in!"

This was not quite the story Destiny had told, E.D. thought. "I'm sorry about this," she said to the mother. "The color on her cheek should wash right off, though."

"No problem," the woman said. "There's bound to be a little rough and tumble with kids this age. But it would be good if we could make sure there's an adult around to step in if necessary."

E.D. nodded. "I'll make sure somebody keeps an eye on them when you're rehearsing."

The woman smiled. "Great. I'm sure it will work out fine. Come on, you two. Let's go find some soap."

"Destiny's in Brunhilda," E.D. told Jake.

"I'll get him and Winston and we'll go for a walk," Jake said, throwing his script on a chair. As he walked away, he looked almost cheerful.

Chapter Eighteen

Jake stood in the cramped "backstage" of the Pageant Wagon and peeked out through the curtains. There were probably forty people already gathered on folding chairs and cushions in the parking lot of the theater, even though the show wasn't to start for another twenty minutes. Brunhilda was parked along the street to shelter them from the noise of passing traffic, and little jars had been hung on strings all around the lot with tiny electric candles in them. It was lovely and magical, especially considering it was a parking lot.

The stage looked terrific. Cordelia had disappeared with Archie to a hardware store and returned with dozens of roll-down window blinds. Then, in a day-long frenzy involving lots of skinny brushes and different shades of gray paint, she had painted them all to look like giant pencil sketches. Doorways, archways, windows, and furniture were all intricately detailed and beautiful to look at, but they looked temporary, like someone had just jotted a quick drawing of them. Destiny had been assigned to E.D.'s stage crew, and they were both wearing all black clothing and the headsets that Destiny called "walkie-talkers." Between scenes they would run out and pull down the right set of blinds to make it look like the actors were in a different room. E.D. was over in a corner, bent over a giant binder with a pack of six different colors of highlighter next to her. Her new hairdo was messed up by the headset, and the little bit of makeup she had started wearing was smudged, but Jake thought she looked entirely happy.

Jake, on the other hand, felt awful. He had a knot in his stomach and his hands were sweaty. This wasn't the excited nervousness that he got before his performance in musicals. *Doom*, he thought. *I have a feeling of doom.*

Rehearsals had gone well for everybody else. Every time Melody read her lines, Randolph would look at her in a kind of distracted amazement, nod at her, and move on to the next scene. Simon Rathbone was cracking everybody up. On the first day of rehearsal, several of Simon's script pages had fallen out of his binder and scattered all over the floor. When he crawled around gathering them up, still in character as the ridiculous Lord Dundreary, muttering to himself and reading bits of the wrong lines off the wrong pages, the cast had laughed so hard they had to take a break. He had, of course, built it into the performance—he had extra pages in his binder just so he could drop them and pretend it was an accident. Even Hal, playing the villain, was doing amazingly well.

Jake had *not* been doing well. For one thing, the character of Asa Trenchard was at least ten years older than he was. For another, he was supposed to be a big, rough, outdoorsy New Englander. Randolph even had him wearing a Daniel Boone cap with a raccoon tail.

Then there were his lines. They were supposed to be funny. He was supposed to *make* them funny. Simon Rathbone managed it easily. But Jake didn't know how to do it. When you sang a song, he thought, you learned the notes and you sang them. Easy. But how did you make words *funny*? Especially when your lines were already goofy a hundred and fifty years ago. His first line was "Wal, darn me, if you ain't the consarnedest old shoat I ever did see." Even when he used the substitute word E.D. had given him for *shoat—piggy*—he sounded like Yosemite Sam, the guy with a big mustache and pistols from the Bugs Bunny cartoons.

"Simpler, Jake," Randolph kept saying. "Don't feel like you have to *do* anything with it. Just let the lines do the work." So Jake would try it again. And it was flat and boring, and nobody laughed. "A bit more spark," Randolph would say. "Really announce your presence. It's a big entrance for a big character!"

And Jake would do his next line big and loud: "I'm Asa Trenchard, born in Vermont, suckled on the banks of Muddy Creek, about the tallest gunner, the slickest dancer, and generally the loudest critter in the state!" and it would sound like Yosemite Sam again. Around the rehearsal room, he could see everybody's polite smiles get more and more strained. This happened again and again, in every scene they rehearsed, and each time Randolph would work with him for a while and then he'd tug at his hair and say something like "Yes, well, keep working on it, I'm sure you'll get there. Moving on!"

But here he was, minutes before the first performance, and he *hadn't* gotten there. He was the lead in the play and he was letting everybody down.

Melody bounced up the Pageant Wagon stairs, holding her script binder. She, like all the women, was wearing just the hoops from a big vintage hoop skirt over her usual jeans and sneakers. That was Cordelia's brilliant idea for the costumes. Each man had an antique-looking jacket over his regular clothes. "They're just a sketch!" Cordelia announced proudly, "like the set!" Melody looked up now from her script and locked eyes with Jake.

"Hey, kid," she said breezily. "You look a little green around the gills. How are you doing?"

Great, he wanted to say. Or *ready to knock 'em dead.* "I'm totally freaking out!" is what came out of his mouth.

Melody gazed at him for a second and then laughed. Right in his face. It wasn't a nice laugh. Then she looked him up and down, which reminded him he wasn't even as tall as she was. "No wonder you're freaking out," she said. "It's a comedy and you haven't gotten a single laugh. Well, there always has to be a first time. Maybe it'll be tonight!" And with that, she gathered up her hoops and slipped out the Pageant Wagon's back door.

"Thanks!" said Jake, as he watched her go. "Thanks a lot!"

"What's the matter?" asked a voice behind him. He spun around to see Simon Rathbone, his hair teased out to hilarious lengths, a scrawny tie knotted around his neck, putting the fake pages into his script so he could drop them later.

"Nothing," said Jake. "I'm fine."

Simon put a hand on his shoulder and squeezed.

"Don't worry," he said kindly. "It will all be all right in the end."

For a terrible moment, Jake thought he might burst into tears.

Simon was wrong, Jake thought later as he sat alone in a booth in the back room of the restaurant they had gone to for their "opening night" party. It hadn't been all right. It was every bit as bad as he had feared, and then some.

Everyone *else* did fine. People in the audience were laughing and having a good time. There were even extra laughs when Destiny pulled down a shade with a window drawn on it instead of the one with a door, and E.D. chased him around to make him fix it. It happened again and became a "bit." The third time they did it, Simon came out as Lord Dundreary and pretended to supervise. The audience loved it.

But when Jake stepped onto the stage, from the first moment he opened his mouth he knew he was doing it wrong. He switched madly between Yosemite Sam and a barely audible whisper, like some kind of malfunctioning actor robot. It was a nightmare. The worst part was, nobody laughed. *I mean,* thought Jake furiously, *they did until I beat it out of them.* Asa Trenchard's garbled, exaggerated version of Yankee English had gotten cautious, polite laughs at first, but the more Jake panicked the fewer there were until he felt as if everything he said was followed by a vast, roaring silence, with occasionally the sound of a car driving through it. And the worst thing, the worst thing of all, was that Archie had been filming every single humiliating moment!

"It wasn't that bad," said Hal, coming over to Jake now with a plate full of chicken fingers.

"It was worse than that bad," said Jake. He noticed that Hal was glancing toward the next room, where the other cast members were babbling loudly over the jukebox music. "Go," he said. "I'm fine, don't worry about me." Hal went.

Yeah, well, Jake thought, *he didn't have to look* so *relieved.*

Melody twirled into the room as Hal was walking out, and even in his funk Jake noticed that she trailed her fingers along Hal's arm lightly as they passed each other. Hal turned to watch her go, his eyes completely moony. Jake put his head in his hands.

"*We're going to the desert next!*" cried Melody happily, plopping down on the padded seat of the booth right next to Jake and slurping her soda through a straw. "The challenge e-mail just came in. We're meeting up with another one of the Expedition groups—the one that's in first place. We're supposed to team up with them. Sure, team up. More like learn their secrets and get out in front!"

Jake didn't say anything. He couldn't even think

about the Expedition right now. Right now, he just wanted to go home. Maybe back to his lavender room at Wit's End. Maybe all the way home to Rhode Island. *I'll just hide out in my parents' basement*, he thought bitterly. *Until they get out of jail.*

Melody was looking at him with one eyebrow up. She bumped her shoulder into his and checked to see if he was smiling. He wasn't, so she did it again.

"Stop it," he said, smiling in spite of himself and then hating himself for it.

"Come on, it wasn't that bad," said Melody. "You've just got to loosen up. Play with it! Do what Simon does—make some of it up. If you just relax and have fun you could be really good in that part. And you've got four more chances!"

Jake couldn't believe his ears. Here was Melody, who told him he was pretty much a total failure right before he went onstage, telling him to relax. He gritted his teeth so hard they hurt.

She got up and stretched, with a big yawn, then looked back down at him. "Jeez, kid," she said quietly. "Where's your *fight*?" Without looking back at him, she walked out of the room.

Some while later, when the party was winding down and people were starting to leave, Simon, drink in hand, peered into the room. "Aha," he said. "Mr. Semple." *Everybody's coming to see the failure*, Jake thought. *It's like I'm in a zoo.* Simon pulled up a chair from a nearby table and sat. He gazed down his long nose at Jake for a moment. "So. You had something of a rough go of it out there, yes?"

Jake sighed. At least there was one person who wasn't telling him it *wasn't so bad*.

"It happens," said Simon. "To everyone. The man who made your role famous back in the day invented the saying, 'There are no small parts, only small actors.' You have a big part and you just need to let yourself grow into it."

"You lied to me," Jake said. "Earlier."

"Did I?" asked Simon, raising his bushy eyebrows.

"You said it would all be all right in the end. And it wasn't. I stank."

Simon nodded solemnly. "You know the rest of that saying, don't you? *If it's not all right*"—he raised his glass to finish his drink—"*it's not the end.*"

Chapter Nineteen

The problem with the Pageant Wagon, E.D. thought, was what to do if it rained. Three nights into the planned five-performance run of *Our American Cousin*, a weather front had moved in and it had rained so hard that Hal had abandoned his rooftop tent and moved to a couch in the storage room at MOST. It went on raining, and the other two performances had to be canceled.

Surprisingly enough, Jake was almost as upset by the cancellations as Randolph. Something had happened after that first night, in spite of the nasty review in the local paper that called Jake "the weak link" in an otherwise "stellar" event. By the second performance Jake had relaxed a little, and by the third, he'd actually added some funny bits of his own. E.D. had the distinct feeling that he'd been planning a couple more. Whatever they were, she was sorry he wouldn't get to use them.

Now, on their last full day in Kansas City, as the rain continued outside, the whole family was crowded into Brunhilda, where Zedediah had called a family meeting.

They were so jammed together that E.D. had the uncomfortable feeling she was breathing oxygen that only moments ago had been in somebody else's lungs.

"It may be time to rethink our participation in this whole thing," Zedediah said. "Now that Jeremy is no longer involved, it has become a media circus. The cart is leading the horse here—the Expedition, the spectacle of it, has become clearly more important than the education. All because some TV people say so! And these Rutherfords are listening to them!" He waved a folded newspaper in the air. "Even this review of Randolph's production devoted half its space to the Expedition."

"It did say our stay here should rocket us to the top," Randolph said.

"Exactly! Nothing about the historical significance of the piece, nothing about the educational value—

nothing about education at all!"

E.D. thought about the video log (she preferred to call it a tutorial) she'd made about Lincoln, and the Civil War, which had just ended when he went to see that play, and about the assassination and what followed. She was really proud of her tutorial. They were in Missouri, so she'd started her research there, and found out that Missouri had declared itself a "free state" when it joined the Union and had a law against slavery in spite of there being a lot of slaves there. People had done raids across the border—between Missouri and Kansas!—killing one another and burning buildings. It was, she thought, the best educational piece they'd sent in yet. But when the standings came out, they were stuck in third place. She desperately wanted to know what the other groups were posting, but her grandfather insisted that they weren't allowed to look.

"And this new challenge," Zedediah went on, "partnering with the Organic School, whatever the name means. It isn't clear what—if anything—that group has in common with the Creative Academy. If they want partnership, why shouldn't *we* choose who to partner with? Worse, we're supposed to do this in a place called Saunders, New Mexico. I've checked out Saunders. It'll take at least two full days to get there and when we do, it's essentially in the middle of nowhere. It's like they picked our destination entirely at random. The whole county has only two towns, three villages and—get this—*three ghost towns*!"

"Ghost towns?" Destiny yelped. "They gots whole towns full of ghosts there? I don't wanna go someplace full of dead people!"

"They're not *towns full of ghosts*," E.D. assured Destiny. She had checked out Saunders, too. "They used to be towns, but they aren't anymore. Just some old empty buildings. Some ruins." It would actually be fun to explore a ghost town or two, she thought.

"The whole county is just desert," Zedediah said. "*High desert*—more than a mile above sea level—with nothing but sand and rocks, and snakes and lizards and scorpions."

"Scorpions?" Cordelia said. "And *snakes*?"

"I've saved the worst for last," Zedediah continued, with an expression like a storm cloud. "They're cutting the whole thing short *again*. Now we're to be in California by mid-October." Murmurs spread through the group. "This was supposed to be a serious, self-directed mission to rethink American education. If there's any rethinking to be done, it should be *us* rethinking whether to keep on with it."

"Of *course* we're keeping on with it," Randolph said. "It is providing publicity for my Pageant Wagon 'Pencil Sketch Tour of America!'"

"*My* name for it, *pencil sketch*," Cordelia reminded him.

"And the sooner it's done," Randolph pressed on, "the sooner we win! And the sooner we can begin our own work!"

"Let me get this straight," Archie said to his father, "you're suggesting that we *give up and quit*?"

"You told *me* quitters never win and winners never quit!" Destiny said.

Zedediah shook his head. "There's a difference between being a quitter and walking away from a bad idea that's getting steadily worse."

"I say we take a vote," Randolph said. "All in favor of continuing the Expedition raise your hand."

E.D., imagining going back to Wit's End when they had managed to get only as far as Missouri, raised her hand immediately, as did Melody, Hal, Randolph, Sybil, Archie, and Lucille. Destiny crossed his arms and shook his head. "I'm scared of ghosts."

"There *aren't* any ghosts!" Randolph said.

"Promise?"

"Promise!"

"How about little kids? Does that Organic thingy have any little kids? 'Cause I'm not playing with little kids ever, ever, ever again!"

"Raise your hand!" Randolph thundered. Destiny did. "Jake? Do you want to get over being a 'weak link' once and for all, or do you want to quit?"

Jake raised his hand, and Cordelia did, too. "Just as long as they aren't *rattle*snakes," she said.

Zedediah sighed. "If the Creative Academy is going to continue this project, I suggest we call the Rutherfords and tell them we at least want to choose a different group to partner with."

E.D. happened to be looking at Melody just then—Melody, who had patted Jake's hand reassuringly when Randolph had mentioned "weak link"—and saw her face blanch. "No!" Melody almost shouted. "Don't do that!" Then she glanced around and said, "I mean, if we're going to do this, we want to *win*. Their game, their rules, right? We don't want to rock the boat."

Zedediah shrugged. "Suit yourselves. Meeting's over." He peered out the windshield. "And so, it would seem, is the rain."

Randolph checked his watch. "If the rain has stopped, maybe we can manage another performance tonight after all. Simon hasn't flown home yet."

E.D. was going to miss Simon Rathbone when he left, she thought, but not half as much as Jake would. If this challenge was about life as education, she thought, Jake had probably learned more than anyone. Simon and Jake had hung out together a lot during the rain break, and he'd helped Jake a ton with his performance. *Mentoring,* that's what it was. A really talented adult sharing his passion with a kid who had it, too. Not something she could get into a tutorial.

When E.D. left Brunhilda to help get this evening's

performance back on schedule, she noticed her grandfather leaning against the back of the Pageant Wagon, his cell phone pressed to his ear.

It turned out that the Organic School's art buses (they had three) were someplace in South Dakota and it was going to take them a lot longer to get to Saunders, New Mexico, than the two days it was supposed to take the Applewhites. "No reason we can't just be regular tourists for a while," Lucille suggested. "We could stay here and explore Kansas City. There's an arts district, and Crown Center—"

But the others were ready to leave what had begun to seem a dreary, rainy place. Jake, in particular, wanted out of Missouri, so when Archie suggested they head into Kansas so they wouldn't have such long traveling days, the family agreed to get back on the road and see what Kansas had to offer.

E.D. found them a nice RV park in Hutchinson, close to the only tourist attraction in the area—an old salt mine that was also a museum. Destiny got especially excited about it because he either didn't understand or refused to believe that there could be any kind of mine other than a gold mine.

When they'd settled in the RV park, and the others had gone over to the rec room to watch a movie, E.D. closed herself into her parents' bedroom in Brunhilda and made a video log tutorial of everything she'd learned online about the geographical history of Kansas, and why there was salt in the state to be mined at all. Amazingly enough it had been laid down 275 million years ago when there was a shallow sea where Kansas was now. She had also researched the use of salt, and how it got from a mine to people's saltshakers. The rest of the family would probably say her tutorial was boring—but she found herself agreeing with her grandfather. This was an expedition of education—it *had* to have some education in it, right?

At the same time, she saw Melody's point. Her Art of Style video helped them move up in the standings. She just needed to find a way to make the educational stuff more *story*-like and appealing. What sort of story could she create around salt? Maybe they could get some really fun and interesting videos in the salt mine. It would help so much, she thought, if they knew what the other groups were doing. Zedediah had forbidden them from looking online. But E.D. was tempted. Very tempted. She looked over at the laptop. *Maybe just a peek?*

The door to the bedroom banged open. "What's up, Eddie?" asked Melody, flopping down onto the bunk next to her.

"Don't call me Eddie," E.D. shot back. Then she leaned toward Melody and lowered her voice. "I'm thinking of going online and looking at the other groups."

"Oooh, naughty," said Melody with a smile. "But don't worry. I already did."

"You what?" E.D. realized she really should have known—there was no way Melody was going to not do something just because Zedediah said not to. "And?"

Melody shrugged. "The old guy was right," she said. "No point watching anybody else's. You can't compare any one to any other. They're all really different, and not that great if you ask me. We're doing fine. We'll pick up in the standings. I just know we will."

"But—"

"Trust me on this," Melody said. "Between my gift for story and your gift for facts, we have it made."

E.D. nodded. She wanted to win as much as Melody, and she knew she was getting better at the educational video logs. She could do this, she thought. She could help them win. And then she could give herself an A+ for the Expedition after all.

Chapter Twenty

As they all waited to get into the elevator that would take them six hundred and fifty feet down (six hundred and fifty!) into the salt mine museum, Destiny kept asking Jake if this mine had gold. Jake assured him that there was so much stuff stored in this mine there was sure to be something even better than gold. "Good, then," Destiny said. "At least I gets to wear a hard hat!"

Everybody had to wear a hard hat, of course, and carry an emergency breathing device. Jake tried not to think about the sort of emergency that might force them to use such a device, or what good a hard hat would do if the roof of the mine collapsed.

The elevator ride was very noisy and so absolutely, incredibly dark that Destiny grabbed hold of Jake's hand with a little whimper and held on during what seemed like way more than the ninety seconds the guide had said it would take.

Luckily, when they got down into the very big, very well-lit mine, it didn't take Destiny long to find something better than gold. "Batman!" he shouted. "They gots *Batman* down here! The realio, trulio, honest-to-goodness *Batman*!" Sure enough, Jake saw, one of the costumes from a Batman movie was on display in a glass case. There was a ton of neat stuff stored in the mine, which was why it was also a museum. It was so deep underground that important things could be stored there to keep them safe.

Melody, who looked sort of wonderful even in a hard hat, he thought, grabbed him by the arm. "Come on. Let's go on the Dark Ride!"

Jake remembered how very dark the darkness in the elevator had been and would have preferred to stay in the well-lit museum part. E.D. had already flat out refused to take the Dark Ride, through completely unlit parts of the mine. But he couldn't let Melody know he was more chicken than she was. He let her pull him over to it.

The ride was like a bunch of electric golf carts all

strung together into a train. He climbed into the nearest car, and Melody swung herself onto the seat next to him, giving his shoulder a playful nudge. Hal climbed in after her. She hadn't had to pull *him* to the ride—he had just followed her, which didn't surprise Jake. Hal had, after all, taken to riding in whichever bus Melody chose, following her like a puppy.

In spite of the darkness, Jake thought, once the train got going it was a pretty neat ride. The cool, dry air blew against their faces, and sometimes they could just barely see the rough tunnel walls sliding past. In the darkest parts, it was so dark that even putting his palm right against his nose, he couldn't see his hand at all.

They were pulling past an alcove, carved into the mine wall and crammed full of antique mining tools, lit with a single electric bulb, when Jake noticed that Melody was resting her leg against his. Firmly. He found his pulse racing. *Maybe it's just an accident*, he told himself, and pulled his leg back just a little bit. He didn't want to crowd her.

She pressed her leg up against his again. It wasn't an accident. *Bump-thump*, went his heart.

All of a sudden he remembered what she had said to him in Memphis. That he would never even try to kiss her. That he wouldn't have the guts.

As they passed another display, Jake glanced down and saw that Melody's hand was lying in her lap. The carts bumped over something and they jostled back and forth. Melody slipped sideways a little and ended up pressing up against Jake even harder. Without thinking any more about it, he reached across and took her hand.

She shifted a little bit so that their fingers were entwined, and closed her hand around his. Jake's heart stopped going *bump-thump* and felt, for a moment, as if it had stopped completely.

Be cool, Semple, he thought fiercely to himself. *It's just holding hands. With a girl. Just 'cause you haven't done it much . . . okay, any . . .* He felt like he was holding on to a live wire, getting just a little bit electrocuted. It was awesome. All of a sudden he didn't mind the dark anymore. She had called him a lap dog. He was *not.* He found himself suddenly fixated on the idea of kissing her. Hal was right there in the car with them, but it was pitch-dark. Melody's fingers gave his an encouraging little squeeze.

Quickly, before he could chicken out, he slid his hand out of hers and reached out to put his arm around her shoulders. He didn't know exactly what he was planning to do, but maybe at least a quick kiss before they hit the next pool of light. He could turn her face toward him, just to show her he had the guts. To show himself, too.

As he reached around her shoulders, he felt something weird. It was bony and muscley. He felt along it until he realized with a rush of sickening mortification that he was squeezing Hal's shoulder. Hal had his arm around Melody. She was sitting there, between them, holding Jake's hand, with Hal's arm around her shoulder.

He heard Melody give a single, dry snort of laughter.

Jake pulled his arm back and pressed himself against the side of the cart, as far as he could go. At the next lit alcove Hal jumped out of the car, which they had been told not to do, and ran ahead to climb into the empty car in front of them, where he slid down into the bench until he almost disappeared.

Seething with anger and humiliation in the darkness, Jake decided he was *done* trying to make sense of girls. He would become a *monk* or something. He couldn't help blessing the deep darkness that hid his burning cheeks and kept anybody—*anybody*—from taking a video of this awful thing, like the video of his first performance as Asa Trenchard. Hal hadn't sent that video to the Rutherfords, he knew, but it still existed somewhere. Now there were two awful, embarrassing things that—recorded or not—he suspected he would never forget.

Between the salt mine and their packing up in Hutchinson to begin the drive to Saunders, New Mexico, Jake kept to himself as much as possible. Hal, he noticed, was fully back to his hermit self, not only not talking, but even taking his food away from everybody else to eat. Jake didn't know whether Melody was avoiding both of them, or whether she had other reasons for wanting to be alone, but she pretty much took over the little room the Hutchinson RV park called a tech center, where people who didn't have their own computer could "get connected while on the road." She hadn't come back to her bunk by the time he'd gone to sleep and was already up and out and helping to pack up by the time he dragged himself out of bed in the morning. Jake was relieved not to have to see her much.

Melody chose to ride in Brunhilda—with Hal—on their way to Saunders, and Jake was not quite so relieved about that.

"Wagons ho!" Archie shouted as the Pageant Wagon roared to life. Just as Archie started to move out, there was a loud thump on the door. He cranked it open and Melody jumped in. "Changed my mind!" she said, and climbed aboard. "Too crowded over there."

"So," she said as she flopped down right next to Jake. "How about that Dark Ride?"

Jake swallowed hard and said nothing, sliding a bit closer to the window.

She punched him on the shoulder. "That was awkward, huh?"

Jake really, really did not want to talk about it. He glared at the floor, clenching his teeth.

"Hey," said Melody, more gently. "Look. I'm sorry about that whole thing. I just—Hal put his arm on my shoulders and he was just so cute and shy about it that I didn't have the heart to push him away or tell him to stop. I didn't want to spend all that time building him up, getting him that makeover, only to wreck it all by hurting his feelings, right?"

He glanced up. She was looking him right in the eye, and she seemed as serious and apologetic as he'd ever seen her. He *wanted* to stay mad at her. He really did. Then she smiled, and he gave up.

"That was . . . ," he started, and she was already giggling, with her hand over her mouth. "That was really, really . . ." He laughed out loud before he could stop himself, and Melody started cackling, with her head rocked back.

"It sure was," she agreed. "It sure was." Jake noticed his hand was sort of near hers on the bench seat.

"Melody!" Lucille called from the back of the bus. "I have a *style* question for you."

Melody jumped up, started toward Lucille, then turned and, with a wink, blew him a kiss.

Bump-thump. Stop that, he told his heart. *Just stop it!*

Chapter Twenty-One

E.D. was having a hard time getting her thoughts in order. It wasn't a feeling she enjoyed. She was sitting at the dinette as Brunhilda rolled on toward New Mexico, trying to process something that had happened in the salt mine. But where to start?

In the mine Lucille had wandered past while E.D. was standing staring at a glass case without even seeing it. "You look a million miles away," she said.

E.D. sighed. "Don't you think sometimes that there's just *too much stuff* in the world to ever get it into any kind of order?"

"I think this trip is turning you all inside out."

"What do you mean?" E.D. asked.

"An adventurous quest, involving the ability to think things through," Lucille said, putting a hand on E.D.'s shoulder. "You like to think things through *before they happen*, because then you can control them—or at least you tell yourself you can. But this is a journey. You've got to let go of control and get into trust. Trust that you'll be able to think things through *after* the fact, and get just as much from them. After all, how could you *plan* for a miracle like the one right in front of you?"

E.D. finally really looked at the display case, wondering what Lucille was talking about. It was a yellowed old newspaper, with the corners gone, and tattered edges. As she read the headline, her heart almost stopped.

OUR LOSS—THE GREAT NATIONAL CALAMITY—DEATH OF THE PRESIDENT, she read. The date on the paper was April 16, 1865. The card next to the case identified it as the first newspaper that was printed after Lincoln was shot. After he was shot watching the very play they had *just* been performing.

It was such an unbelievable coincidence that it *did* feel like a miracle, she thought. *Trust,* E.D. thought now, bouncing along in Brunhilda. Could trust really be the opposite of planning? That newspaper clipping was going to be a great addition to her video log—it would look like she did it on purpose, like she'd pulled the whole thing together, like she'd turned their trip into a curriculum. But she hadn't! She hadn't known she would find a connection to the Lincoln assassination in that salt mine—it was just chance. How could she rely on chance? She didn't want to *hope* they would find educational connections and things to learn. She wanted to *know*.

After stopping for lunch in Dodge City, Kansas—which was billed as a "wild frontier town of the Old West," where Zedediah bought a cowboy hat for himself and one for Destiny—E.D. settled back in, with Winston at her feet under the table. Cordelia had brought Hal a hamburger. He hadn't gotten out to see Dodge City. Had his makeover worn off somehow? E.D. wondered. Ever since the salt mine Hal had been his old, most reclusive self.

She began recording in her notebook the bits of history she'd managed to collect from signs and pictures on the walls at the restaurant. In another coincidence, she had learned Fort Dodge, the fort the city was named for, had been built in April 1865, the same month Lincoln was assassinated. She underlined that bit.

They had traveled through the panhandle of Oklahoma, which E.D. had shown Destiny on a map to explain the word *panhandle*, and had entered New

Mexico when Randolph called out to alert them to the fact that they were passing the border to Texas. "That's Texas, right over there." He pointed to the left. "Biggest state in the lower forty-eight."

"Doesn't look any bigger than this one," Destiny said.

Ahead of them, the Pageant Wagon started flashing its parking lights. "What's Archie doing that for?" Randolph wondered out loud.

E.D. sniffed. A familiar smell was wafting through Brunhilda's windows. "What is that?" she asked.

"French fries!" Destiny hollered. "Somebody's making french fries!"

The Pageant Wagon swung into the passing lane and Brunhilda followed. Three extraordinary buses were ahead. The one in back had an entire field of pinwheels mounted on the roof, which were spinning madly in the wind. It was painted a vigorous, electric green.

"It seems," Randolph said, "that we have located the Organic School." As he pulled up next to the green pinwheel bus, Sybil and Cordelia all waved to the driver, who waved back. Up ahead, the other buses started to pull off the road with the Pageant Wagon now in the lead. The pinwheel bus backed off to let Brunhilda into the lane ahead of it, and they all turned into the big, dusty parking lot of a truck stop that had gone out of business and was shuttered and faded in the sun.

Everyone—except Hal—climbed out of Brunhilda, and the guy with the flattop who'd been driving the pinwheel bus came striding over to them. "The Applewhites' Creative Academy, I presume?" he said.

"And you must be the Organic School," Randolph said.

"Organic *Academy*," he corrected, waving one finger from side to side. E.D. heard a *whuff* behind her and turned to see Winston on the bottom step, looking suspiciously toward the newcomers. "Ah," said Flattop. "Wasn't aware you had a dog. Yeah, um . . . some of our kids have allergies. So, can you just . . . keep him in your bus? Thanks. Great."

E.D. grabbed Winston's leash from Brunhilda's door pocket and clipped it to the dog's collar. Destiny, in his cowboy hat, was staring fixedly at the pinwheels on the roof of the bus when four small children came tumbling out of it. Not one of them was older than seven.

Uh-oh, E.D. thought.

Destiny hadn't noticed them yet. Jake was on his way over from the Pageant Wagon and E.D. waved at him frantically. He raised his eyebrows questioningly, and she pointed to the little kids. She looked down at Destiny, back at the little kids, and mouthed "Do something!" at him. He understood immediately, as she knew he would, and swooped down on Destiny.

"Hey, cowboy!" he shouted, turning the little boy

around and hoisting him onto his shoulders. "How about a rodeo ride? See if you can stay on the bucking bronco!"

He bounced around E.D. with Destiny squealing in delight and grabbing at his hair. "You get Winston inside," Jake said to E.D., as he galloped around behind Brunhilda and out of sight of the little kids, neighing like a horse.

When she'd closed Winston into Brunhilda, E.D. walked along beside the other two amazing buses. One was done up like Vincent van Gogh's painting *The Starry Night*, with a swirly blue night sky full of stars and a moon and a tall, dark tree. The other was so interesting she just stopped and stared at it for a minute. She realized her mouth was hanging open, and closed it. The bus was covered all over in shiny metal scales, like a fish, and had a big fin that looked like it was made out of folded metal on the roof, and smaller fins on the sides. There was even a tail—it was a couple of feet long, stuck on the back of the bus and hinged in sections so it could sway back and forth as the bus went down the road. E.D. began to feel a little embarrassed about Destiny's purple possum on the side of Brunhilda.

A pale, freckled woman wearing a long skirt made out of cut-up pairs of jeans emerged from the fish bus. She had what looked like a stretchy fabric seedpod around her waist—a baby, all curled up in a sling. "Hi, *hi*," she said in general, to the whole family. "I'm Michaela, great to *meet* you. You must be the *Applewhites*, we are *so* looking forward to working with you on this *challenge*."

More kids had come out of the Organic Academy buses now and were wandering around, staring at the Applewhite buses, or trying to peer into the boarded-up windows of the truck stop. A couple of the littler ones, with light brown skin and soft curly dark hair, came pelting over and flung themselves onto Michaela's legs, where they peered out suspiciously from behind her skirt.

Jake came around Brunhilda just then and Destiny, still on his shoulders, saw the little kids. "Oh, *great*," he said, kicking Jake in the chest. "Put me down!" he demanded. The moment his feet touched the ground, he ran to Brunhilda and shut himself in with Winston.

Introductions and greetings were exchanged—Michaela's husband, Gary, a balding dark-skinned man with wire spectacles, nodded but didn't speak. They were joined briefly by Flattop, whose name E.D. missed. "So, those are actual *windmill generators*?" Archie asked, and Flattop nodded. "That's the Green Machine. Of course the bus itself runs on recycled restaurant cooking oil."

"So that's why it smells like french fries!" Randolph said as Archie and the man headed toward the back of the Green Machine.

There were two more families traveling with the Organic Academy, but one couple was buried in their electronic devices and barely mustered a wave, and the other couple was bickering quietly but intensely, and after a quick, awkward handshake with everybody, they headed off to the far side of the parking lot to continue their argument.

"We'd love to meet the rest of the children, as well," said Lucille brightly. "They look like a great, exuberant bunch!"

"Well, *sure,*" said Michaela, "but they're all over *there* just now. I can't exactly *gather them up* in some kind of *formation* like they're in the *army*, can I?" She barked a quick laugh.

Melody came over to E.D., leaned in, and whispered behind her hand. "Check that out!" E.D. looked across the parking lot where Melody was pointing. There was a boy, about fourteen or fifteen, with long wavy blond hair. *Like a surfer,* E.D. thought, though she had never in her life met a surfer. A very, very good-looking boy. He was laughing about something. He ruffled one of the little kids' hair and started over toward the assembled grown-ups.

"Hi," he said, extending his hand confidently to Sybil and then making his way down the line of the Applewhites. "I'm Tyler." When he got to E.D. he took her hand and held on to it for just a moment. "Well, *hi,*" he said. E.D. felt her cheeks get suddenly hot. She was very, very glad that she had taken the time to do her hair and put on some blush and lip gloss after they'd eaten at the restaurant in Dodge.

Sybil proposed that the kids start getting to know one another by riding the rest of the way to Saunders, about an hour and a half away, in each other's buses.

"Hooray!" shouted a few of the little kids, and headed off toward Brunhilda, where Destiny was holed up. Jake hurried after them.

As he climbed the steps Destiny was yelling from inside, "No, you GET OUT! This is MY PIRATE HAMMOCK!"

"Let's you and me take Winston to the Pageant Wagon, cowboy," E.D. heard Jake say.

She brushed her hair back into place, tugged her shirt down over her jeans, and followed Tyler, who was shepherding some of the other kids to the fish bus. *Why not?* she asked herself. Wasn't that what *trust* was all about? Taking the chances that the journey put in front of you.

Chapter Twenty-Two

Jake was warming his hands around a cup of coffee as everyone gathered for breakfast around the rickety picnic tables of the only campground in Saunders, New Mexico, wearing jackets against the high-desert October-morning chill. Whoops and shrieks from the other buses had wakened them not long after sunrise, and even Lucille had been less than cheerful as she took her turn fixing their scrambled eggs and toast.

Hal climbed down from his tent and told them they'd received their next destination. As desolate as

Saunders seemed, it did at least have cell service. "Sedona, Arizona, next," he said, "after we're done with the challenge here in Saunders."

Lucille positively shrieked at this news, startling Winston, who whuffed grumpily from under the table. He had been unceremoniously tied to the leg of the picnic table so he wouldn't accidentally wander anywhere near any of the allergy-ridden French Fries, as Archie had started calling the kids from the Organic Academy.

"I have *always* wanted to go to Sedona!" Lucille said, one hand on her heart, her face lit with enthusiasm. "It's famous for its vortexes of spiritual energy—it's got some of the best psychic vibrations in the world!"

"What are we supposed to do there?" Randolph asked. "I intend to organize another reading no matter what it is!"

"No challenge yet," Hal said. He grabbed the cup of coffee Cordelia had poured for him and settled onto a bench as far away from Melody as he could manage. He had not, Jake thought, recovered from the Dark Ride. He wanted to tell Hal that his skill in editing the video logs, and the way he'd played the villain in *Our American Cousin*, said way more about who he was than that one embarrassing moment in the awful dark.

"I, for one, intend to visit the vortexes and commune with the spirits of the place," Lucille said, looking positively rapturous.

Randolph gulped his second cup of coffee. It was earlier than he liked to start the day. "I'll need to organize the next reading, and make plans to put a cast together. What the rest of you will do here in Saunders I have no idea. It isn't as if we'll have anything in common with this bunch of organic farmers."

"I doubt that they're farmers," Zedediah said. "They're from Brooklyn."

"Urban farmers, then. Rooftop gardens of okra and chard. Why else would they name their school Organic?"

"It's irrelevant to me," Sybil observed. "I shall be working on my *final* revision."

Just then, Tyler came ambling over from the Organics' campsite. Melody elbowed E.D., Jake noticed, and E.D. sat up straighter, pulled off her jacket's hood, and ran a hand self-consciously through her hair. E.D. was a sucker for a pretty face, he thought.

"Excuse me for interrupting your breakfast," he said, "but Michaela has asked if you could join us in half an hour for a joint conversation about what we'll all be doing at Saunders Elementary. She's organized it with the principal, but in the spirit of partnership, she would like your input. The videographers are setting up at the campfire circle now."

Videographers? Jake thought. That sounded like a

lot bigger deal than just Hal with his lights and tripod. Maybe that had something to do with their being in first place.

A few minutes into the rather chaotic "joint conversation"—which was being filmed by two of the Organic adults, who turned out to be professional filmmakers—Archie and Zedediah went off somewhere with Henry, the man who had invented the Green Machine's windmills. Jake would have liked to go with them. Hal, he saw, was standing with one of the videographers. The two were carrying on a whispered conversation. Clearly, what *Michaela* called a conversation consisted of her talking and everyone else listening as best they could over the noise the children were making.

"If you've been watching our *videos*," she said, "you'll know that the Organic philosophy at the heart of our academy is all about raising *free-range children*." At the moment, Jake noted, two of the French Fries were dismantling the fireplace circle, dragging the rocks away and piling them into a heap. As far as he could tell, the philosophy actually meant that the adults never said no to the children, about anything.

"Free-range parenting is actually quite a splendid movement," Jake heard Lucille whisper to Cordelia, as a little boy began to use a bit of charred wood from the remains of a previous campfire to make black charcoal smears on the side of the closest of the buses, which happened to be the Pageant Wagon. "But they do seem to be taking it to extremes. . . ."

Tyler hurried over and conferred with the boy for a moment, after which the child rubbed his hands on the charred end and then began making black handprints on his own sweatshirt instead. Jake saw Tyler catch E.D.'s eye, give her a thumbs-up sign, and grin. E.D., of course, grinned back.

Michaela, standing in the sun that had begun to warm the morning air, her baby snuggled in his pod against her stomach, went on talking, undistracted by the children. Jake heard something about her *epiphany* on the way to New Mexico about their challenge, and something about the *indigenous fauna* of New Mexico. Her strange way of speaking, Jake thought, at least emphasized the most meaningful words.

"What's ind . . . indid-juh-nus fauna?" Destiny asked Jake. He had chosen to sit between Jake and E.D. in order to be protected on both sides from marauding small children.

"The animals whose natural habitat is New Mexico," E.D. told him.

This led to a side discussion between E.D. and Destiny about whether New Mexico had any possums, so Jake missed quite a bit of the next part of Michaela's talk. He did hear something about *catching* and something about *cages*.

"There is such a *rich biosphere* here in the desert," Michaela was saying now.

"*High desert*," E.D. said under her breath. "There's a difference!"

"And, of course, our *children* have been so *focused* on the *creatures* of the desert . . ."

Jake remembered one of the children had been hollering about finding a lizard at the truck stop and right now one of the boys who'd been piling rocks had started stomping on ants.

". . . and it is *so* important to allow ourselves to be *guided* by the interests of the *children*. . . ."

A cluster of French Fries had begun to sing a song about a bunny bopping field mice on the head, and even though Michaela raised her voice to be heard over the singing, Jake missed the next part of her one-sided conversation. Nobody, of course, hushed the children. Archie, Zedediah, and Henry came ambling back just as the kids finished their song, in time to hear Michaela's triumphant conclusion, "So *that's* my thought about our partnership *challenge*. We'll call it *the Zoo of the Desert*!"

Zedediah stepped into the circle. "A zoo? You expect us to create a zoo?"

Michaela nodded. "For the students of Saunders Elementary. The principal said we could engage them in any project we chose."

"A zoo isn't a little *project*, it's a massive

undertaking! The facilities required to care for animals, to display them properly . . ."

Michaela waved her hand dismissively at Zedediah and he fell quiet, dumbfounded. "Not a *zoo* zoo, obviously, just a *temporary* one. A *pop-up* zoo, if you will. Catch them one day, display them one day, let them go the next. Then on to the next challenge."

"Excuse me," Lucille interjected, "but if your philosophy about raising children is to allow them *free range,* doesn't it seem a little—a little *contradictory*—to set out to catch and cage wild creatures?"

Michaela again made that dismissive gesture. "Children's inquiring minds are surely of *greater consequence* than the brief *inconvenience* of a few mere *animals.*"

At the words *mere animals,* Lucille flushed pink, stood up, and left the campfire circle. Jake saw that her lips were moving, but he couldn't hear what she was muttering to herself as she went. He suspected they had just lost another adult member of this so-called partnership.

"The creation of this zoo will give all the children involved a *greater appreciation* for the *diversity* of nature," Michaela went on, apparently unmoved by Lucille's leaving, "and the *videos* will expand that appreciation to children across the country who might never have the *opportunity* to visit the desert!"

"*High* desert," E.D. whispered again.

"Even a one-day zoo is still a massive undertaking,"

Zedediah protested again.

"Oh, I'm more than happy to leave the details to you"—she looked him up and down, and then circled her hand in the air, including Archie and Henry this time—"you *handy* types."

The baby in the pod began to cry.

"Who's going to find and capture the specimens for this zoo?" Zedediah asked.

Michaela was bouncing the baby now, and shushing it. She looked up, in apparent surprise at the question. "The *students* of *Saunders*, of course. They'll know a lot more about where to look for them and how to catch them than any of *us*." As the baby began to cry louder, she announced that she needed to feed it and she'd leave the organization of the rest of the project up to others. "My work here is *done*!"

And everybody else's is just beginning, Jake thought.

Chapter Twenty-Three

High desert! E.D. thought again, as Michaela took her crying baby away and the meeting, such as it had been, broke up. The whole idea for this so-called partnership challenge had been invented and steamrolled into existence by a woman who didn't know the enormous difference between desert and high desert!

Hal was deep in conversation with the Organics' videographers. Archie and Henry, having accepted the label of "handy types," were talking about getting to a hardware store and what equipment they would need to build cages and habitats for indigenous fauna, and Zedediah had stuffed his hands into his pockets and gone off toward the Pageant Wagon by himself. Melody came over to E.D. and gave her a nudge with her elbow. "I saw that!" she said.

"What?" E.D. asked, coming back from an impossible vision of cages full of coyotes and mountain lions and snakes. Anyway, little kids wouldn't catch stuff like that.

"The way Tyler Organic was showing off for you. I'm thinking it's time you expanded your horizons. I know you have a thing about Jake"—E.D. opened her mouth to protest but Melody just held up a hand and kept right on—"but think about it. He's practically your brother." There it was again, E.D. thought. The *practically-your-brother* thing. "He's also been following *me* this whole trip like a puppy."

It gave E.D. a pang not just to hear what she knew to be true, but to have Melody call Jake a "puppy," as if she had no respect for him at all!

"Your real brother's been doing the same, which is totally not going anywhere, by the way. But at least Hal's older."

It doesn't bug me that Hal has a crush on Melody, E.D. thought. *Just Jake.*

"Which brings us back to the topic at hand," Melody said, reaching out to rearrange E.D.'s hair. "Cute little Tyler Organic!"

Tyler was the first guy who hadn't instantly become besotted with Melody, and E.D. was pretty sure Melody had noticed this, which was why she had called Tyler both cute, which he definitely was, and little, which he *wasn't*! But Tyler was the first boy other than Jake who had paid any attention to E.D. at all.

"So here's my idea. We make Tyler your personal project—think of it as a sociology assignment. I'm going to show you how to hook this guy. He won't know what hit him. Boys are real pushovers, and it's high time you found out how to push 'em! Hell"—she punched E.D. on the shoulder—"you can write a report afterward, and give yourself a grade!"

"Ow," said E.D. Melody had punched her kind of hard.

"And I know," said Melody mysteriously, "what your final exam can be."

"Final exam?"

"I went online to check the hype for the big awards ceremony out in California, and guess what they're having after the winner's announced! You know, after the celebrities and entertainers and all they're doing to make sure people tune in to watch . . ."

"What?" E.D. asked.

"The Rutherford Arts and Education Ball. A great big *dance*!"

E.D. had never been to a dance. The last grade she had gone to in regular school was third. Third graders didn't have dances. The whole idea of it made her dizzy.

"And here's what you're gonna do to get yourself an A on this sociology assignment. Before we're done here in this friggin' high desert, before the Applewhites go one way and the Organics go another, you are gonna get Tyler to ask you to go to that ball with him. Like Cinderella and Prince Charming," Melody said, "except for the glass slipper and the midnight deadline."

"I don't know."

Melody looked at her like a cat eyeing a mouse. "Trust me on this."

It was the second time Melody had told E.D. to trust her. But on this subject, E.D. thought, she pretty much could.

"You're good at learning stuff. You can learn this, too."

The next day, when Brunhilda and the Organic buses all pulled up outside a low, dust-colored public school building, Melody, camera in hand, stood for a moment before stepping out onto the gravel parking lot. "You ever noticed that most schools look like prisons?" she said to no one in particular.

A small, thin, balding man wearing a suit and a bow tie—apparently the school principal—was coming out the front doors toward a baby-pod-less Michaela, who was advancing on him with her usual passionate intensity. She grabbed his hand and shook it vigorously. From the rather worried expression on the man's face, E.D. guessed Michaela had already called him to explain her idea for the Zoo of the Desert.

"I've checked the weather forecast," he said, "and you're in luck. This unusual warm spell is expected to continue for another week or so. Most years we'd be having hard freezes at night by now and most of our wildlife would have gone underground."

"We've taken that into *account*, of course," Michaela said smoothly. E.D. suspected that was a bit of a fib. "Have you *gathered* your *student body*?" she asked.

"The children and their teachers are waiting for us in the cafetorium." He moved out of the way to let the videographers and their equipment through the doors.

The French Fries had begun spilling out of the Organic buses, some of them carrying the butterfly nets Cordelia and the two other Organic mothers had made out of sticks and coat hangers and fabric. Cordelia had tried to get Lucille to help but she had utterly refused to have anything to do with catching and caging living beings. "No matter who, or what, or how small, they have as much right to live their lives as we do!"

E.D. spotted a little boy with one of the rather lopsided cages she and Tyler had built, and she shuddered. That had been part of Melody's plan for E.D. to get

Tyler's attention—she was supposed to act less capable than she was and let Tyler show her how to do things.

She *hated* that and said so, but Melody assured her that it was only a starting point. "You can be your whole supergirl self later, once he's well and truly hooked. Remember, this isn't *truth*, it's a useful *story*." Even so, E.D. wished she'd built the cage herself. Tyler was no carpenter.

The principal cleared his throat. "You did say this project might get us a mention on national TV?"

"And all over the *Internet*," Michaela said.

"It would be quite a feather in Saunders's cap. We're a very small district."

Michaela was already heading toward the building, so he scurried to get in front of her to open the doors. Everyone else trooped along after them, except for Destiny, who had stayed with Winston in Brunhilda because there would be even more little kids at Saunders Elementary.

After the introductions, Michaela launched into a full description of the Zoo of the Desert. "Your job during the *school day today* will be to gather as much *information* as you can about the sorts of *animals* you might search for and what they will *need* during their brief period of *captivity*. This is a *pop-up zoo* and they will be on display for only a day. After school you will begin *collecting*. And first thing tomorrow *morning*, you will bring in whatever *specimens* you have managed to *capture*. We are interested in *all kinds* of wildlife: reptiles, insects, even small *rodents* and other mammals if you are able to handle their *humane capture*. You will, of course, avoid capturing any major *predators* that are indigenous to this area, *ha-ha*." None of the assembled students laughed with her. "We have brought some *nets* you can use for the smaller, or *winged* specimens."

E.D. felt somebody come up beside her. It was Tyler. "They say you're good at organizing stuff. I haven't got a clue what we need to do."

E.D. could almost see the wall chart for the Zoo of the High Desert that was taking shape in her head. *Less capable*, she thought. She looked into Tyler's pretty blue eyes, smiled, and gave her head a little toss the way Melody had shown her. "*Between* us, we'll figure it out."

When they headed back to the campground later, Tyler rode in Brunhilda over Michaela's protest that he was needed with the "little ones." E.D. had thought they might talk about organizing the zoo, but Tyler asked her what her favorite books were. Every title she mentioned turned out to be one of Tyler's favorites, too. Better yet, he knew some books by some of her favorite authors that she'd never heard of, and had one of them in his bus that she could borrow.

Back at the campground, Tyler hurried off to find the book for her. E.D. noticed her grandfather heading for the Pageant Wagon, his phone in his hand. "E.D.," he said when he saw her, "I'm thinking I owe you an apology."

"What? Why?"

"I've always told you to follow your joy, and it has occurred to me that I haven't been doing that myself."

"So," she said after a moment. "You don't like Michaela's idea for a pop-up zoo?"

Zedediah laughed, and E.D. realized she hadn't heard him laugh in a long time. "The point is, do *you*?"

"I kind of do," she surprised herself by admitting. She was wondering what kinds of animals the kids would find, and whether some of them might be ones she'd never even heard of. In a world as different from North Carolina as this was, it wasn't just possible, it was *likely*. And besides, there were zoos all over the world that were working to help save species that were endangered in the wild, and helping to make people care more about the wildlife around them. She wasn't as sure as Aunt Lucille that the idea of a zoo was *automatically* bad. She nodded. "I like it. I really do."

He put his hand on the side of her face, and she could feel the scratchiness of his calluses. "That," he said, "is all that matters. Find a way to make it actually work." He went into the Pageant Wagon.

"What was that about?" she wondered aloud to herself, as Tyler came back, waving the book in the air.

Chapter Twenty-Four

Jake had been named the "specimen-intake supervisor," and the next morning he found himself thinking this whole thing had been a tremendously bad idea. He and E.D. had talked about it when they'd gotten back to the campground yesterday and for a little while it had felt like old times, before the Kiss, when the two of them had worked really well together to save the Applewhites' camp from being shut down. E.D. had asked him to help her work up a list of the kinds of animals the kids might find and the things that might be needed to keep them properly cared for over the day and a half they'd be caged—the kinds of food they might need. The kinds of habitats. But then Tyler had come over to the Applewhite side of the campground, and E.D. had hurriedly closed up her spiral notebook and asked the kid if *he* could help her organize. Before she'd gone all gooney about Tyler, she'd made Jake think Michaela's project was sane and educational, but now . . .

Up the sidewalk in front of the school stretched a long line of Saunders Elementary students, waiting patiently (or, in some cases, impatiently) with the fauna they had collected.

So far, the dozen or so specimens he'd checked in had all been bugs: crickets in cottage cheese tubs, wolf spiders in matchboxes, grasshoppers in milk cartons. One second grader proudly held up a ziplock bag full of ants. Jake didn't see any movement in the bag.

All the cages that had been built for the zoo—in the few frenzied hours they'd had to build them—were sitting empty, while armies of insects already jammed the two glass terrariums they had dug out of a science room's closet. An emergency call had gone out to residents of Saunders for any empty jars that could be called into service for bug display.

A couple of kids back in the line was a little girl holding a big pet carrier. *Now that looks promising,* Jake thought. He assigned the next three kids—grasshopper, crickets, ladybug—to the two oldest

French Fries, who were helping him at the specimen-intake table, and waved the little girl forward.

She stepped up, struggling to get the big heavy carrier up on the table. Then she tucked some of her stringy brown hair behind her ear, opened the front of the carrier, and dumped the contents out. Jake found himself staring at a pile of fur, mostly light brown but with lots of dark red.

"'S'a jackrabbit," the girl said, wiping her nose with the back of her hand.

"I see it—wait, is that blood?" Jake asked.

"Well, sure. I winged him with my pellet gun, in his leg."

Jake waved frantically for Lucille, who had come along not so much to help as to oversee the *humane treatment* requirement. "Why did you do that?" he asked.

The little girl looked at him in disbelief. "I'm not quick enough to run him down otherwise!"

Lucille gave a yelp of dismay at the sight of the wounded rabbit, scooped it up in her arms, and ran into the school to apply first aid.

"I do okay?" asked the little girl, looking suddenly concerned. "It was the only way I could think of to catch one! I didn't kill him like my dad does when we have them for supper."

These kids, Jake thought, had a *seriously* different way of life than he was used to. "You—no, it's okay.

Just try not to . . . um . . . shoot anything else, all right?" The girl nodded and scooted aside just as a boy who looked about eleven slapped a squirming pillowcase onto the table in front of Jake.

"Snakes!" he announced proudly.

It took them all morning to get the animals squared away in something like livable conditions. The collection was still mostly bugs, with some truly unsettling variations: large centipedes; two tarantulas, all bristly legs and beady pinpoint eyes; three small scorpions, which seemed to mostly want to hide under rocks; and a horrific creature called a vinegaroon, or "whip scorpion," which Jake was sure he would have nightmares about all night. It was like a fatter, uglier, mutant scorpion with one long string for a tail. He had put it in the far corner of the "zoo," but he shivered just thinking about it.

They had some bigger animals, too: the jackrabbit, looking much better now that he'd been cleaned up and bandaged (the pellet had gone cleanly through his leg, Lucille had assured everybody); two turkeys that a little girl had brought out from her farm ("We need them back," she said seriously as her dad got them out of his pickup, "they're for Thanksgiving"); the snakes, which turned out to be harmless garter snakes and were now in a cracked aquarium one of the teachers had gone home to find. There was a kangaroo rat, peeking suspiciously out from the hidey-hole shoe box they had put in its cage. The prize of the zoo was a young javelina, a bushy-haired wild pig that a girl in the fifth grade had brought. "My uncle is a trapper," she explained.

Then there were the "rejects," which had been left out of the zoo exhibit. A girl brought her cat, but Michaela told her to take it back home ("We're looking for *wild* animals, dear, plus our children are *quite* allergic. . . ."). Jake had opened a plastic kitchen container with daisies on the lid and found it full of cockroaches—he'd secretly given those to Destiny, to carry out into the field and release. He didn't think they qualified as wild animals, either, and anyway, they were gross. The best, or *worst*, of all, was the boy who dragged up a heavy burlap bag, which didn't seem to be moving.

"Whatcha got?" Jake asked.

"Possum!" said the boy proudly.

Jake looked at the sack. It still wasn't moving. "Um," he said. "Where did you get it?"

"Side of the road!"

Grateful that Destiny was nowhere to be seen, Jake waved for the custodian.

When the students of Saunders gathered at the tables for lunch, having spent most of their morning watching the zoo being set up around the edges of the cafetorium, except for the javelina that was in a pen outdoors, Michaela called for a "brief meeting" in Starry Night, the Organics' classroom bus. They called the fish bus Pisces, and the windmill bus the Green Machine—whatever they might do differently, it comforted Jake somehow that the Organic Academy had named their buses, too.

Inside, the French Fries were running around, hollering at one another, getting out puzzles, walking away again and leaving them all over the floor, finger-painting on a big easel, and creating general havoc. Michaela and the other Organic parents seemed barely to notice, and made no move to settle the kids down. Melody was filming the chaos with her phone, Jake saw, and Archie flexed his fingers as if, like Jake, he was imagining banging their heads together.

After a while, Tyler pushed his long blond hair back out of his face and cleared his throat. He turned to E.D., who was sitting next to him, and said in a voice loud enough to be heard over the din, "Man, those lizards in the bushes out front were cool, weren't they?"

E.D. looked confused, but one of the older French Fries pulled up short in the middle of a lap around the classroom. "Lizards?" he asked. "What lizards? We looked all morning and didn't see lizards!"

"Oh yeah, cool ones," said Tyler. "Under the bushes. But you have to be very still and quiet to see them."

"COOL!" the French Fry shouted, and tumbled out of the bus with the rest hot on his heels.

"They're allowed to go wherever their curiosity leads them," Tyler said to E.D. "Sometimes you just have to point their curiosity in the right direction."

"*Excellent* work on the zoo, everybody," said Michaela. "As we *go forward* this afternoon we turn to the *educational* portion of the project—"

"Michaela," Tyler said, actually interrupting her, "I've been thinking about that. Do you mind?" Jake noticed he talked to her like he was another one of the grown-ups. Frowning, Michaela waved him on.

"The regular way would be to have the kids *research* the animals. Gather all sorts of *facts*." He said those two words in a tone that implied they were totally ridiculous. Jake looked at E.D., ready for her to argue with this, but her mouth was firmly shut. "But!" Tyler continued. "We figure, they could look all that up themselves."

"So you are *suggesting* . . . ?"

"We're suggesting we let the kids tell their *stories* about them. How they caught them. When they first remember seeing one. You know, we'd *listen*, not talk."

"It would make a good video," one of the videographers said. That seemed to carry a lot of weight with the Organic folks. Few of the Applewhites had an opinion one way or another—Archie was absently picking splinters out of his thumbs from the cage-building. Melody was nodding. Jake was sure E.D. would object—how could she go along with an educational program that didn't include any actual information?—but she sat quietly, watching Tyler, and didn't intervene. With general agreement all around, the meeting broke up. Michaela looked oddly disappointed.

As he headed for the door, Jake became aware of a low rumble, like thunder. Outside, the desert sky was clear and blue. The rumble built and built into an ear-splitting roar, and Jake headed out to see what was going on.

Two big, gleaming motorcycles pulled into the school parking lot. The one in front had tall handlebars with leather dangling from the ends. Riding the bike was a hulking figure with a lush white mustache streaming out on either side of him, mirrored sunglasses shining under a tiny motorcycle helmet.

The roar of the bikes echoed off into silence as the riders turned them off. "Ahoy, Applewhites!" cried the rider in front.

"Bill? Bill Bones?" called Archie, ambling over from where he'd been tightening the gate on the javelina's pen.

"Archibald," said Bill with a serious nod. "Jake."

"What on earth are you doing here?" Archie asked.

"Your father called me! We been keeping in touch—always had an eye toward meeting up somewhere."

Right on cue, Zedediah came out of the Pageant Wagon. He had on his cowboy hat and a heavy jacket, and there was a backpack over one shoulder. "Good to see you, Bill," he said warmly. "You're sure about the loan of the bike?"

Bill nodded, smiling. "Betsy here"—he nodded toward the other rider, a woman about his age in a weather-beaten leather coat—"can ride on with me."

"Wait, you're leaving?" Jake asked.

Zedediah nodded. "It's for the best," he said. "E.D. can explain. I think it's time I had an expedition of my own."

"We're gonna get old Zedediah here some of his cowboy back," Bill said, winking at Jake.

"Don't worry," said Zedediah, putting a hand on Jake's shoulder. "I'll be back with you all soon enough." He picked up the spare helmet, took off his cowboy hat, and handed it to Jake. "Take care of this for me." When he'd tied his backpack down, he flung a leg over the bike as Betsy climbed up on the back of Bill's. He checked out the controls, working the handles and the foot pedals once or twice. Then, with a few revs of the engine and a thumbs-up to Jake and Archie, he was off. The motorcycles spat gravel as they pulled out onto the road, and the roar faded as they disappeared into the long distance of the New Mexico high desert.

Jake and Archie stood side by side, totally flummoxed. "Well," said Archie at last. "I'll be." Shaking his head, he headed back to the school.

Jake couldn't picture what the Expedition was going to be like without Zedediah. He went over to Brunhilda to check on Destiny, to take Winston for a walk, and to give himself time to get his head around it. He found Destiny drawing a series of bright green cockroaches on a big pad of paper at Brunhilda's dinette table.

"Brunhilda is like our house for this 'spedition, right, Jake?" asked Destiny as soon as Jake came in.

"Um, right, buddy."

"And those cockroach guys live mostly in houses, right?" Jake agreed that they did, and Destiny nodded in satisfaction. "Good. I got them back into their right hab-in-tat, then." He went back to drawing.

In front of him, the daisy-covered lid lying on the table next to it, was an empty plastic kitchen container.

Chapter Twenty-Five

It was not quite six o'clock, the sun wasn't up yet, and E.D. had closed herself into the small bathroom in Brunhilda. It was the only time she could get any privacy. She'd been awake for about half an hour, and had been obsessing the whole time. She sat on the closed toilet with the brand-new spiral notebook she had picked up at one of their stops on the way from Saunders to Sedona, Arizona, where they were now, set up in the only campground in Sedona that could accommodate their buses. The cover of the notebook had the word *Journal* in flowing script. She had never in her life kept a diary or a journal—had never seen any reason for such a thing. She had her charts, her calendars and timelines, her curriculum notebook, her plans for every day and every week—what was there to write about afterward?

She thought about Tyler. In the four days they had spent in Saunders, New Mexico, something had changed. Charts and calendars and plans were all about *doing*. She was really, really good at doing, and she knew it. Melody had given her an assignment, and as much as she hated the idea of Melody ordering her around, she'd taken it on. After all, the style stuff Melody had helped her with had been sort of fun, and she'd really learned some things—about hair and makeup and choosing clothes. So as much as she could, she'd tried what Melody had told her to do.

It worked. She could give herself an A on this sociology assignment. Tyler had not only invited her to the dance, he'd kissed her when she said yes! And she had kissed him back.

Now she understood what journals were for. Not for recording what you *did*. Journals were about sorting out how you *felt* about it. And maybe why. This wasn't something she could talk to anyone about, or say out loud in front of a camera. *Dear Diary,* she wrote now, at the top of the first page. Then she crossed it out. She felt silly writing to a spiral notebook as if it were a person.

Dear me— (that was more like it—it really was her own self she was writing to!)

I did it. I got my stupid A. And ever since Tyler asked me to the dance and I said yes, I've been kind of sick to my stomach. How come I'm not glad about that A? How come I'm feeling so icky and kind of mad at myself?

It isn't that I don't want to go to that dance with Tyler. I do. He's cute and he's nice and he's the first boy (besides Jake, my almost-brother) that I've kissed. It wasn't quite as good a kiss as Jake's, but that isn't Tyler's fault. It's mine.

He's nothing at all like David Giacomo. He's truly, honestly, a supernice person. He's outgoing and friendly and he likes kids and he's not afraid of standing up to the Organic grown-ups. He has pretty much everything you could want in a boyfriend. It isn't Tyler who's the problem here. It's me. What the heck does he see in me? Who does he think I am?

There was only one time during that whole four days—at least once Melody gave me my assignment—that I wasn't pretending when I was with him. I pretended to need help building cages. I pretended I didn't care if we gave the kids the real scientific information about all the wildlife in the zoo. But we left those kids in Saunders not even knowing that something with six legs is an insect and something with eight is an arachnid!

The one time—the only time—I was being my real self with Tyler was when he asked me about my favorite books. And that talk was the only real fun I had with him.

Here's the thing about having an almost-brother. Jake really knows me. When he kissed me it was because he wanted to kiss me, not some fake version of me. He knows I'm smart and I like to organize and I'm a lousy actor and I'm not very creative, and he still kissed me.

There was an urgent knocking on the bathroom door. "E.D.?" It was Cordelia, speaking in an intense stage whisper to avoid waking anyone. "Aunt Lucille's got an appointment with some spiritual guide for a sunrise hike into the most intense vortex in Sedona, and I'm going along. I need to use the bathroom before the guide gets here to pick us up. Are you almost done?"

E.D. looked down at her journal. Almost done? She was just beginning. "I'll be out in a minute," she said.

It's Melody, she wrote, hurriedly.

There's a reason I felt what I felt the first time I saw her. She isn't real. She even admits it—is proud of it. All that stuff about telling a story all the time. You can't trust anything she says or anything she does. And I got caught up in that.

The trouble is, E.D. thought as she closed her journal and flushed the toilet, Melody's method *worked.* That was pretty scary. She wrapped her journal in the towel she'd brought in with her, and opened the door.

"Thanks!" Cordelia said as they squeezed past each other. There was a loud call from outside that sounded to E.D. like *quork*! A raven, E.D. thought, peering through the windshield. She shivered as a large, dark shadow flew up into the slightly graying darkness outside.

After she had grabbed breakfast in the screen house and helped everybody else embark on their activities for the day, E.D. sat at the picnic table to organize the tutorial she was going to film later, and started making a log of what everyone was doing. The Rutherfords had said everyone needed to have a thirty-minute final video, summarizing the whole Expedition, for the judges. Only the top three teams' videos would be shown to the whole world at the awards ceremony.

E.D. got a little surge of pride. On the way to Sedona they'd learned that they were now—finally,

finally—in first place. It must have been her video tutorial that got them into the lead. It was really thorough and filled in all the stuff with real educational value the Organics had left out of the zoo project at Saunders. She felt as if her own work was maybe about to win them the whole thing.

She could see Jake wandering over by the campground's playground, talking out loud to himself, his script for *Our American Cousin* tucked under his arm. Randolph had announced that they would be doing another several readings at some point—without, E.D. noticed, any regard for the Expedition's schedule or the challenges they'd be sent. Jake had been diligently working on the role of Asa, and from what E.D. had overheard, he was actually starting to get really good at it.

Otherwise, the campsite was peaceful and quiet. It almost felt like the Expedition was finally coming together the way it was intended, and E.D. couldn't believe there was less than a week left! Everyone was finally following their own interests and getting something rich and meaningful from it. Lucille and Cordelia had set off at the crack of sunrise for their vortex hike—Lucille had been raving about the intense psychic energy all around from the moment they arrived.

"There had better be good energy," Sybil said. "I sent *Petunia Possum, Detective* off to my editor last night, so this will be the birthplace of my new career!"

With her manuscript submitted and nothing pressing to do, Sybil had gone off with Destiny to the local historical museum. Archie was planning to spend his day in the art galleries that seemed to line all of Sedona's streets, Hal took off on his own for a hike after breakfast, and Randolph, having been up well into the night making phone calls about his upcoming performances, was just now waking up, banging around in the back of Brunhilda. Even from out here, E.D. could hear him grumbling about his desperate need for coffee. E.D. sighed, and got up to turn on the camp stove and heat up what was left in the pot.

Through the hissing of the gas, she heard a holler from Brunhilda. "Cockroaches!" her father shouted. And then she heard a string of parrot words accompanied by banging and smashing. E.D. had no idea how roaches had suddenly become a problem, but she suspected Jake knew more than he was letting on—he got a weird gulpy look every time one was spotted.

As soon as the bus was quiet again, there was a shriek in the distance, and Melody came running into the campsite. She was waving her cell phone in the air and slid to a stop, dust rising around her sequined sandals.

"Change of plans," she shouted. Her face, E.D. noticed, was incredibly pale. "Change of plans! We have to drop everything and get on the road. There's an e-mail from the Rutherfords' TV guy!"

Randolph banged open the door of Brunhilda, looking groggy and rubbing his eyes. "What's all this noise? And where's my coffee?" E.D. wordlessly pointed him toward the stove.

"We've got to head for California immediately," Melody insisted. "This morning. All further stops canceled. They've pushed up the whole schedule! They're shooting interviews with everybody, which will air during the award show, and they're shooting them *this weekend*. We've got to go!"

Randolph stared at her, then shook his head. "Not possible. I've got plans for two more performances in California, on our way to the Rutherfords. The actors are flying in tomorrow to start rehearsal while we're here in Arizona." He waved dismissively. "We can't just change plans like that."

"Jeez, Dad, talk about changing plans," E.D. objected. He hadn't given her any warning! And now she had actors to coordinate and rehearsals to schedule?

Jake had, by now, come over to see what was going on. Melody's hands were in fists. "Look," she shouted, "this is it. This is the part where we get famous! Where people find out who we are! You want to be famous, right, Randy?" Randolph choked on his coffee as Melody plunged ahead. "We're supposed to get there—with our finished, edited video for the final presentation, which is basically the most important part of the whole competition, by *noon tomorrow* so they can start shooting behind-the-scenes, human-interest, interview stuff. All the other expeditions are closer—it'll take us over twelve hours! Really, really, we have to start now!"

"Preposterous," said Randolph, impatiently drumming his fingers on the side of his coffee mug. "I will not have my performances jerked around for some *television shooting* schedule."

Melody stared at him in utter disbelief. "B-but . . . ," she sputtered, "we just took the lead! We're finally in first place! We can *win this thing*!"

"Exactly," said Randolph, sipping confidently from his mug. "You saw those *lunatics* in the other group! I'm certain we're going to win. And no small part of that victory," he added with a humble bow of his head, "will be the performances that I am putting together. We will still arrive in time for the award ceremony. We are not leaving early, and that's final."

The fight escalated from there. Melody wondered, loudly, who cared about his "stupid little play." Randolph pointed out, even more loudly, that he, the rest of the family, and the cast all cared quite a lot about it. She said some mean stuff about theater people in general and Randolph in particular. He said some mean stuff about "selfish, spoiled little girls," and Melody, trembling and shouting, held her hands up at him like claws. For a moment E.D. thought Melody was going to jump on Randolph and try to rip him apart like a wildcat. *I have to do something!* E.D. thought.

So she got in between them, even though it was the last place she wanted to be, and held her hands up in both of their faces.

"ALL RIGHT," she hollered. "THAT'S ENOUGH! Jake!" Jake snapped to attention, and E.D. fought down a sudden rush of annoyance that he had just been standing there watching while E.D., as usual, was doing something. "Take Melody someplace and find out what's really going on. Dad, take a breath and let's talk about these extra performances that you never even bothered to tell me about."

Chapter Twenty-Six

When E.D. told Jake to take Melody away, Melody shouted, "Nobody's *taking me* anywhere!" and grabbed Jake by the arm, dragging him toward a hiking path that led off from the campground into the red rock hills.

"Twelve hours, it'll take to get there," she fumed as they walked. "Twelve at least! The TV crew will be there in the morning. They want to start filming in the afternoon. This is it! The big deal. He's going to ruin *everything*! *We have to go NOW!*" She was walking fast, and Jake found himself struggling to keep up with her.

He didn't know what to say. He didn't know what to do. At least, he thought, when a lion tamer went into the ring with a lion, he had a whip and a chair with him. The path went around the side of a hill and started to climb. Soon they reached a ledge that overlooked a really breathtaking view, dark green bushes climbing up the red and tan cliffs and towers of rock, across a little valley and off into the distance. Jake thought it looked like a landscape that dinosaurs should be walking through, not people.

Melody stopped walking. She wasn't looking at the view, she just seemed to have run out of steam. She sat down on a big rock that had tumbled down near the path. Jake sat about a foot away.

"If we waited until everybody got back from what they're doing this morning, and we got on the road right after lunch—*right after!*—we could still get there when they want us. This family is like some kind of democracy, right?" she said, picking up a pebble and winging it down the hill in front of them. "So, he can't just make the rules. If everybody else wants to go right now so we can get there when the filming starts . . ." She trailed off and flung another rock. She was probably thinking the same thing Jake was: that the odds were against her. He wondered if Melody had ever felt completely at a loss before.

"I know getting interviewed and being on TV would be cool," he said carefully, "but even if we were a little late, maybe—"

"Being on TV would be *cool?*" she asked witheringly. "Are you *crazy?*"

"What do you mean crazy?"

"Are you *happy*? Are you *happy* being just *what you are?*" To Jake's astonishment, she had tears in her eyes. "How many people—how many people on the whole planet—even know you exist? Like, how many people, if somebody said 'Jake Semple' to them, would even say, 'Oh yeah, that kid'? A couple hundred? A thousand? In the whole world?"

Jake had never really thought about it before. He thought now about everybody he'd known in school, and his family, and the Applewhites. He thought about everybody he had performed for, in *The Sound of Music* and *Oliver!* and the other shows he'd done. Did any of them remember his name? But then again . . . "What difference does it make?" he asked. "If people know who I am? I mean, it would be nice, but what would be different?"

"Everything!" Melody shouted. "Everything would be different! Nobody could treat you like just *some kid*. You wouldn't be just some dumb anybody, like all those other dumb anybodies. Think about them! Think about those millions of people we've driven past on this Expedition! They're like *ants*! There are so many of them and they're all exactly the same!"

That didn't seem right to Jake. Very few of the folks they'd met on this Expedition seemed much like anybody else at all.

Suddenly she reached out and grabbed his hands. "You're on my side at least, right? About leaving? I mean, we *have* to be there for the filming. We have to be on TV, and we have to win. We absolutely have to!"

"Maybe Randolph's right," he said, "and the timing really doesn't matter that much. The Rutherfords aren't going to just dump the leaders because they get there a little bit late. They can do the human-interest stuff and the interviews and all that with everybody else till we get there."

"We can't take that chance!" she said. "They've turned it all over to the *television* people. And all *they* care about is numbers—they *fired* Jeremy! I need—*we* need to be there for *everything* they're planning! If we can get the family to vote, are you with me?"

Melody was leaning in close and staring right into his eyes. For one wild moment, he felt sort of sorry for her. And then he heard himself saying yes.

Her face lit up. "Really? You'll vote that we dump Big Randy's stupid play and go today?" When she put it that way, he was pretty sure that was the wrong decision. But he found himself nodding anyway.

"Come on," she called, "let's go see if Lucille and Cordelia are back yet!"

After lunch, once everybody had returned to camp, a family meeting was called to discuss what they would do. It was surprisingly civilized, Jake thought, given that Melody on one side and Randolph on the other had both dug their heels in.

When the vote was called it had pretty much come down to a battle between the Applewhites' desire for winning and good publicity, and their intense dislike of being told what to do. And it was way closer than Jake had expected—Archie, Cordelia, Melody, and, reluctantly, Jake, voted to leave immediately. Hal didn't want to be interviewed, he said—ever—and Lucille wasn't ready to leave Sedona yet, so they both voted with Randolph and E.D. to stay.

Then Sybil, the deciding vote, announced that she was going to abstain.

"What's that?" asked Destiny.

"It means I'm not voting," Sybil said. "I see both sides and I can't make up my mind." She held up a hand toward Randolph as he opened his mouth to start arguing with her. "I abstain," she repeated firmly.

"So it's a tie," said E.D. "Now what?"

"It's not a tie," said a little voice. "I hasn't voted."

Melody and Randolph both turned to Destiny in disbelief. "You don't get a vote!" they both shouted.

"Why not?" asked Destiny indignantly.

"You're five," they said, then glared at each other.

"I'm an Applewhite," Destiny insisted, putting his hands on his hips. "I gets a vote!"

"Talk some sense into him, Jake, he'll listen to you," Melody whispered urgently. Jake hesitated, and then it was too late.

"I wanna stay," said Destiny decisively. "I likes it here. I wanna visit a vortex. I wanna take a cowboy ride. I wanna stay."

Randolph whooped in triumph. Melody went very, very quiet. It seemed like everyone was holding their breath.

"Fine," she said after a long, long while, her mouth tight. Then she flipped her hair out of her face. "Whatever. If we're doing these shows, I need to work with my script." The fire seemed to have left Melody like a thunderstorm disappearing from a summer sky.

That evening, Lucille went into Brunhilda to start getting dinner together. Minutes later, screeching and smashing sounds split the early-evening air. Jake and Archie jumped up and ran for the bus. Inside they found Lucille standing in the aisle by the kitchen, staring at her hands and quivering. Her hair was wild. She looked at them with big, horrified eyes. "I . . . I killed them." She held her hands up, palms out, and there were brown- and cream-colored smears on them. "I killed them with my *bare hands*. . . ."

Jake edged toward her. He saw a leg, an antenna, part of a wing. Her hands were covered in chunks of mashed up cockroaches. Archie grabbed a dish towel and started wiping her clean. Lucille was shivering violently. "I asked them to leave," she told Archie pleadingly. "SO many times, yesterday—and the day before. They wouldn't leave! I came in and opened the cabinets and they just fell out all over the counter . . . And I *killed* them!" Archie led her down the aisle and out of Brunhilda.

Hal and Archie took over dinner, which was a giant vat of pasta and sauce. "Any more roaches?" asked Jake quietly as Hal carried the big steaming pot out to the picnic table.

"Couple," said Hal. "I don't think any made it into the pasta. Let's not talk about it."

After dinner, Melody raised a hand to speak. "Everybody," she said, "I'm sorry about today." Jake was stunned. "You've all taught me so much about teamwork, and how any group works best when it works together." Lucille came out of her cockroach-murder trauma long enough to clasp her hands over her heart and look at Melody with misty eyes. "Let's all go watch the sunset. All of us. In, like, *togetherness*. There's an overlook Jake and I found today with a beautiful view."

"Well, Melody," said Sybil. "I think that's just lovely. I could do with an after-dinner walk. Destiny, go find Winston's leash."

Randolph grumbled. "It'll get dark. I'm sure to trip on a rock and break my neck."

"Togetherness!" Sybil reminded him.

Halfway up the path to the overlook, Melody stopped short. "My camera," she said, smacking her forehead. "I want to record this. I'll be right back," she said, and scampered back down the path in the gathering dusk.

There was just room for the whole family at the overlook. It really was a beautiful view, and the sunset was copper and gold on the cliffs across the valley. At moments like this, Jake thought, for all the cramped quarters and bouncing around on country roads, and pasta with possible cockroaches in it, and weird challenges, and changing schedules . . . at moments like this, the whole Expedition made sense.

"Melody," said Lucille, "this was a lovely impulse. Thank you." Silence. "Melody?"

Everyone looked around. Melody wasn't there. "Did she ever come back with her camera?" asked Sybil.

They headed back down the path, having to go more slowly in the dark, now that the sun was down. "What if she fell off the path and broke her neck and *died?*" Destiny said.

"Nobody died!" said Randolph. But he walked more slowly and carefully. There was no Melody along the way.

There was no Melody back at the camp.

There was no Pageant Wagon, either.

Melody and the Pageant Wagon were gone.

Chapter Twenty-Seven

"My *Pageant Wagon!*" Randolph shouted at the top of his lungs. "This is grand theft RV! Call the state police and have them set up roadblocks. Helicopters! Bloodhounds! She can't have gone far. When they catch her, I fully intend to press charges!"

E.D. stood with the rest of the family staring at the place where the Pageant Wagon wasn't anymore. What was there instead was a blanket, piled with clothes and random belongings. In the light that shone from Brunhilda's front windows, she saw one of

Lucille's ruffled skirts and a matching blouse, a couple of pairs of jeans and some socks and underwear that could have been Archie's or Jake's, and on the very top, lying open, Jake's thoroughly dog-eared and highlighted script for *Our American Cousin*.

"Her phone goes right to voice mail," said Jake, his phone to his ear.

"After her!" cried Randolph, leaping into Brunhilda's driver's seat. "All aboard! We're going after her!" With that he turned Brunhilda's key, and her engine turned over with a groan. And again. And again. But she wouldn't start.

E.D. worried her father might have a stroke. "*She's done something to Brunhilda!*" he bellowed, tearing at his hair. "Archie! Fix it! Make it work!"

"I don't know much about this engine," Archie admitted. "We're going to have to wait for roadside assistance." After a few minutes on his phone, he hung up and shook his head. "They can't send anyone until morning," he said.

Randolph turned purple and lost the ability to speak. He just opened and closed his mouth, making furious gasping noises.

"You don't suppose she's planning to drive all the way to the Rutherford Art Center by herself?" Sybil said.

Lucille picked her blouse out of the pile on the blanket. "It was thoughtful of her to leave us something to wear. I can live without pajamas tonight."

"I don't see my shaving kit," Archie said.

"You can use this opportunity to grow a beard," Lucille told him. "I've always thought you'd look rugged and manly with a beard."

Jake was picking through the pile of clothes. "There's a lot of stuff I don't see," he said. "She didn't clear out the whole bus, it looks like—just a couple of armfuls." E.D. realized he was right. There was no way the pile was big enough. She didn't see anything but clothes and Jake's script—no books, no papers, no electronics.

"We'll chase her down in the morning," Randolph said, having recovered somewhat.

"We don't know which way she went," E.D. said. She looked over at Jake, and at Hal standing next to him. "Unless she told one of *you* what she was planning."

Hal shrugged and shook his head.

"Why would she tell one of us?" Jake asked.

E.D. narrowed her eyes at him suspiciously. "Good question."

Jake frowned. "All I know is that she was absolutely determined to get herself on television. I mean *determined.*"

"Good thing she didn't take Brunhilda," Destiny said. "I still gots all *my* stuff. And my pirate hammock."

"Good heavens!" Lucille said, clutching Archie's

arm. "She's taken our bed! And Jake's."

It was only then that they all fully realized what it meant that the Pageant Wagon was gone.

No one but Destiny got much sleep that night. Jake spent the night in Hal's tent. Archie and Lucille crowded into the dinette bunk, which meant that E.D. had to share the couch with Cordelia, who *flailed* in the night, and kicked. *Maybe she's choreographing in her sleep,* E.D. thought at two o'clock in the morning after taking an elbow to the ribs. Eventually, she gave up and snuggled in a comforter on the hard, cold floor with Winston.

The family began to gather in the campfire circle not long after dawn. When Jake got there, milk and cereal and the coffeepot had already been put out on a picnic table.

"Daddy's been on the phone, saying he wants to see the car fix-it guy by the time the sun gets up over those hills," Destiny said, nodding in the direction of the mountains as he dug into his bowl of Cheerios. "But when we go, Aunt Lucille's not going with us."

"I'm staying here with Madame Amethyst," Lucille said, from the boulder where she was sitting, staring into the steadily lightening sky and breathing in the steam from her coffee cup. "She's the guide who took us out into the vortex yesterday, and she will be here any minute to pick me up. She's offered me a place to stay for a few days to center myself in Sedona's calming energies. I need to recover from whatever it was that sent me into a murderous rage against those poor, innocent cockroaches. Never in my life . . ."

"Her name is *Madame Amethyst?*" asked Archie. "Really?"

Lucille took another breath of steam. "Her birth name was Colleen Finklebaum. She used to be an advertising copywriter in New York, but she came here on vacation about ten years ago and never went back. She took her spirit name from the most spiritually resonant crystal. She's very wise. And she flies her own plane, do you believe it? She's going to fly me out to California in her Cessna to meet up with all of you, on her way to a gathering of shamans at Mount Shasta."

E.D. wished *she* could go by plane instead of in Brunhilda, which Archie and her father were planning to take turns driving straight through to the Rutherfords, twelve hours away, to try to catch up with Melody. Even without Lucille, it was going to be a long, crowded ride.

"Hey, has anybody seen my computer?" Hal asked. "The tent's packed, and it wasn't with any of my stuff."

"Last time I saw it was when we were working on the Saunders video in the Pageant Wagon," Jake said.

"I'm sure I took it to my tent after."

"Melody took it," E.D. said. And even though she

had not the slightest shred of evidence, she knew it was true. "Does that mean all the video files are gone?"

Hal shook his head. "Whenever we've had Wi-Fi I put everything into online storage. And it's all backed up on flash drives, too."

"Do you gots all mine?" Destiny asked.

"You've been making videos?" E.D. asked. "Since when?"

"Since always! I got lots and lots of pitchers, but Melody said they weren't good enough to be in the film you guys was working on. She says I'm too little to do good pitchers, but I'm not!"

"Bring your camera to me," Hal said, "and we'll get all your stuff uploaded."

"Onto what?" Jake asked.

"Mom's computer. I put all my editing programs on it, too, just in case. And Archie's, but that'll be gone with the Pageant Wagon. You know the geek motto, *back up, then back up the backups*."

"The sun is over the hills!" Randolph shouted, emerging from Brunhilda. His phone rang, and he answered, yelling, "Where is my blasted roadside assistance?" He listened a moment. "Ah, Govindaswami, sorry, I thought you were someone else. How is everything in—"

He stopped then, his face first going pale and then flushing red as he alternately listened and spoke, his voice growing louder and more incredulous with each response. "Flagstaff? I didn't even realize they *had* an airport—*What? Impounded?*" He ran a hand through his hair. "Homeland Security? What do they have to do with it? What do you mean they asked you about explosives? Don't be silly, you do *not* have a suspicious accent. Don't think another thing about it. I'll get over to Flagstaff right now and straighten it all out. They threatened you? How dare they? You're a citizen. *I'm* a citizen! They have no right—Well, *immediately*. I'll call you as soon as—Yes, of *course* we'll get it back. They can't keep it; it's private property!" By the time he hung up, Randolph was seething with fury.

"The Pageant Wagon's been impounded?" Sybil said.

"Melody *abandoned* it in the middle of the taxi lane at the Flagstaff airport! So they impounded it and traced the license number. That's why they called Wit's End. For some reason Homeland Security got involved. Something about a suspicious vehicle. Something about homemade mechanisms of unknown but suspicious purposes. Govindaswami thinks because of his accent they may have thought he was a terrorist."

Archie slapped a hand to his forehead. "Unbelievable," he said.

"They actually threatened him with deportation. I've got to get over to Flagstaff now! Archie, you come along to drive the Pageant Wagon back."

"We're still waiting for the mechanic," Archie reminded him. "Plus, I don't think you should take

Brunhilda. If they thought the Pageant Wagon looked suspicious, what are they going to make of her?" E.D. looked at the big bus—she was so used to it she had forgotten how outlandish it looked. "And, Randolph," Archie continued, "given your . . . issues with authority figures, maybe you shouldn't be the one to go at all."

"Issues with authority?" demanded Randolph. "Ridiculous. I have no issues with authority! I am merely steadfast in the defense of my rights." Archie rolled his eyes. "Anyway, it is *my* Pageant Wagon, it is *my* stage, for *my* show. I am going. End of discussion."

Archie held up his hand. "Fine. But leave Brunhilda here. Lucille's new friend—Lady Crystal, or whatever—should be here any minute. Maybe she'll be willing to drive you up to Flagstaff."

E.D. looked at her mother. "Archie's right. You know how Dad gets with people in uniforms," she said. "We can't let him go alone."

And so it was that Lucille's new friend, a woman with a mane of curly red hair, wearing feather earrings and a gold dream catcher pendant with an amethyst in the middle, drove off half an hour later with Randolph in the front seat of her bright yellow VW bug and Cordelia in the back, sent along to try to keep her father under control, or, if necessary, to bat her eyelashes charmingly at whatever authority figure he was insulting. "Remember, dear," Sybil called to Randolph as the car pulled away from the campsite, "whatever you do, don't *yell* at anyone!"

Just after they left, the roadside assistance truck pulled up. The guy had Brunhilda running again about thirty seconds after popping the hood. "She just pulled the wire off of one spark plug. All you hadda do was stick it back on. Don't any of you know *nothin'* about engines?" Jake and Archie stared off toward the mountains, blushing, and E.D. thought it was high time she learned about cars!

"Let's get a look at Destiny's videos," she said to Hal, then. She needed something to keep her mind off what might be going on at the airport.

"I'll get Mom's computer. I must have left mine in the Pageant Wagon and Melody just took it by accident. I doubt she even knew it was there."

Right, E.D. thought disgustedly. Whatever there was about testosterone, it appeared to make guys go totally brainless. Archie called the Rutherford Foundation to tell them there had been an unavoidable delay in leaving Sedona, but they would be on their way soon. Four hours later, just about the time E.D. had hoped her father would pull into the campground in the Pageant Wagon, the yellow VW came back instead. Cordelia climbed out of the passenger side as the family gathered around.

"Is your father on his way?" Sybil asked.

"Dad's in jail," Cordelia said, and burst into tears.

Chapter Twenty-Eight

It took them a while to figure out exactly what had happened, with Cordelia wailing and blubbering. Madame Amethyst came over and dropped a set of keys into Archie's hand. "That's about all that's left," she said.

"What does she mean, that's all that's left?" Sybil asked Cordelia.

"It's gone!" cried Cordelia, dabbing carefully at the corner of her eyes so that she didn't smear her eyeliner. "The Pageant Wagon! They . . . they . . ."

Sybil put a hand on Cordelia's shoulder. "They what, dear?"

"They *took it apart*!"

"Don't tell me they took the stage off the side!" said Archie. Jake groaned, and thought about how much work it would be to reassemble the mechanism, especially without Bill Bones and his metalworking expertise.

Madame Amethyst was leaning against her car now, shaking her head. "The term they used was 'dismantled.' For the purpose of national security."

"You wouldn't believe it!" Cordelia wailed. "The hood was over here, the engine was over there, all our stuff was just lying around in piles, totally shredded. They took the windows out! They took the tires off the wheels! It looked like a used-bus-parts store! They thought there was a *bomb* in it somewhere!"

Sybil was rubbing her temples. "No wonder your father is in jail. I'd better make some phone calls."

"Well," said Archie, shaking his head. "So . . . that happened." He wandered off toward the cooler they'd put out on the picnic table and started making himself a sandwich.

Lucille stood for a moment, watching him. "Want a hug?" she asked him. He shook his head. She went over to Madame Amethyst. "I guess if they shredded our stuff, I don't have much left but what I'm wearing," she told the woman. "If you're still okay with having me stay with you for a while . . ."

Madame Amethyst nodded and opened the door for her.

Lucille stopped before getting in, and turned to the rest of them. "I'm really sorry about deserting you like this. But you know what the airline people say—put your own oxygen mask on first. I have full faith in this family. We will all come through this ordeal one way or another. I'll catch up to you all in a couple of days. Blessings on you!" She got into the car, then, and firmly shut the door.

When the Volkswagen had driven off, and the rest of the family had gone back into Brunhilda, E.D. wheeled around at Jake, her face furious. Jake stepped back a foot and put his hands up. "Why are you glaring at me?" he asked, annoyed at himself for blushing.

"What do you know? What did Melody tell you?"

"Do you think I knew she was going to steal the Pageant Wagon and fly to California? Well I didn't! Don't you think I would have done something to stop her, or at least told somebody?"

"I *don't know*!" E.D. shouted back. "I don't know what you would do when it comes to her!"

"What is that supposed to mean?"

"It means you're not *yourself* when you're around her."

Jake tried to convince himself that wasn't true, but he knew better. "You mean the way *you* aren't yourself when Tyler Organic's around?"

He saw E.D. flinch.

"Fine," said E.D. after a moment, walking away to the picnic table and sitting with her back to him.

"Fine. Whatever. It's none of my business."

Jake wished he hadn't lost his temper, but he didn't know how to take it back. E.D. wouldn't even look at him. He realized suddenly how very much he missed having her to talk to. Before he had even thought about her being his girlfriend, E.D. was his friend, and since Melody showed up she hadn't been either one. It was strange to think about, since he had been traveling in such close quarters with so many people for so many weeks, but Jake realized what the odd feeling he had in his stomach was. He was lonely. Had been lonely since the Expedition started.

All right, Semple, he thought. *What do you do when you don't get what you want?* Was he supposed to sit around moping about it? Of course not. But what was he supposed to do? He couldn't very well just *tell* E.D. that he missed talking to her.

Right?

He went over and sat next to E.D. She still wouldn't look at him.

"So," he said. "This is awkward. I, um . . ." He took a deep breath. "I miss talking to you," he mumbled. She didn't react. Maybe she hadn't even heard him—he hadn't managed much more than a whisper. He cleared his throat. "I know things have been weird. I'm sorry. I guess. Or whatever." *Smooth, Semple.*

She sighed. "Yeah," she said at last. "This has all been pretty weird. But, thanks. You, too. Or whatever," she added with a tiny bit of a smile.

"So what do we do now?" he asked.

"We go after her. We finish the Expedition."

They heard scuffling in the dust behind them and turned to see Hal, shifting awkwardly from foot to foot with Sybil's laptop hanging from one hand. "You guys done fighting?" he asked. They nodded. "Good. You've got to see this."

"What is it?" asked E.D.

"Just watch," said Hal, setting the computer up on the picnic table. He hit play on a video. The camera panned across Brunhilda and the Pageant Wagon, parked by the barn at Wit's End.

"I've seen this," said E.D. "This is what you used for the start of our final presentation."

"Just . . . watch," Hal repeated. The shot on-screen changed—there were the Applewhites trying to take a photo in front of the buses. It was chaos. Everybody was arguing, jostling one another into different positions. Randolph was yelling, Winston was barking. Off to the side stood Melody, in a vivid turquoise halter and hot pink shorts, her hair falling alluringly over one eye. She turned to look right into the camera, and winked. The shot froze with Melody smiling slyly, and over the picture appeared a title:

Surviving the Applewhites—
by Melody Aiko Bernstein

"Where'd you get this?" E.D. asked.

"Online! Melody posted a bunch of videos. It's not just this one—everything that's been posted in our name for *weeks* has been videos that *she* must have made!"

"What about ours?" E.D. asked desperately. "Your summaries? My tutorials?"

"I don't know," said Hal. "They're not there. They're not anywhere. I don't know where they went! I sent them to the right place, I've checked! And everything she posted . . . that first one is bad, but it gets worse. *Much* worse!"

Jake swallowed hard as Hal pulled up video clip after video clip. If he hadn't been so completely mortified, he would be really impressed. Melody must have been filming a lot more often than she let on. And she'd included only footage that made the Applewhites, and Jake, look like total, complete idiots. Loud, opinionated, arrogant idiots.

There was quite a lot of Randolph yelling at people. Every time he yelled she would cut to somebody looking sad—even if it wasn't from the same time, or even the same stop on the Expedition. Rehearsal footage was all about Melody getting laughs, and Randolph yelling, and Melody rolling her eyes. At the stop in Clayton, Tennessee, it showed Sybil totally losing control of a roomful of small children. Then in swept Melody to the rescue, as if it had been she, and she alone, who saved the day. Jake realized that she couldn't have done that filming—she had just stolen bits from Hal's video. And she'd included snatches of Destiny's tantrums, which made it seem that he was always out of control. Hal came off looking like the world's most awkward recluse. You'd see the back of his head or get a glimpse of him ducking into his tent on the roof of the bus. There was Hal blushing and turning away. Then came Melody's makeover—the whole unveiling of the "new Hal" was included. Melody the hero.

There were a few clips showing E.D. bossing people around, but mostly Melody had managed to make her look clueless and lonely. "What's wrong with how I dress?" she was asking in one clip, wearing a tattered T-shirt and a faded pair of baggy jeans. E.D. yelped in fury at that part. "She must have hidden the camera behind her *backpack*!" There were shots of Melody coaching E.D. on how to fix her hair and talk to Tyler Organic. There was even a shot, from behind a bush, of E.D. and Tyler kissing on the steps of the Organics' classroom bus. Jake felt so awkward about it he closed his eyes for that part, but he could hear E.D. making little strangled noises as she watched. Lucille looked daffier than she really was, Cordelia snotty and stuck-up, Archie clueless, and Zedediah bossy and just plain mean.

The hardest for Jake were the bits she'd included of

Jake's worst moments in *Our American Cousin*, interspersed with images of audience members not laughing. He felt totally gutted.

"It's bad," Hal said. "Every one of these was up on the competition website. And you can tell she was learning the whole time, just like Jake and I were. The editing gets better and better at making us look bad. She even stole a lot of it from *my* video logs!"

"What about my tutorials?" E.D. asked. "They're just *gone?*"

Hal shrugged. "Not one has been posted since Valley View. This is why she borrowed my laptop so often late at night," he added apologetically. "She said she had insomnia. How could I be so stupid?"

"Believe me, Hal, it wasn't just you," Jake said, and felt himself blushing. He had thought maybe he understood Melody at least a little bit, but no. He had no idea what she'd been capable of all along.

Just then Sybil emerged from Brunhilda, her phone in hand. "Family meeting!" she called. When everyone had gathered in the campfire circle she told them that Randolph would be in jail for "a few days at most." All of the charges of suspected terrorism had been dropped when the dismantling of the Pageant Wagon revealed nothing threatening, but he was still in trouble for blowing his top at the airport security folks and the Homeland Security people and resisting arrest.

"So what are we going to do now?" Archie asked.

"We'll have to get on the road as fast as we can and get out there to the Rutherford Art Center. There is no telling what she's going to be doing—or saying—there."

Jake thought they ought to tell the rest of the family about Melody's version of their video logs. "Um . . . ," he said, but then saw E.D. glaring at him and ever so slightly shaking her head. So he bit his tongue.

"If you find a hornet's nest outside your back door," she said quietly while everyone was finding a place to settle in Brunhilda for the drive, "are you gonna whack it with a stick? Or are you going to sneak up on it at night when the hornets are sleeping? Tell Hal to bring Mom's computer and we'll take it back to the bedroom. I don't know how she got these videos posted, but I do know this: Anything she can do? We can do better."

As they thundered along the highway, Brunhilda's engine roaring with the strain of Archie's heavy foot on the gas pedal, E.D. and Hal and Jake worked on a video to upload to the Rutherford website. They titled it *The Real Melody Bernstein*. Destiny's videos helped a lot—"I got lots of pitchers of Melody," he said, and he was right. While nobody was paying attention, he had managed to capture Melody in all her glory. There was plenty of yelling, sulking, insulting people. There, in living color, was her withering sarcasm, her endless negativity.

When Archie finally insisted they stop at a restaurant so he could take a break, Hal took the computer in with him and used the free Wi-Fi to upload their final product directly to the Rutherford site. "It's done!" he said as they all piled back into the bus.

Chapter Twenty-Nine

"Wow!" E.D. breathed the next morning as Archie steered Brunhilda from the two-lane road named Rutherford Boulevard into the wide, long, upward-sloping driveway beneath a vast, spectacularly ornate iron archway that was part sign—*Rutherford Art Center* in looping script—and part contemporary sculpture. The grassy, shrubby hillside stretched away in front of them with ranks of hills on either side, all dotted with tall, wind-twisted trees. No buildings were immediately visible, so the grounds had to be vast. The sky beyond the hills was utterly empty in a way that suggested the possibility that the ocean lay beyond.

"Guess this is it," Archie said. "Not exactly what I was expecting."

E.D. wasn't sure what she'd been expecting, but maybe a slightly bigger, more elegant version of Wit's End. This place had absolutely nothing in common with Wit's End. It could be a national park!

"Jake!" E.D. called. "You gotta come see!"

Archie had wanted to drive straight through from Sedona, but Sybil insisted on stopping at a motel so that everyone would be rested when they got there. "We need to be at our best," she pointed out, "if we're going to counteract any negative impression the Rutherfords might have gotten from Melody!" *Any negative impression,* E.D. thought. Little did her mother know!

In spite of the stop, though, none of them were really at their best. The motel had been cheap and uncomfortable, with a restaurant so bad Archie said the term "greasy spoon" would have been an upgrade. Jake, who had gone to the back to stretch out on the bed, came out now, rubbing his eyes. "We're there, huh?"

They reached the top of a hill, and the center revealed itself—a sprawl of low, elegantly rustic stone and wooden buildings, scattered across a long, narrow valley and up the sides of other hills. Archie braked to a stop and they sat for a moment looking down at the destination they'd been pushing themselves through the long, miserable drive to reach. Hal and Cordelia scooted out of the dinette and came forward to see.

The largest of the buildings, situated in the center of the valley, had a peaked roof rising at least three stories high, its front all glass. It was entirely encircled by decks, with tables, chairs, benches, and lounges, some of them with sheltering umbrellas of vibrant colors. Television crews, with lights and sound equipment set up, were occupying one of the decks. The other buildings were smaller, each a different shape and size, but somehow all matching with their wooden shingles and stone foundations. People were coming and going on wide footpaths between the buildings, some on foot, some on bicycles.

The driveway ahead of Brunhilda plunged down the hill and looped in front of the main building around a garden with a collection of flagpoles, their large, brilliantly colored flags waving in the wind, and then branched to either side, to encircle the whole collection of buildings. Golf carts moved on the drive between the series of broad, paved parking lots that stretched out wherever the ground was level enough for them.

"Well," Sybil said, "we've come to the right place!" The biggest parking lot held a flotilla of weird and colorful expedition buses. All around the buses TV vans sporting satellite dishes and cherry pickers for filming from above were circled. Like hyenas around a herd of zebras, E.D. thought.

"Looks like the expeditions are all here," Archie said. "There's Pisces down there, and Starry Night and the Green Machine."

She'd be seeing Tyler soon, E.D. thought. The beautiful boy the whole world had seen her kissing.

Destiny, who had been sleeping in his hammock, was now peering over the side and out through the windshield. He pointed to the left, where two hills made a kind of greenish-brown *V*, which was filled in to the horizon with a deep, sparkling blue. "Is that the other ocean over there?" he asked. "Is it as big as the one at Haddock Point?"

"Bigger, I think," Jake said.

"Do we gets to go to the beach? I wanna go to the beach."

Archie stepped on the gas and Brunhilda started downward. "There's the biggest, fanciest motorhome in the known universe by the main building, and the Art Bus beside it."

"The Art Bus, the Art Bus! I wanna blow the big horn," Destiny said.

"I don't think so," Archie answered. "Jeremy's not there anymore."

"Where'd he go?"

"Nobody knows. He's been off the grid."

"I worry about him," Sybil said.

Archie drove around the flag garden and stopped

in front of the main entrance, and what was left of the Creative Academy's expedition team climbed wearily out. Moments later, a lanky guy in khaki slacks and a turtleneck, wearing aviator sunglasses and a backward baseball cap, strolled out through the big double doors and down the steps, followed by a man and a woman E.D. recognized from the television interview back at Haddock Point. Larry and Janet Rutherford.

"Hail to the leaders!" the man in sunglasses said, raising a hand that held a glass. "Welcome, Applewhites. I'm Hector Montana, the producer. Glad you managed to get here. Quite a little tempest you've got going on."

"Tempest?" Sybil asked. "What sort of tempest?"

"Not to worry," the man said. "It's getting more buzz than anything about the Expedition so far! Practically viral! The world loves a good villain. My interviewer is out on the south deck with the 'Real Melody Bernstein' as we speak."

Sybil and Archie looked puzzled. Jake winked at E.D. *So they got our video,* she thought as Hal gave her a thumbs-up. She wondered what Melody was saying in this interview.

The Rutherfords came down to the bus and shook hands all around. "I understand there's been a small glitch with your Pageant Wagon," Mrs. Rutherford said.

Small glitch. Apparently, E.D. thought, unlike everything else about their lives recently, that story hadn't gotten out to the whole world yet.

"My brother's working on it," Archie said. "It'll be taken care of in no time."

"Since you'll be a bit crowded with only one bus," Mrs. Rutherford said, "we've arranged for lodging in one of our cabins where Miss Bernstein is already in residence."

"*That's* awkward," Jake whispered to E.D.

Mr. Rutherford clapped his hands together. "I hope you've been considering the details of the Creative Academy charter-school franchise. Not that we're making any promises. No one can know for certain until the award ceremony tomorrow night when the judges announce their decision."

"It's looking very good for you," Hector Montana said, whipping off his ball cap and smoothing his lustrous black hair. "You guys have been climbing straight up the charts. Keep doing what you're doing, and . . . well. Enough said. Right now we're filming the human-interest stuff for the award ceremony broadcast. So once you're all set up, we'll send a crew over." He waggled his eyebrows at them. "We're eager to get the view from the other side, so to speak."

"So," Archie said, "where should we take Brunhilda to set up?"

* * *

While Archie and the boys were getting Brunhilda hooked up next to the Art Bus in the lot by the main building, a young woman came in a golf cart to show them where the cabin was. "Mom and Cordelia," E.D. said, "why don't the two of you—and Destiny—take the cabin with Melody. Jake and I can stay here. I'm pretty used to the dinette, and Jake can take the couch."

Her mother frowned, considering this. "I assume there are *private rooms* in this cabin," she said stiffly to the young woman. "We will *need* private rooms!" That, thought E.D., was how Melody had managed to make her mother look cold and aloof in the videos. Even if the others didn't know—yet—everything Melody had done, E.D. felt a little guilty about sending them off to stay in the cabin with her. But there was no way on earth she herself was going to share a space with Melody, private rooms or not!

Chapter Thirty

While Archie was finishing Brunhilda's hookup, and Hal, with Destiny's "help," was putting up his tent, Jake sneaked away past the Art Bus and around the main building toward the deck where the TV crew was interviewing Melody. He wanted to hear what she was saying, preferably without anybody noticing he was listening.

The south deck was high enough off the ground and had enough bushes planted around it that Jake could get close without being seen if he crouched a bit. Melody and the woman who was interviewing her were seated at a table beneath a canopy, with lights positioned on their faces, while two videographers filmed the interview from different perspectives. The air was too chilly for Melody to get by with one of her skimpy outfits, but she was wearing the brilliant silk blouse and black jeans she'd bought in Valley View, with a warm scarf draped artfully over her shoulders. As he inched closer, bending down and pretending to tie his shoes, Jake could hear voices but couldn't make out what was being said.

One of the crew members had an electronic "clapper board," which he clacked as Jake moved in even closer. "Bernstein interview, take three!" he shouted. Moving very slowly Jake crept close enough to the railing to hear what they were saying as the interviewer spoke.

"As the people of America know, Melody," the interviewer said, "you aren't just a pretty face. Your videos have told the story of the Creative Academy's expedition powerfully enough—and, it has to be said, *entertainingly* enough—to edge out all the competition. Across the country people have been following your story. You have certainly become an . . . artful editor. But as we learned last night, there may be reason to believe you haven't been entirely fair, or truthful. What do you say to that?"

The interviewer paused, waiting for an answer, but Melody didn't respond. Jake raised his head long enough to see her staring off into the distance, as if she were composing her thoughts, then he ducked back down again and began pretending to tie his other shoe.

"We were there last night when you watched *The Real Melody Bernstein* video the other members of your team sent in, and you seemed upset. Would you like to tell America what you were *feeling* as you watched?"

Another pause. When Melody spoke, her voice had a tone Jake had never heard before. Apologetic. Contrite. Very nearly tearful. "I mean, I was devastated. These are the people who took me in and brought me along on this incredible trip. To see what they thought of me? It forced me to take a hard look at myself. They really feel like I betrayed their trust." There was another pause. A sniff. "It's just that . . ."

Pause.

"Yes?" the interviewer said.

When she spoke again, Melody was fighting back tears. "My middle name, my Japanese name, is Aiko." Her voice was trembling but got stronger as she spoke. Jake had never heard her sound like this before. "It can be interpreted to mean 'beloved.' And I guess . . ." There was a choked sob. "I guess I've just never *felt* beloved! I've never felt like anyone truly saw me, and loved me for *who I was*."

There were some sniffles, and a quiet "thank you."

Jake guessed someone had handed her a Kleenex.

"I know how it sounds, really I do, and I don't want to seem arrogant after everything that's happened, but I'm really, really smart. I always have been. It made me a target. I was *gifted*, I guess you'd say, and a *girl*, and that makes it hard to be taken seriously. *You* must have experienced that . . ."

"Well," the interviewer said, "I suppose I have."

"That's what's killing me about this whole thing," Melody said, her voice growing louder. "I've been so hurt in my life—*so hurt*—that I didn't recognize kindness when I saw it. I never even gave them a chance. I turned against the only people who have *ever* understood me, believed in me, the *only people* ever to give me a chance to use my talents to the fullest. I want to apologize to the Applewhites and to Jake, and to *the people of America* for deceiving them. I am so, so, so *sorry*!"

Jake's stomach had been clenching up more and more as Melody went on. She made it sound so real—he had to fight to keep from believing it himself. Could it all have been a big misunderstanding? Had Melody attacked them—*used* them—because she was afraid of being hurt? *No way*, he thought. *No way*.

He couldn't help himself—he had to see how she was managing to keep a straight face. He stood up and turned toward the interview. Melody spotted him immediately.

"Jake!" she cried.

"Quick!" the interviewer said to the crew. "Get this!"

One of the videographers turned quickly to focus his camera on Jake, while the other stayed with Melody, who had jumped up, throwing her chair over backward. "Oh, Jake! Jake, Jake, Jake!" She ran across the deck and down the stairs toward him. By the time she reached him, she was sobbing giant, heartrending sobs. Before he could back away, she flung her arms around his neck and started weeping piteously into his shoulder.

Now both videographers had managed to get their cameras off their tripods and were closing in on them. Jake hunched his shoulders, doing his best to dislodge Melody's grip. She clung like a leech. She went on crying for one long, agonizing minute. She was shaking with tears and holding him with such intensity that, in spite of himself, he thought it *had* to be real, it just *had* to be. Then she paused to catch her breath. "Thanks," she whispered directly into Jake's ear, calm and cool as a cucumber. "You guys are geniuses!" And then she was sobbing again.

There was an enormous *aaah-oooo-gah* from the direction of the Art Bus, which startled everyone. "Cut!" shouted the guy with the clapper.

"Got it!" the ones with the cameras both said.

"Perfect!" the interviewer said. "Good work, everyone."

Destiny came running around the building, then.

"Hi, Melody!" he said. "Didja hear the horn? I gots to do it again, even without Jeremy here." He stopped then, and looked at the scene in front of him. "Wha'cha been cryin' about, Melody? Did Jake tell you they 'dismantled' the Pageant Wagon?" One of the videographers had his camera trained on Destiny now, Jake saw. "Daddy's pretty mad at you for stealing it, don'cha know? I guess *everybody's* really, really mad!"

As soon as the crew announced that the interview was finished and they were free to go, Melody latched on to Jake's arm and dragged him off to a secluded corner of the center's coffee shop. He could have broken loose, he knew, but something in him wanted to hear her story. He figured it would be at least half fiction, but he had to admit there was something true about what Hector had said. Jake might not "love a good villain," but he was intrigued. How did she get so very, *very* good?

"Listen," Melody said, when she'd swallowed her first sip of mocha and wiped the whipped cream off her lip. "I'm not much at admitting I screwed up, but I did when I took off in the Pageant Wagon. *Besides* nearly totaling it—and me—on that awful curvy, steep road up to Flagstaff!" She paused, shuddering as if reliving that trip. "Everybody here was really *suspicious* when I showed up without the rest of you. I tried to make it seem like I'd had enough of the 'crazy

Applewhites' and just had to get away, but I don't think Hector, at least, was buying it. It was starting to look, once the Organics got here with all their brilliant video stuff and the cute kids and the beautiful Tyler, that they might just win this thing after all. Nobody seems to care if the kids are all brats and hellions, as long as they can bat their eyelashes and flash their dimples and look adorable on camera! And then you sent in that video that made me look like a total creep. You told the whole family, I guess."

"Just E.D. and Hal. Nobody else knows you're a total creep, they just think you're a thief and a vandal."

Melody chuckled.

"So how come you called us geniuses?"

Melody look a long, slow drink and swallowed. Then she smiled her most electric smile. "*Art saves the bad kid!* That was the Creative Academy's edge from the start—the whole reason Uncle Jeremy convinced my parents to let me come along on this little adventure. Not that they needed much convincing! They were plenty ready to have me out of the house." She took another sip of her drink. "I have to admit I was pissed when I saw your video—nice work, by the way, you guys did better than I would have thought. But then I realized. All I needed to do was be *saved.* Piece of cake! The Creative Academy is *for sure* going to win this thing! And here I am in California, like I wanted from the start. Better yet, without Uncle Jeremy!

Happy ending all around."

"So now what?"

"Now nothing, as far as you're concerned. Take a little vacation." She waved her hand around at the center. "It's a great place to hang out. Better than that spa! And the Rutherfords pay for everything." She blinked slowly a couple of times, batting her eyelashes. "We're a shoo-in. I had Hal's computer with me on the flight, and I made the thirty-minute 'summation video' the judges are going to see. Hector says he's going to edit it a bit, to include the film of me watching the *Real Melody* video. And I guarantee you he'll put in that stuff they got just now. I guess that's technically cheating? But who's counting! He knows winners when he sees them. You and me and the hug and the tears! Genius!"

"Don't you care about the rest of us at all? We worked really hard on this whole thing, and you just—you just took it over! What about Hal's videos and E.D.'s tutorials? What did you do with them?"

"They're fine, they're in a folder on the computer. Those dummies never changed the password on the e-mail account Uncle Jeremy used! And if you think I didn't get that off him the first day, well then I really am hurt. Whenever Hal would send your videos, I'd log on to that account, folder them, and upload my own instead!" Melody finished her coffee. "What's the problem? First of all, we win, which is what everybody wanted. And besides, you still *have* those videos. E.D. can collect all her ever-so-earnest educational tutorials and sell them to all the Creative Academy franchises. She'll be rich and famous. Meantime, *she*'s learned it all! Mark my words, that girl's going to get into Harvard someday. If she wants to go there. See? Everybody wins."

She reached out and put her hand on his. His heart didn't go *bump-thump* at all. He reached across with his other hand, lifted hers off, and set it on the table. Then he got up and walked away.

Chapter Thirty-One

E.D. knew Jake was trying to get a chance to talk to her—alone—but the whole rest of the day went by without a single moment for them to go off by themselves. It had been a hectic and highly emotional day. When the TV crews came to do the human-interest interviews for the awards ceremony show, nobody could find Hal, or Destiny, or Winston. "They must be together," Sybil said. "Winston's gotten so out of shape on this trip that they won't be able to go far. They're bound to be back soon."

The TV people agreed to put Hal's and Destiny's

part off till they showed up, but they were pressed for time, so the interviewer—a young man with the same sort of earnest focus Jeremy had when he first showed up at Wit's End to interview Sybil—gathered the rest of them into Brunhilda. How this went would depend, E.D. thought, on what questions he asked. "The Creative Academy," he began, speaking at the camera, "has the advantage of extremely successful and well-known artists taking the role of educators. You've been educating the Applewhite children—and Jake, here—successfully, for some time." So far, so good, E.D. thought, catching Jake's eye.

The young man took a deep breath, then, and leaned in toward Archie and Sybil, who were crowded together with Cordelia on the couch. "So how does it feel to have your reputations destroyed by a fifteen-year-old girl you so generously included in your Expedition's team?"

The next forty-five minutes were a positive firestorm of Applewhite outrage, as Sybil, Archie, and Cordelia learned for the first time what Melody had done.

It was then that Hal wandered in with a glazed look in his eyes and a goofy grin on his face. Hal? E.D. thought—with a goofy grin?

"Where's Destiny?" Sybil asked. "And Winston?"

Hal seemed to wake up then. "Destiny? Winston? How would I know?"

A search was organized, and after another hour of trauma and commotion, Destiny, Winston, Tyler Organic, and three of the French Fries turned up at Brunhilda's door. "We been all the way to the beach!" Destiny shouted. "Tyler took us all. This ocean's big, like Jake said. And pretty. And Winston doesn't like waves." He pointed to the French Fries. "These guys is Jack and Austin and Cricket. That's a great name, huh, Cricket? These guys is my *friends*!"

So it wasn't until after a multicourse dinner in the center's main dining room, where Melody sat with the television people rather than the Applewhites—and during which Archie and Sybil kept jumping up to make or answer a number of emotional phone calls—that Jake and E.D. finally were able to close themselves into Brunhilda's bedroom for a few minutes to talk.

Jake explained what Melody had told him about her fake confession and apology. And about the final video that was going to represent the Creative Academy in the judging, which Melody was so sure would be a winner.

E.D. listened, aware that her mouth was hanging open in a way that would have been embarrassing on video. "She can't. We c-c-can't l-l-let her—" She was suddenly stammering, she realized. "*Art didn't fix her.* What'll we do?"

"We could just let it go," Jake said. "She's right. We'll win."

E.D. found herself rocking back and forth, her arms clamped around her middle. "But it's all a *lie*!" She thought very hard for a moment, and then looked up at Jake. "I want to make our own final video. I want to put in the good stuff, all the stuff we worked so hard on. My tutorials from Valley View. And the salt mine. And *Saunders*! I did fifteen minutes of great stuff about the *indigenous fauna*! Really great stuff!"

"You've got probably *hours* of tutorials," Jake said. "It's *all* good if it's education they want. But we've only got thirty minutes! We'd have to include some good clips from the stuff that went well—the museums, and the shows, and the kids all working together at the Clayton library and . . ."

"It's supposed to be a *summation*, right? Giving just a sample of all the wonderful things we've been doing. Bits and pieces, all edited into a video collage. The fainting goats!" she said, then. "We can't leave out the fainting goats."

Jake made a face. "Yes we *can*!"

"Well, four seconds of them with their legs in the air, then. I want to record the *truth*. The amazing experiences we've had on this trip. How much we've learned. *Us*, not her. We could go to Hector Montana and make him trade our final video for Melody's. We could tell him he'll be sued if he doesn't. . . ."

"Melody's right, though," Jake said. "About people not really caring about education and art. This is *television.* People like drama! Ours wouldn't have drama. Not Melody's kind. It would just be kind of . . . nice."

E.D. felt her eyes filling up with tears. "Remember the great spangled fritillary?" she asked.

Jake blinked a couple of times. "You mean that butterfly I found for your Butterflies of the Carolinas report?"

"Remember how mad I was at you?"

"I never really understood why."

"Because if I gave myself an A on that report, when I hadn't found it myself, I wouldn't really have earned it."

"So you didn't give yourself an A?"

"I don't remember," E.D. said. "That's not the point. The point is that Zedediah was right all along—education isn't about competition. *Winning* isn't everything. Especially when the win is based on a lie. Melody's is a *lie,* Jake! And the *truth* is we had a really good expedition, and we all learned stuff. Even Mom and Dad and Archie and Lucille. *Everybody!*"

"Even Zedediah," Jake said quietly. "He got his cowboy on again."

"See? He left the Expedition to stay true to what he believes. All we'll get out of this if Melody's video wins, is that. Just *winning.*"

"And lots of money," Jake reminded her. "Plus all of us would still have everything we learned! Just like you still have all your tutorials."

She sighed. "Yeah. I guess in a way, we'd be letting our family down if Melody's right and our video can't win." But E.D. couldn't get that fritillary out of her mind. "Let's make it anyway. Just for us. Just so we know we did it."

"Okay," Jake said. "Just so we know we did it."

So the next morning, early, they asked if they could have a place to work for a while, and one of the Rutherfords' staff members provided a small technical studio, where they took Sybil's computer. They looked for Hal, but once again he had disappeared. They looked everywhere they could think of, and then finally saw him, sitting on a bench under one of the big, twisted trees, his hoodie zipped almost all the way up, turned just slightly away from a girl who was also wearing a hoodie, a long braid sticking out from it, and looking straight out in front of her. E.D. started toward them, but Jake grabbed her hand and pulled her back.

"Don't," he said. "Don't disturb them."

"What? Why?"

"Look," Jake said then. "Check out their hands!"

E.D. looked. Though neither of them was looking at the other, and she didn't think they were talking to each other, she saw that their fingers were entwined on the seat between them. Hal was sitting with a girl, holding hands.

"She's one of the mimes," Jake said quietly.

He was right, E.D. saw. What little she could see of the girl's face was unusually white in the shadow of her hood. "Amazing!" she said.

Three hours later, Jake closed Sybil's computer. "Done. If we didn't care about winning, this would be a *terrific* final video."

E.D. said nothing. She just looked at the closed computer. Then at Jake. Then at the computer again. "Let's do it," she said. "It's noon. The presentations don't start for another couple of hours. Let's take it to Hector Montana and get him to trade it out."

"What'll we tell him?"

"The truth. We can say it's the *official* Creative Academy summation."

"You think he'll buy that? He seems pretty invested in us winning."

"I trust us," E.D. said, "to figure something out. One way or another, we can make sure ours is the one the judges see."

"And then we lose."

"To quote a famous cowboy, *winning isn't everything.*"

E.D. held her breath, waiting for Jake's answer.

"Let's do it!" he said.

Chapter Thirty-Two

If nothing else, Jake thought, he could feel good about how accurately he had predicted what would happen. Hector didn't want their version of the final video. Not after he had spent all that time editing Melody's and carefully including all the human-interest drama she had provided.

But then Jake remembered that he was a kid who didn't always follow the rules.

And so, they waited until Hector disappeared back into the control booth, and took the memory stick with their final video to a frantic-looking production assistant who was clearly trying to get through a very long list of tasks on a clipboard. "Hector says it's absolutely critical—*urgent!*—that the judges get this final video he just finished reediting," E.D. said.

The poor guy looked doubtful. "I dunno," he said, "he gave me the one he said was final cut last night."

E.D. turned to Jake with big eyes, as if to say, *What do we do now?*

So Jake stepped right up in the guy's face, took a deep breath, and lowered his head like he was Wolfie about to charge the fence. "He gave you one *last night*? So you think the edits he made on it till two in the morning aren't important?" He glanced dismissively at the assistant's name tag. "Tell me, *Dan*," Jake went on with icy calm, "do you want to *lose your job* today? What do you not understand about the word *urgent*? You want the judges to have the *old* one? You want the whole audience—the *whole country*—to see the *old one?*"

With a shaking hand, the assistant took the memory stick.

And that was how it came to be that Jake and E.D. sat, in the third row of the Rutherfords' glistening, gleaming, state-of-the-art auditorium, trying not to look at Melody or Hector when their version of the final video played for the judges, the audience, and the television cameras instead of Melody's.

Jake could *feel* Melody's rage burning from where she sat on the other side of Hal. But in the end she kept up appearances. She didn't make a fuss about it.

He supposed even Melody Aiko Bernstein knew when she was beaten.

Their video was really good, he thought, his and E.D.'s. It was educational, it was touching, it was well put together, it was smart. It lost.

The Organic Academy's final video—on which their videographers really had outdone themselves—won with a unanimous vote from the celebrity judges, which meant, once all the standings had been tallied, that they easily won the Rutherfords' Education Expedition, and all that went with it. As she led the entire Organics group up onstage to accept the award, Michaela didn't even pretend not to gloat.

Jake didn't much feel like going to the big ball that night. Part of him just wanted to slink back to Brunhilda, curl up in a bunk, and go to sleep. Except, of course, he didn't *have* a bunk and E.D. would be there, too, getting ready for the ball. Besides, he didn't want Melody—or *anybody*—to think he was hiding. So, while E.D. was closed into the bedroom, muttering to herself as she dressed, he did his best to shake the wrinkles out of his nicest shirt, spiked up his grown-out Mohawk as far as it would go, and headed over to the ballroom. He wasn't sure if Melody would show up at the dance, and he wasn't sure he wanted to see her if she did.

Hector Montana was outside with a film crew. Jake held his head high and went right over to him.

"Jake Semple," said Hector. "Ah, buddy, what could have been."

Jake just shrugged.

"No, but I get it. You Applewhites. You're *artists*." The way he said it, Jake could tell it wasn't entirely a compliment. "I could have done a lot with you guys. But you had to want it. And I guess in the end, you just didn't want it."

I guess that's right, Jake thought. *Selling a story, putting on a show, living what people wanted to see. I guess we didn't want it. In the end, only Melody really did.*

That gave Jake a thought, though. "Hey, Hector," he said. "About Melody . . ."

The ball was actually pretty fun. E.D. and Tyler Organic danced once or twice. He seemed unfazed and humble about their victory. Jake had worried that seeing them together would make him jealous, but it wasn't as if they were all that romantic. Mostly they were just talking. Destiny and Cricket and some other French Fries formed a conga line and snaked their way in and out of the crowd, stomping and kicking and laughing. Hal and the girl from the mime troupe weren't dancing, but they were sitting at a table together, with their hands on the table and just their pinkies overlapping. She was still wearing her white makeup with little black dots above and below her eyes, even though she was also wearing a very pretty little dress. They weren't looking at each other or talking, but they both looked unbelievably happy.

One of the little French Fry girls came over to him—a cute kid in a red velvet dress who looked about Destiny's age—and asked him to dance. Laughing, he said yes, and she held his hands and stood on his feet while he rocked back and forth. She kept throwing her head back and giggling, which made Jake giggle, too. Suddenly there was a tap on his shoulder and he turned to see Melody, her jet-black hair covering half her face. "My turn," she said to the little girl. She slipped her hand into Jake's, her other one around his waist. She looked into his eyes, serious but amused, and then put her head down on his shoulder and started swaying back and forth in time to the music. Not knowing what else to do, he put his hand around her back and followed her lead.

"Hector came and talked to me," she said after a while, not looking at him, her head still on his shoulder. "He said he *liked my style*. He wants me to come to Los Angeles with him, for an internship. He's going to get me a tutor so it counts as a home school, but mostly I'll just be working with him and his crew. Making real TV shows." A little shiver went through her body, but she didn't stop dancing. "He said"—and she squeezed Jake's hand—"you told him that's what he should do."

Jake nodded, with his head against hers. "It didn't take any convincing," he said, feeling he needed to be straight with her. "I'm pretty sure he was already planning something like that."

"Well," she said. "Thanks." She stopped dancing and straightened up. It still annoyed Jake that she was taller than he was. Her eyes were bright and as intense as always. "You," she said at last, "are a pretty good kid."

Jake laughed in spite of himself. "Yeah, thanks," he said. He had to ask, he thought. "So. Mel." She raised an eyebrow at him. "Melody Aiko Bernstein." There was a time that holding her, saying her whole name, dancing with her, would have had Jake's heart tap dancing all over the place. But he knew the *bump-thump* was gone forever. "That stuff you said in the interview. About never feeling loved. Was that . . . was any of that true?"

She smiled radiantly. "As true as it had to be," she said. But just for an instant—and then it was gone—he saw something flash behind her eyes. Something quiet, and still. And sad.

Then, with a last squeeze of his fingers, she turned and walked away.

Chapter Thirty-Three

Something very loud and vaguely familiar intruded on E.D.'s dream and—whatever that dream had been—zapped it out of her memory instantaneously. Today, she thought, struggling to sit up in the dinette bed as a great roar continued outside, was the day after she and Jake had sort of cheated and let the Organics win. It was the day after the ball where she had danced with Tyler. It was the day after Hal had the first *date* of his life. The roar that had wakened her had faded away. Winston roused himself finally, and barked.

"AHOY, Applewhites!" a voice boomed. *Bill Bones*, E.D. thought. *Motorcycles*. No wonder that sound had been familiar.

Jake had just swung his feet over the edge of the couch, and Archie, in his pajama bottoms, was making his way down the aisle from the bedroom when the pounding started on Brunhilda's door. "Open up! Open up!" Bill Bones yelled. "The prodigal has returned!"

It was supposed to be prodigal *son*, not *father*, E.D. thought as Bill pulled open the door and Randolph dragged himself up the steps, bent over, with one hand on his back. His hair was sticking out all around a motorcycle helmet that didn't fit very well, and his face was a grimace of pain. "Never!" he said. "Never again, not even if my life, *not even if the fate of the entire world* depends on it, will I put my rear end down on a motorcycle, no matter *who* is driving it." He shoved Jake over and sank down onto the couch, groaning. Behind him came Zedediah, looking only slightly less miserable than Randolph.

From outside came Bill Bones's voice, as two motorcycles started up again. "Betty and me are off to Portland! We both enjoyed all the drama! Let us know, Z, if you're ever in mind of another adventure! Ride 'em, cowboy!"

Zedediah waved and the motorcycles roared away. "Well," he said then. "It seems we missed the ending of this Expedition altogether. Tell us about it."

Randolph shook his head. "That can wait. I need some aspirin, some sleep, and some food, in that order."

"Breakfast starts at nine," E.D. said.

"Where's everyone else?" Zedediah asked.

"In a cabin over that way," Archie said, gesturing toward the other end of the parking lot. "You do know we *lost*, right?"

"I might not have come back if we hadn't," Zedediah said. "Can you even *imagine* trying to duplicate the Creative Academy around the country under the direction of the Rutherfords—and their television team?"

"I'm sorry about the Pageant Wagon," E.D. said to her father, who had taken off his helmet and was sitting now with his elbows on his knees, his head in his hands.

He looked up and, surprisingly, smiled, his eyes becoming suddenly bright and awake. "It's all good! Wait till you hear my news. It's the only thing that kept me alive on that ghastly, bug-shot, wind-ravaged, backbreaking ride from Arizona. By the way, sleeping in a *bag* on the bare ground is one other thing I will never, never, never do again. There is *no* cowboy in me!"

Zedediah sat gingerly down in Brunhilda's driver's seat. "Death and rebirth," he said. "My cowboy's *dead*.

It remains to be seen what will be reborn."

"I have some ideas about that," Archie said.

Neither Randolph nor Zedediah turned up for breakfast. A few of the other losing expeditions had already started home, but the Rutherfords came to the dining room to announce that there was no rush to leave. Mrs. Rutherford also pointed out, much to E.D.'s dismay, that every video that had been sent in from every expedition was now the property of the Rutherford Foundation, and there was a television series in the works that would make good use of the material. "Does that mean they *own* my tutorials?" E.D. asked her mother, who was the family's expert on copyright.

"Only what got to them before Melody took over, and the bits from the one you and Jake made yesterday."

Archie received a text from Lucille midmorning, saying she had decided to stay in Sedona for a two-week shamanic poetry workshop. There was a photo attached, and E.D. barely recognized her aunt. She was wearing embroidered jeans, fringed moccasins, and a batik T-shirt decorated with a multicolored spiral design, and had strung wooden beads on strands of her hair. There were feathers stuck in among the beads. And she was holding a round, skin-covered drum with a bald eagle painted on it.

"This, too, shall pass," Archie said.

The Organics were staying on at the center for several weeks to plan for franchising their academy. Free-range education, Michaela was saying to anyone she managed to corner, was going to change the face of childhood in America. The baby pod no longer appeared to be a part of her body. E.D. saw Tyler at one point, the baby pod slung over his shoulder, walking one of the white stone paths with a guy from the Da Vinci School.

Whether the Organics would change the face of childhood or not, they had in some mysterious way changed Destiny, E.D. thought. Every single time she caught sight of him that morning, he was surrounded by a small herd of French Fries. "I gots friends now!" he explained when the family gathered in the dining room for lunch. "Even the girl ones."

Randolph had commandeered a large round table in the corner for the Creative Academy Expeditionary Force, as he had started calling them. When everyone was there except, of course, Melody—E.D. fervently hoped she would never have to lay eyes on that girl again—he tapped a spoon against his glass for attention.

"The Pageant Wagon may be no more," he said, "but I am pleased to announce that its spirit lives on! You may remember my meeting with George in Memphis?" Sybil groaned. "I sent him the best of the videos of *Our American Cousin*." E.D. glanced at Jake, who was looking fixedly down at the tablecloth. "He has shared it with other theater people around the country and they are so taken with the whole 'pencil sketch' concept that they all want me to direct readings for *them*. And they're asking to have Cordelia come along to design costumes and window-blind sets. It will be my Pageant Wagon tour—without the wagon!"

"But what about my ballet?" Cordelia asked.

"You can work on it in your spare time. We have reservations to fly to Seattle tomorrow."

"As it happens," Sybil said then, "I am flying out tomorrow as well."

"What? Where?" Randolph said.

"Home," Sybil said. "*Petunia Possum, Detective* has been—" There was a long silence, while she closed her eyes and swallowed hard. "It has been *rejected*."

"Does that mean I don't gets to draw a possum for the cover?" Destiny asked.

"Sadly, it does," she said, patting Destiny's hand. "My editor has suggested that writing for children is not my greatest strength, and she wants me to go straight home and start on a new Petunia Grantham novel."

"But she's *dead*!" Randolph reminded her. "You refused to resurrect her before, even to save your family from starvation."

"The sign of a great mind is the ability to change it," Sybil said. "It appears that the publicity of the

Expedition has raised a clamor for a new volume, and who am I to deny my fans?"

Jake caught E.D.'s eye. While they were working on their version of the final video, they'd talked about what they hoped would happen next, and agreed that what they wanted most of all was to travel back across the country, stopping wherever anyone wanted to stop and "mining the territory" for interesting possibilities.

She nodded at him now. "The Great Dismal Swamp," she said. Everyone stared at her uncomprehendingly. "We didn't get to go there after Haddock Point," E.D. said. "I want to go! Jake and I think we should do our own Expedition, from this coast to the other one, just the way we want to, seeing what we want to see, stopping where we want to stop, and learning whatever there is to learn along the way."

"Sounds good to me," Zedediah said.

"Me, too," Archie agreed. "I've been thinking you and I should go back to the Metal Museum and find out about building ourselves a smithy at Wit's End. Metalworking may be the wave of our future."

"Rebirth!" Zedediah said.

"Lucille can join us along the way, after her workshop," Archie pointed out.

Randolph raised his coffee mug. "The Education Expedition is dead. Long live the Education Expedition!" They all cheered.

Hal cleared his throat then. "Would it be okay if

Trudy went with us?" he asked. "Only as far as Indiana . . ."

"Trudy?" Randolph asked. "Who's Trudy?"

Hal blushed. "My girlfriend. She's sixteen. She's a mime. And a computer geek."

"Will wonders never cease?" Archie whispered.

"Well? Can she?"

"If it's all right with her family," Zedediah said, "I don't see why not."

Hal pumped his fist in the air.

"If Trudy goes, can my friends go too?" Destiny asked.

"No," Sybil said. "Your friends have to stay here with the Organics."

Destiny let out a shriek and burst into tears. He flung himself down, beating on the floor with his fists and his feet. "I wanna have *friends* with me!" he yelled. "Or I wanna stay here with them."

At that moment Melody appeared, her backpack over one shoulder. Everyone stared at her in stunned silence, except Destiny, who kept wailing. "I thought I should come and say good-bye," she said at last. "I'm off to LA. What's with the squirt?"

"I wants to have my friends go in the bus with us and *they all say I can't*! I'm never gonna have friends never ever never!"

Melody stood for a moment, looking from one Applewhite adult to another. "Haven't you people ever heard of *kindergarten*?" she asked.

And so it was, E.D. thought later, that Melody's last interaction with the Applewhite family made a permanent change in Destiny's life.

Jake, she noticed, as Melody turned to go, simply raised one hand and waved. But after she left, he walked out onto the balcony to watch them pull away.

It was time, she thought, to start figuring out what it meant to have an almost-brother. She got up and went out on the balcony with him.

"I never asked," she said after Hector Montana's SUV disappeared over the hill. "How'd that go? With Melody, at the dance?"

"Weirdly fine, I think," said Jake.

E.D. nodded. "I think she'll really like it in LA."

"How'd it go with Tyler Organic?" Jake asked.

"Weirdly fine," said E.D., grinning. "I told him I thought we should just be friends. He was okay with it! To be honest, he seemed almost relieved!"

Jake smiled and brushed his hair out of his eyes. "Just friends, huh?" he asked, and nudged E.D.'s shoulder. "That seems to be kind of a habit with you."

E.D. laughed. "Yep," she said. "Kind of a habit."

"Well," said Jake, sticking his hands into his pockets and squinting off across the valley the way Zedediah might have stared across the prairie in his cowboy days. "Friends are good."

"Yep," said E.D. "Friends are good."